H

NO MAN'S NIGHTINGALE

Center Point
Large Print

Also by Ruth Rendell and available from
Center Point Large Print:

The Vault
The St. Zita Society

**This Large Print Book carries the
Seal of Approval of N.A.V.H.**

NO MAN'S NIGHTINGALE

An Inspector Wexford Novel

RUTH RENDELL

CENTER POINT LARGE PRINT
THORNDIKE, MAINE

This Center Point Large Print edition is published
in the year 2014 by arrangement with Scribner, a division
of Simon & Schuster, Inc. and Doubleday Canada, a
division of Random House of Canada Limited.

The text of this Large Print edition is unabridged.
In other aspects, this book may vary
from the original edition.
Printed in the United States of America
on permanent paper.
Set in 16-point Times New Roman type.

ISBN: 978-1-61173-953-4

Library of Congress Cataloging-in-Publication Data

Rendell, Ruth, 1930–
No man's nightingale : an Inspector Wexford novel / Ruth Rendell. —
Center Point Large Print edition.
pages ; cm.
ISBN 978-1-61173-953-4 (library binding : alk. paper)
1. Wexford, Inspector (Fictitious character)—Fiction.
2. Police—England—Sussex—Fiction.
3. Sussex (England)—Fiction. 4. Large type books. I. Title.
PR6068.E63N5 2014
823'.914—dc23

2013027862

1

Maxine was proud of having three jobs. These days more and more people had none. She had no sympathy for them but congratulated herself on her own initiative. Two mornings a week she cleaned for Mrs. Wexford, two mornings for Mrs. Crocker, afternoons for two other Kingsmarkham women, did gardening and cleaned cars for Mr. Wexford and Dr. Crocker and babysat every evening where she was wanted for those young enough to need a baby-sitter. Cleaning she did for the women and gardening and car-washing for the men because she had never believed in any of that feminism or equality stuff. It was a well-known fact that men didn't notice whether a house was clean or not, and normal women weren't interested in cars or lawns. Maxine charged maximum rates for baby-sitting except for her son and his partner, who got her services for free. As for the others, those who had kids must expect to pay for them. She'd had four and she knew.

She was a good worker, reliable, punctual, and reasonably honest, and the only condition she made was payment in cash. Wexford, who after all had until recently been a policeman, demurred at that but eventually gave in the way the tax inspector up the road did. After all, at least a dozen other households would have paid almost anything to secure Maxine's services. She had one drawback. She talked. She talked not just while she was having a break for a cup of tea or while she was getting out or putting away the tools, but all the time she was working and to whoever happened to be in the room or upstairs in the kitchen. The work got done and efficiently while the words poured out on a steady monotone.

That day she began on a story of how her son Jason, now manager of the Kingsmarkham Questo supermarket, had dealt with a man complaining about one of Jason's checkout girls. The woman had apparently called him "elderly." But Jason had handled it brilliantly, pacifying the man and sending him home in a supervisor's car. "Now my Jason used to be a right tearaway," Maxine went on, and not for the first time. "Not in one of them gangs, I'm not saying that, and he never got no ASBOs, but a bit of shoplifting, it was like it came natural to him, and out all night and underage drinking—well, binge-drinking like they call it. As for the smack and what do they call them, description drugs—mind Mr. Wexford can't hear me, hope he's out of hearshot—all that he went in for, and now, since him and Nicky had a kid, he's a changed character. The perfect dad, I still can't believe it." She applied impregnated wadding to the silver with renewed vigour, then a duster, then the wadding once more. "She's over a year old now, his Isabella is, but when she was a neonettle, it was never Nicky got up to her in the night, she never had to. No, it was my Jason had her out of her cot before the first peep was out of her. Walked her up and down, cooing at her like I've never heard a bloke go on so. Mind you, that Nicky never showed no gratitude. I call it unnatural a mum with a new baby sleeping the night through, and I've told her so."

Even Maxine sometimes had to pause to draw breath. Dora Wexford seized her opportunity, said she had to go out and Maxine's money was in an envelope on the hall table. The resumed monologue pursued her as she ran out to the conservatory to tell her husband she'd be back in an hour or so.

Wexford was sitting in a cane armchair in autumn sunshine doing what many a man or woman plans to do on retirement but few put into practice, reading *The Decline and Fall of the Roman Empire*. He had embarked on it expecting to find it heavy going, but instead becoming fast enraptured and enjoying every word. Reaching the end of the first volume, he was happy to anticipate five more and told Dora she'd picked her moment to desert him.

"It's your turn," she whispered.

"I didn't know we had a schedule."

"You know now. Here starts your tour of duty."

As Dora left, Maxine swooped, pushing the vacuum cleaner and continuing to hold on to it while she peered over his shoulder.

"Got a guide to Rome there, I see. Going there on your holidays, are you? Me and my sister took in Rome on our Ten Italian Cities tour. Oh, it was lovely but hot, you wouldn't believe. I said to my Jason, you and Nicky want to go there on your honeymoon when you get around to tying the knot there's no untying, only these days there is of course, no point in getting married if you ask me. I never did and I'm not ashamed of it." She started up the vacuum cleaner but continued to talk. "It's Nicky as wants it, one of them big white weddings like they all want these days, costs thousands, but she's a big spender, good job my Jason's in work like so many's not." The voice became a buzz under the vacuum's roar. She raised it. "I don't reckon my Jason'd go away on a honeymoon or anything else come to that without Isabella. He can't bear that kid out of his sight for his eight hours' work let alone a week. Talk about worshipping the ground she treads on, only she don't tread yet, crawls more like." A pause to change the tool on the end of the vacuum-cleaner hose. "You'll know about that poor lady vicar getting herself killed and me finding the body. It was all over the papers and on the telly. I reckon you take an interest though you're not doing the work no more. I had a cleaning job there with her up till a couple of weeks back, but there was things we never saw eye to eye on, not to mention her not wanting to pay cash, wanted to do it on line if you please and I couldn't be doing with that. She always left the back door open and I popped in to collect the money she owed me and it gave me a terrible turn. No blood, of course, not with strangling, but still a shock. Don't bear thinking of, does it? Still, I reckon you had to think of things like that, it being your job. You must be relieved getting all that over with . . ."

Standing up, clutching his book, "I'm going to have a bath!" Wexford shouted above the vacuum's roar.

Maxine was startled from her monologue. "It's ten thirty."

"A very good time to have a bath," said Wexford, making for the stairs, reading as he went the last lines of volume one, describing another murder, that of Julius Caesar: . . . *during the greatest part of a year, the orb of the sun appeared pale and without splendour. This season of obscurity, which cannot surely be compared with the preternatural obscurity of the Passion, had already been celebrated by most of the poets and historians of that memorable age. . . .*

His mobile was ringing. Detective Superintendent Burden, known to the phone-contacts list as Mike.

"I'm off to have a look at St. Peter's Vicarage, taking Lynn with me and I thought you might like to come too."

Wexford had already had a shower that day. A bath at 10:30 a.m. wasn't needful, only seized upon as a refuge from Maxine. "I'd love to." He tried to keep the enthusiasm out of his voice, tried and failed.

Sounding surprised, Burden said, "Don't get excited. It's no big deal."

"It is for me."

He closed the bathroom door. Probably, Maxine wouldn't open it but would perhaps conclude that he was having an exceptionally long bath. The vacuum cleaner still roaring, he escaped out the front door, closing it after him by an almost silent turning of the key in the lock. Taking an interested member of the public—that, after all, was what he was—on a call or calls that were part of a criminal investigation was something Wexford had seldom done while he was himself an investigating officer. And his accompanying Superintendent Ede of the Met on the vault enquiries was a different matter as he, though unpaid, had had a kind of job as Ede's aide. This visit, this opportune escape from Maxine, was undergone, he knew, because, once senior and junior officers, over the years they had become friends. Burden knew, none better, how much Wexford would wish to be involved in solving the mystery of who had killed the Reverend Sarah Hussain.

All Wexford knew of the death, apart from what Maxine had mentioned that morning, was what he had read in yesterday's *Guardian* and seen on the day-before-yesterday's regional television news. And seen of course when passing the vicarage. He could have seen more online, but he had cringed from its colourful headlines. Sarah Hussain was far from being the only woman ordained priest of the Church of England, but perhaps she was the only one to have been born in the United Kingdom of a white Irishwoman and an Indian immigrant. All this had been in the newspaper along with some limited biographical details, including information about her conversion to Christianity. There had been a photograph too of a gaunt woman with an aquiline nose in an academic cap and gown, olive-skinned but with large, deep-set, black eyes and what hair that showed a glossy jet-black. She had been forty-eight when she died and a single mother.

Her origins, her looks—striking but not handsome—her age, her single parenthood, and, above all, that conversion made him think that her life could not have been easy. He would have liked to know more, and no doubt, he soon would. At the moment he wasn't even sure of where the murder had taken place, only that it was inside the vicarage. It wasn't a house he had ever been in, though Dora had. He was due to meet Mike and DC Lynn Fancourt in St. Peter's Church porch, the one at the side where the vestry was.

The vicarage was some distance away and he had no need to pass the church to reach it. Heading for the gate that led out of Queen Street, he passed a young man pushing a baby buggy, a not particularly unusual sight these days, but he recognized this one as Maxine's son Jason. As industrious as his mother if not as vociferous, he must be having a day off from his job as a supermarket manager. Curious to see the child whose father worshipped the ground she crawled on, Wexford looked under the buggy hood and saw a pretty, pink-cheeked blonde, her long-lashed eyes closed in sleep. Wexford hastily withdrew his head from Jason's glare. No doubt the man was wary of any male person eyeing his little girl. Quite right too, he thought, himself the parent of girls who were now middle-aged women.

He was a little early and by design. In his position it was better for him to be waiting for them than they for him. But Burden was seldom late, and the two of them appeared almost immediately from the high street. All the years he had known him, Wexford had never ceased to marvel at Burden's sartorial elegance. Where did he learn to dress like that? As far as he knew, Mike went shopping no more than any other man of Wexford's acquaintance. And it couldn't be the influence of his wives, neither of whom, Jean, long dead, or Jenny, the present one, had had much interest in clothes, preferring in their own cases no more than attention to "neatness and fashion," as Jane Austen has it. But here was Burden today, his abundant but short hair now iron grey, his beige jacket (surely cashmere) over white shirt with beige-and-blue-figured tie, his beautifully creased trousers of denim, though discernibly—how? How could one tell?—not jeans.

"Good to see you," Burden said, though he had seen him and eaten lunch with him three days before.

Lynn, whom he hadn't seen for as much as a year, said in a respectful tone, "Good morning, sir."

They walked along the path among gravestones and rosebushes towards Vicarage Lane. It was October and the leaves had only just begun to fall. Green, spiky conkers lay on the grass under the chestnut trees.

"I don't know how much you know about this poor woman's murder, Reg," Burden said.

"Only what I read in the paper and saw on TV."

"You don't go to church, do you?"

"I hesitate to say my wife does, though it's true, and you know it already. She knew Sarah Hussain but through church, not socially. Where was she killed?"

"In the vicarage. In her living room. You tell him, Lynn. You were one of the two officers who were the first to see the body."

2

Lynn spoke in the same respectful tone as before. "I expect you know this, sir, but it was a woman called Maxine Sams who found her. She'd been the Reverend Ms. Hussain's cleaner, and she came in to collect some money that was owed her. She's not a suspect."

"I know her, Lynn. She cleans for us."

"She says she rang the back-door bell, and when Ms. Hussain didn't answer, she came in. Apparently that had happened before. If the vicar was upstairs, she might not hear the bell. The back door was left unlocked in the daytime. Maxine called out to her, called her by her Christian name, which most people did."

"Which I think you should do with me. It's the way we live now."

"Yes, sir, I know, but I couldn't. It wouldn't be respectful."

"Try," said Wexford. "Go on about Maxine."

15

"When she didn't seem to hear her, she looked in the study, then went into the living room and found her body on the carpet. She'd been strangled."

"It was," said Burden, taking up the narrative, "as she kept on saying, a terrible shock. She phoned us—well, she called nine nine nine—and we got there in under five minutes. I must say, she acted very properly apart from talking too much. The shock hadn't deprived her of her voice. It was such an unusual killing, such a dramatic event you might say, that I went along with Lynn and Barry Vine. And in a few minutes Mavrikiev turned up. Remember him?"

"How could I forget the prince of the pathologists? A white-blond creature of moods, ice and incandescence. He got the news of his first child's birth while he was poking about with some corpse here and it changed him for the better."

"He's got four kids now and I don't notice much of a change. He wouldn't say much beyond telling me she'd been killed sometime between two and five in the afternoon and the strangling was from the front. Her killer facing her, in fact. It was half past six when Maxine Sams called us. He'd maybe be more precise later on, and there followed some rude remarks about how the police 'in their ignorance'—his words—expected pathologists to be clairvoyants."

They had come in sight of the vicarage, a

Victorian building, dating from the ugliest architectural phase of the nineteenth century, now festooned in blue and white tape round its front garden and the temporary porch of battens and tarpaulin covering its front door. The back door, in fact on the side of the house, stood open and PC Copeland was on the top one of the three steps leading up to it.

He said, "Good morning, sir," and it took Wexford a second or two to realize that this relative newcomer to the force wasn't addressing him but Burden. This was something he must get used to and perhaps increasingly in the next few days.

They went inside, finding themselves in a kind of vestibule at the end of a passage. This Victorian Gothic house was one of the few vicarages or rectories which hadn't been sold off to wealthy people wanting weekend houses, but retained as incumbents' homes. As they moved along into a hall large enough to be the entire ground floor of a modern house, Wexford thought of the family that would have lived here 150 years before, the paterfamilias on a stipend of perhaps eight hundred a year if he was lucky and had a good living, his wife old before her time, worn-out with childbearing, and their progeny, seven or eight of them, all the boys expensively educated at public school because these people were gentry, the girls learning French, music, and needlework at home from mother, another task for the parson's wife to perform. And now the incumbent was or had been a woman with one child.

Burden opened the door to the study. "It's all of it still as she left it, desktop computer, printer, tablet or whatever you call it. A good many books and not all them theological by any means."

"That isn't her, is it?" Wexford indicated a framed photograph on the desk. It looked about the same age as the woman in the *Guardian* picture or a little older but far better looking, even beautiful. He couldn't recall ever having seen the Reverend Sarah Hussain, but this was no forty-eight-year-old woman.

"Her daughter, Clarissa, sir," said Lynn.

"Does she live here?"

"She did," Burden said. "We were afraid she might arrive while we were all here and the cars outside and—well, you can imagine. Lynn here found the dead woman's mobile and Clarissa's number on it."

"She wasn't answering and I couldn't leave a message on her voice mail, not a message like *that*. Maxine told us there was a man called Dennis Cuthbert, who's something called the vicar's warden, and I phoned him, but when he heard what had happened, he got in such a state he was useless. In the end I rang a friend in Kingsmarkham to earth and got her to agree to leave a message for Clarissa saying her mother had had an accident and come to her house. She's a woman called Georgina Bray, who was a friend of Sarah Hussain, and Maxine gave me her number. I went round to her place later, it's in Orchard Road, so I was there when Clarissa arrived. It was pretty awful—well, like Mr. Burden says, you can imagine, sir."

The living room, where the body had lain, was even bigger than the hall, a huge chamber with a vaulted and beamed ceiling, windows with peaked tops that faced the front, a pair of French windows, evidently a fairly recent addition, and a good deal of heavy, dark brown woodwork. There was no longer any trace of what had taken place there, but that would have been true once the body had been removed. Strangling is as fatal as shooting or stabbing and in a dreadful way, Wexford thought, cleaner. He looked away from the floor where she had lain and up to the wall above the fireplace, where there hung a portrait in oils of the girl in the photograph.

"She looks less Indian than her mother," Lynn said. "I suppose I shouldn't say that, it's maybe politically incorrect. Actually, she's very attractive, isn't she? She looks like someone in one of those Bollywood films."

Wexford noticed how fair-skinned the girl in the portrait was and beautiful rather than "attractive." "Where is she now?"

"Still with Ms. Bray, sir. She's at school here,

Kingsmarkham Comprehensive. They're one of those schools that have kept a sixth form. Mr. Burden will know all about that."

"Jenny's her form teacher," Burden said. "Clarissa's still off school and will be for a week or so, I suppose."

They did no more than put their heads round the doors of the dining room and other downstairs rooms. The kitchen had been refitted at about the same time as the French windows put in. It hadn't aged as well as the windows and with its wood-grain cupboard doors and mottled blue-and-white tiling now looked antique. Letting Lynn go before them up the stairs, Burden said quietly to Wexford, "Can you make it for lunch tomorrow? I'd like to give you some details."

"Of course," Wexford said, relieved because he was asked and didn't have to ask.

"I remember how you used to say, 'We will talk further on't,' which you said was a quotation from Shakespeare."

Wexford laughed. "I expect I did."

Sarah Hussain's bedroom was bleakly furnished, not exactly a nun's cell but conspicuously austere: a single bed, one small mirror rather high up, a wicker chair, and a small, round-topped wicker table serving as a bedside cabinet. The books on it were Herbert's collected poems and Newman's *Apologia Pro Vita Sua*, Sarah Hussain's place marked with a folded letter. Another book that threatened to be dull but was anything but, thought Wexford, who had read it. While Burden was opening the door to the built-in cupboard, Wexford put the letter in his raincoat pocket. After that bedroom, the cupboard's contents were, with one exception, no surprise to him. Two dark trouser suits, two dark skirt suits, a black wool dress, two cotton dresses, a cotton skirt, two cardigans, and two pairs of Indian dress trousers and two patterned tunics. On a shelf above the hanging clothes were some neatly folded sweaters.

"What was she wearing when she was killed?"

Burden seemed surprised at Wexford's question. "Lynn? I'm afraid I don't remember."

"The salwar kameez," Lynn said. "Very much like one of those in there, sir. And a necklace of coloured stones, the kind they call sea-glass."

"Did she often dress like that?"

"Never in church, apparently. But sometimes when she was at home."

Clarissa's room was exactly what one would expect of a seventeen-year-old's, highly coloured, a blind instead of curtains, a duvet without a cover, clusters of photographs on the walls and two posters, Blur on one and Lady Gaga on another. Wexford picked up a framed photograph off the IKEA desk.

"She was close to her mother?"

"It would seem so, sir."

If the daughter looked like a Bollywood star,

the mother was more a younger version of Indira Gandhi, the face gaunt, deeply intelligent, dedicated.

"She looks clever, doesn't she, sir?"

"Stop it, Lynn," said Wexford. "I'm not 'sir' to anyone anymore. If you can't bring yourself to call me Reg or, come to that, Mr. Wexford, when I was a young copper my contemporaries used to call me Wex."

Lynn only smiled and they went downstairs.

Burden said to her, "Time to get over to Orchard Road. Clarissa's expecting you. She may feel more able by now to talk about Thursday, how much she knows of what happened that day starting with breakfast."

"I'd like to go with her," Wexford said rather tentatively. "It's on my way home."

"I don't see why not," Burden said. "I don't have to warn you to go easy with her, I know that."

Except that saying it was itself a warning. Their route took them along Vicarage Lane past a big house called Dragonsdene, whose garden, Burden said, abutted on the vicarage garden. There were no others nearby. "At first I thought the way everyone else did, certainly the way the media did, that this was the work of some lunatic-at-large, some nut without a motive. The kind of character newspapers love who goes about the country killing women and elderly couples, the people who leave their doors unlocked because nothing ever happens in the country, the country is safe. And it may be so, but I'm not thinking that way anymore. She wasn't that sort of victim, her past was too—what shall I say?—too involved, too exotic."

"You're going to tell me more tomorrow?"

"I am," said Burden, leaving them to return to the police station.

The woman who opened the door of No. 14 Orchard Road had been crying and began crying again as soon as she saw them. Not the best kind of carer for an orphan whose mother had just been murdered, Wexford thought, but he could be wrong. This kind of overflowing sympathy might be just what the girl needed.

"I'm so sorry," said Georgina Bray. "I can't seem to stop crying. It's all so awful. Clarissa's in here, she doesn't cry, I really wish she would."

Sarah Hussain's daughter was at least as beautiful as her portraits. She had a calm, still face, perfect features, and ivory skin. Nodding to Lynn, she turned her large, blue eyes on Wexford.

He glanced from one woman to the other. "I'm not a police officer, though I used to be. If you'd rather I wasn't present when DC Fancourt talks to you, I can easily go." He smiled. "You don't have to put up with me."

"No, please stay." Georgina Bray looked at Clarissa, and Clarissa nodded her head once more.

Suddenly, having been absolutely silent, she spoke. "It's not just that it's devastating, what happened to my mother, not just that it's so horrible, but that it's so *unfair.* She'd had such a hard life, such a lot of things to make her unhappy. Now she was like due for some sort of *compensation,* and what she got was being—being choked to death."

Whatever those things were that had happened to Sarah Hussain, he thought, now was not the time to ask about them. But perhaps Lynn or Burden or Karen Malahyde knew already. Lynn was waiting as if she knew Clarissa would go on talking, that she would need no prompting, and she was right.

"I don't believe in God. I haven't for years, though I never told Mum. I didn't want to make her unhappy, not now when she'd come here and was—well, she called it serving God. It didn't matter her getting those filthy letters and being told she wasn't fit to be a priest and her parishioners turning their backs on her and that man Cuthbert disapproving of her, she could bear all that because she had the love of God." Tears welled in the girl's eyes but her voice remained steady. "She thought God had deserted her when her parents died and then when her husband died and then more awful things happened, but God came back and told her to study theology and get ordained and she did and she was happy at last because God loved her. But He didn't, did He? He doesn't love anyone. He never told her anything because He doesn't exist." Wexford thought the tears would come now and overflow but they didn't. Her face had grown stony white and hard as marble. "I was the one good thing in her life apart from God." She turned to Georgina. "I think I'll go up to my room now. I'm tired, I'm tired all the time."

They sat in silence as she left the room and closed the door quietly behind her.

Wexford was the first to speak. "Ms. Hussain was a good friend of yours, Ms. Bray?"

Wexford didn't really know if they were Miss or Mrs. or one of each, but he seemed to have got it right as Georgina didn't correct him. Her eyes were wet but the weeping had stopped. "I met her at university. That was thirty years ago and we lost touch, sent each other Christmas cards, that sort of thing. Her coming here to St. Peter's was a bit of a coincidence, she'd no previous connection with Kingsmarkham, and I was living here because my husband's work is here. I don't go to church but I do take part in local activities, and we met at the Mothers' Union." She stared defiantly at Wexford. "Don't laugh. The Mothers' Union does lots of good work, especially in the area of domestic violence, something I know a lot about."

"I wasn't going to laugh," said Wexford mildly. "You campaign against domestic violence?"

"I don't campaign against anything. I just know about it."

The way she said it made her seem personally involved. Wexford thought he had said enough for now and left the field to Lynn.

"You said last time I saw you that you were her only friend."

"That was what *she* said, though she did have a friend in Reading where she once lived. Oh, and she said she seemed to have missed out on the knack of making friends. She didn't know how it was done, but I did, she said, and our reunion came about through me. But still I felt guilty. I've got a husband, as you know, and three children, but they're grown-up and gone. I do voluntary work. I didn't have the time for her I should have had. I keep saying to myself that I should have been at the vicarage that afternoon, I should have been with her, poor darling Sarah. . . ."

"You had made no arrangement to call in at the vicarage, had you?" For a moment Lynn hoped she might be onto a lead.

"Oh, no, no. If only I had. I would have been there and none of it would have happened. I shouldn't blame myself but I do, I do." And Georgina Bray burst into noisy tears, soaking handfuls of tissues.

•••

When he walked in, Dora was at home and Maxine, on the point of leaving, never a swift process, was telling her the tale of his perfidy. "Well, like I said, I'm sure I'm very sorry but I couldn't clean the bathroom. If you find a nasty tidemark round the bath, Mr. Wexford has only himself to blame. Mind you, the idea of having a bath when you've got two showers in the house seems very peculiar to me, not to say weird. But to cut a long story short, I went upstairs with the Mr. Muscle and the sponge et cetera and found the door shut as I expected. He'd been a long time in the bath, but if people are going to use all that water when we've got a drought on the horizon, they may as well make the most of it, is what I say." Here a long stare at Wexford, lips temporarily compressed. "Well, I went back after a good twenty minutes and the door was still shut. Locked, I suppose, though I wasn't going to try it, was I?"

"I don't know why not," interrupted Wexford.

A humourless laugh. "Well, if you don't know, I'm certainly not going to tell you." Maxine proceeded to do so. "Naturally, I presumed you was in there in the altogether, though I must say an hour and a half had gone by. It was all of twelve, past midday, and then Mrs. Wexford come in and I felt I was called upon to explain,

27

not that she did call upon me. I hope I know my duty, that's all."

Dora placated her, checked that she had taken her money, exchanging those smiles of wonder and exasperation women typically produce at the incomprehensible behaviour of men, and hurried her out.

"Why did you have a bath at ten thirty in the morning?" Dora asked.

"I didn't. I said I was going to. But maybe I will on Maxine's days in future. If I hadn't escaped, I think I'd have sacked her."

"Oh, for God's sake don't do that, Reg."

Maxine spent ten minutes chatting without respite to Dr. and Mrs. Crocker while they tried to watch a DVD of *Mad Men*, season three. She had given them a biographical account of her son Jason from his breech birth—an agonizing labour, they nearly lost him and her—until the present day, so now embarked on her horrible discovery at St. Peter's Vicarage. Dr. Crocker was an altogether tougher customer than Wexford when it came to being forceful with women and told her to get on with her work, he and his wife were concentrating on the television. Maxine left them alone for about a quarter of an hour, she had to while she swept leaves from the front path and the patio, but then returned to remark that some people said you shouldn't watch TV in the daytime, it was bad for your health, not to mention your eyesight, and she'd never allowed her kids to watch it before 6:00 p.m.

"I'm the health expert, not you," said Dr. Crocker. "You leave our eyesight to me. Now off you go and shut the door behind you."

It wasn't the way she was accustomed to her clients' talking to her, as she told Jason and Nicky when she dropped in on them on her way home.

"Is that what you call them? Clients?" Nicky didn't dislike her mother-in-law—well, as good as a mother-in-law or as bad as—but she kept up a mild feud with her because you weren't supposed to get on with your husband's mother, it was a well-known fact. "That's really weird."

Maxine was a worthy adversary for she too approved of mother-in-law versus daughter-in-law discord. "Don't you use words like that to me. I happen to know you left school without no GCSEs."

"Knock it off, Mum," said Jason. He was watching television with Isabella on his knees. "*Weird*'s not a bad word. Nicky wouldn't use one of them in front of Issy. Go on about Dr. Crocker."

So Maxine went on about Dr. Crocker, her audience expressing the opinion that his conduct was likely the onset of Alzheimer's, the same applying to Wexford when the tale was told of his bath or nonbath.

"I saw him this morning when I was out with

Issy. He's aged since he retired. Going into the churchyard he was with a cop and a lady cop and then on to take a look at the vicarage, I reckon. Well, I don't know, but that's what it looked like, didn't it, Issy?"

"Dada, Dada," said Isabella, repeating the only word she so far knew.

"That's my sweetheart," said Jason, kissing the top of her head. "She's talking very early. It's a sign of intelligence. I'll not be surprised if she gets to uni, maybe Oxford. Unless she does modelling. Why not both?"

No one argued. This was a subject on which they were unanimous. "Time for bed, my honey," said Jason, and took her upstairs himself. "Mum will come up and say good-night."

Left alone with Nicky, Maxine reinstituted the bickering. "You don't know how lucky you are, getting hold of a fella like him. You don't have to do a stroke for that baby."

"Leave it out, will you?"

Nicky went off upstairs to say good-night to Isabella, and without waiting for either of them to come down, Maxine started for home. On the corner of Peck Road and Khouri Avenue (named after a local council leader of Asian parentage), she met Jeremy Legg, who was Jason and Nicky's landlord. Maxine and Legg had never been on good terms—no one except his girlfriend was on good terms with Legg—but they spoke, they even maintained a show of politeness.

"Good evening," said Maxine, a greeting uttered in a scathing tone that she wouldn't have used to anyone else.

"Hiya," said Legg. "Been to see your son, have you?"

"There's a broken window in the front bedroom needs seeing to. Little job for you when you can spare the time from your busy schedule."

Everyone knew that Legg, who had suffered from a mysterious back complaint since he was twenty-nine, subsisted on the Disability Living Allowance, his rents, and his girlfriend's income. "Tenant does repairs, not landlord," he said, remembering to limp a bit before getting into his car. He drove home to Stringfield, to Fiona's cottage.

3

The one property Jeremy Legg owned was in Ladysmith Road and had been left him by his mother when she died five years before. This was let to an immigrant couple. His other house, the one in Peck Road, was not his at all but belonged to Kingsmarkham Borough Council. He had lived there for years with his wife, now long departed with another man. No more social housing was available in Kingsmarkham or the villages or was likely to be in future, so the sole recourse open to young couples who could only dream of getting a mortgage to buy a house was to rent. The pretty cottage he lived in with Fiona Morrison belonged to her. They had met in a pub where Fiona was drinking whisky and Jeremy orange juice. As far as anyone knew, he didn't drink or smoke, while she did both. She drank so much that night that he had to drive her home. He was quite a bit older than she, nothing special to look at, and he had that limp, which came and went when it suited him, but she fell in love with him. That also suited Jeremy. If he could move in with her, he could let the Peck Road house he was living in on the Muriel Campden Estate. He could and he did.

Fiona had it all worked out. She wanted a baby, and at forty-one she reckoned she had about three years left in which to conceive. Jeremy was the ideal partner and putative father of this dream child. He had his Disability Living Allowance plus two lots of rent, each of which amounted to about twice as much as the DLA, he had a car, and—this was as important as anything else—he stayed at home, was a househusband, idle, and had no desire ever to get a job. As a result, she could return to her work as an optician's receptionist after the baby was born. In a property-owning nation, as the United Kingdom once was and possibly still was, inevitably a great many people lived in houses or flats which had become theirs when their parents died.

"Best to be an only child," as Wexford remarked to his wife that evening. "Behave so horribly as an infant that they don't have any more. Later on make sure that your parents own their house and that you get on with them. What could be worse than that you fall out with the surviving one on his or her—probably her—deathbed? Then it all goes to donkeys or kids in a developing country."

"What a cynic you are."

"No. Just a realist."

"We had two, though," said Dora.

"Yes, but we're the exception. Neither of our children is in need of a house."

Fiona Morrison had been in need of a house, and the one she got on her grandmother's death was a pretty thatched cottage at the end of Church Lane, Stringfield. She attended to the front garden because that was the bit visitors and passersby saw. The back garden was less pretty; Fiona got too tired to do this as well as receive the optician's patients and send out the optician's bills, while Jeremy was too lazy to pull out weeds or mow the lawn. She didn't reproach Jeremy because she was fond of him and he was going to give her a baby. Jeremy's suggestion, made out of the blue, that they could adopt a baby, rather upset her, the way he said it as if it were an easy option open to anyone. "Or foster one like a sort of trial, see how we get on."

"What, and send it back if we don't like it?"

She had never until recently questioned the rightness of her choice of Jeremy, though she recognized that her decision to share her home with him had been hastily taken. Now, as he walked in, she was again conscious of a remoteness that came over him when he entered the house or came down the stairs or even simply sat in an armchair opposite her. It was as if he enclosed himself inside his head, seeing nothing, hearing nothing, unaware particularly of her. He could move while in this condition, did move, and the only state she could compare it to was sleepwalking. Was autism like this or could it be? She didn't know and didn't know whom to ask. Now, as several times before, she asked him if he was all right.

He answered her in what she imagined might be a sleepwalker's voice, the same slow monotone as when he'd suggested they adopt a baby. "Fine. I'm fine. How are you?"

His fugue, if that was what it was, lasted perhaps five minutes and then was over.

Restaurants of every nationality had opened in Kingsmarkham ever since—sometime in the sixties—the death of the English café where fish and chips, sausage and mash, toad-in-the-hole, boiled ham, and pork chops had been served. Fish and chips had never gone out of fashion, while sausage and mash had come back into it, and Detective Superintendent Burden had ordered this in the restaurant called Spirit of Montenegro, while Wexford would be having grilled sardines and couscous.

"What do they eat in Montenegro, anyway?"

"What we're having, I suppose," said Wexford. "But don't imagine the sausages are going to taste like the bangers you were brought up on."

"You can have a glass of wine but I shan't. It doesn't look well."

Both were thinking of the time Wexford, taking a well-earned respite from hard work, had been photographed in a pub garden with a tankard in his hand, a shot which later appeared on the front page of the local paper. He had never forgotten that photograph, though it no longer mattered.

"I suppose a picture of me could be in the *Courier* lying in the gutter overcome by chardonnay and no one would turn a hair."

"I wouldn't say that," said Burden. After all these years he still wasn't always sure when Wexford was serious. "Anyway, you don't care for chardonnay."

Their food came with a glass of claret and a jug of tap water. Burden said, "When the body was first found by that cleaner of yours, I made an assumption I shouldn't have made. I almost took it for granted the perpetrator was one of those nutters who go about quite a wide area killing lone women. But I've told you about that. There'd been a woman who lived alone in a cottage outside Myringham a couple of weeks ago, and I was foolish enough to think Sarah Hussain might have been another one of his victims. Of course I was wrong. The Myringham psycho was caught the following day, and he was being questioned by police at the time of her murder."

"Anyway," said Wexford, "Sarah Hussain wasn't a lone woman, was she?"

"You mean she had her daughter living with

her? Yes and no. Seventeen-year-old girls, as you must know, don't usually spend their evenings at home alone with their mothers. Whoever did this may have known Clarissa lived there, but also that she either came home from school and went out again pretty soon or went straight from school to whatever she did."

"So you gave up your stranger-as-killer theory?"

"I'd moved on to a new one. We'd no possible witnesses, you see. It was odd. We'd done a house-to-house, looked at all the CCTV—not that there's much, though there is a camera on the church porch. It was installed because of the increase in metal theft from churches. Nothing that was on the tape would have helped with finding whoever went into the vicarage between two p.m. and five that afternoon."

Burden nodded doubtfully. "How's your fish?"

"Not at all bad. Why is it that fresh sardines are so different from sardines in a tin? They might almost be a different breed of fish. It's the same with pineapple."

Burden knew Wexford well enough not to have to ask for elucidation. "These sausages are overspiced and vastly overgarlicked. The mash comes out of a packet." Burden gave a small sigh and shook his head. "The vicarage furniture— well, you've seen it—is nearly all what old Mr. Kirkbride left behind. We got a lot of finger-prints off it: Sarah Hussain's, Clarissa's, Maxine

37

Sams's, no men's. A woman could have killed her, of course. A lot of women are strong enough for that these days."

"I take it you got nothing from the house-to-house?"

"Well, there aren't really any houses to call at, are there? Vicarage Lane is mostly deserted unless someone's calling at the vicarage—as of course someone was that afternoon."

"The man in the gloves."

"I'm sorry?"

"He must have worn gloves, mustn't he? Just to enter the house, just to be there. If, that is, the killing was premeditated."

"True. We did a house-to-house in the lane at the back. St. Peter's Path. That meant calling at the most six cottages because the rest of it is all lock-up garages. No one saw a stranger in St. Peter's Path. The most important witness in a negative kind of way is the chap who was working in the garden of the nearest house to the vicarage, whose land has a boundary with the vicarage garden in fact. That's the place called Dragonsdene—don't ask me why—we passed yesterday. The gardener, who's called Duncan Crisp, was planting bulbs in flowerbeds in a big paved area close to the vicarage fence. He's only been living here for a month or so, and he's only been doing the Dragonsdene garden for two or three weeks. He told Barry Vine he saw no one come into the vicarage garden from St. Peter's Path all the time he was there."

"And that was when?"

"The relevant time. He started at one and knocked off at four thirty. Barry Vine had a good look at the next-door garden, and if anyone had come into the vicarage garden, he would have seen them. It was a fine, sunny day. Crisp is an elderly man but there's nothing wrong with his eyesight."

"What's your definition of *elderly?* It's a sensitive point with me as you may imagine."

"Oh, I don't know. Sixty to eighty."

"And what happens after that?"

"Ask me again when you get there," said Burden, laughing. "Do you want a dessert?"

"No, I want a *pudding* but I'm not going to have one. Coffee, please. So when you'd abandoned your wandering-psychopath theory, what did you light on next?"

"Well, I do try to be politically correct without being ridiculous," said Burden, "but the fact is she was half-Indian and there's a lot of sort of apologetic racism around here. I can say *Indian,* can't I?"

"You can say it as far as I'm concerned, but *Asian* might be wiser."

"A whole lot of people objected to her being half-Asian and—well, being a woman. Including, apparently, Dennis Cuthbert, the vicar's warden.

But he objects to everything in the Church that's different from what it was a hundred years ago. You'd think they'd have got used to women clergy by now. God knows how many women vicars there are in this country."

"My wife would say He does know, but I don't expect that there are a lot. I know because Dora has told me that there was a good deal of feeling against poor Sarah Hussain, but I thought that had died down. She also mentioned Cuthbert. With the sort that do have that kind of feeling, they seem to have disliked her a lot less once it became known that she'd converted to Christianity from Hinduism when she was very young, in her teens, I think."

"When she was fifteen, according to the *Guardian*."

Burden turned his attention to the cappuccino he had ordered, scooping foam from its top and pronouncing it not bad considering it came from Montenegro. "That's what I call 'apologetic racism,'" said Wexford. The more austere double espresso that was his own choice he tasted without comment. "But you've given up on race and religion and gender possibilities?"

"I wouldn't say 'given up.' I've not given up on anything."

"What did you mean yesterday when you said her past was involved?"

"Well, I suppose she'd once been married, but

what happened there I don't know. I think her husband died in a car crash. Clarissa must be the result of a subsequent arrangement. If she knows who her father was, she hasn't told us. Sarah had been a teacher at a school in Reading, and it was while she was there that Clarissa was born, then while her baby was small, she lived by teaching English to immigrant Urdu-speakers. Apparently she was fluent in Urdu or Hindi or something, and she had some sort of qualification in teaching English to foreign students. After that she went to live in India with her grandmother for a couple of years. She'd gone to Nepal originally with an aid agency, taking the baby with her of course, but she couldn't stand some of the sights she saw—or that's what Clarissa said—had some sort of breakdown, and it was after that she and the child went to her grandmother's in Darjeeling.

"She seems to have come into contact with a good many of those Christian missions of the kind we associate Mother Teresa with, but apparently there are lots of them all over the place, rescuing the dead and dying off the streets, we know the kind of thing. The two of them came back here when Clarissa was four. She went on teaching English to migrants for a while—you'd have thought there'd have been ample scope for that considering the number there are—and maybe lack of decent accommodation contributed to her decision, because she got herself ordained. Her

first—what d'you call it? Incumbency? Living?
—was a curacy in Colchester, and when old Mr.
Kirkbride died, she was sent here. That's about
it? Detailed enough for you?"

"It's not the details that are the problem," said
Wexford.

"That means something else is."

"The whole spiel is riddled with apologetic
racism."

"Well, thanks a bunch."

"Never mind, it was a nice lunch. Thank you."

"We'll talk further on't," said Burden drily.

"One more thing. Can I talk to Dennis Cuthbert?
It would be quite informal. Off-the-record."

"All you like," said Burden without much
interest.

Wexford was an atheist fascinated by religion; a
not uncommon position, he had found. As he
walked home, he thought how interesting it was
that Gibbon and Newman, from whose autobiography he had appropriated the letter, were
deeply critical of superstition in other faiths while
exempting Christianity from their strictures.
Rational, enlightened, and with a splendid sense
of irony, Gibbon could write about the darkness
that fell over the earth at the time of Christ's
crucifixion as if it were historical fact, the laws of
nature suspended. Had Sarah Hussain believed
that sort of thing? Or was it something to which
present-day Christians no longer gave credence?

4

Wexford and Dora had a second home in London. It was in Hampstead, a pretty little converted coach house in the grounds of their daughter Sheila's home, a "mansion," as the media had it and its kind, on the edge of the Heath. Wexford called this second home "a grace and favour apartment" because it was elegant and charming, they paid nothing for it, and it was theirs owing to Sheila's favour and graciousness.

They spent the weekend there, going to the National Theatre on Saturday night to see Sheila in *The Changeling* and on Monday morning walking across the Heath to Highgate. Warned by his wife that Maxine would be in the house when they got back to Kingsmarkham, Wexford asked why they couldn't leave two hours later, only to be told that this was impossible as Dora had to speak at a lunch organised by a children's charity of which she was chair.

Not for the first time, Wexford objected to the term. "I'm not going to say a human being can't be a piece of equipment for sitting on. We've been there before. But if it's offensive to call a woman a bicycle, and it is, why isn't it to call her a chair?"

"I don't know, darling. I don't make the rules. To change the subject a little, couldn't you look on Maxine as a possible source of information? Before you retired you used to have to question possible witnesses, but now people like Maxine come to you. You don't have to ask."

"True," said Wexford, "but it isn't necessarily the information I want."

In this case, though, it was. And no probing was needed. He was back with the *Roman Empire* and Dora had gone to her charity lunch when Maxine trotted briskly into the conservatory with a basketful of cleaning fluids, sponges, dusters, and glass polish but without the vacuum cleaner. Lifting his eyes from his book, Wexford noted its absence, always a bad sign. The Hoover left behind in its cupboard, Maxine had no competition, need not even raise her voice or repeat herself, but could launch into a flowing riverine narrative, uninterrupted by the need to draw breath or clear her throat.

"I thought I'd give this place a spring-clean. Not that it's spring, that's a long way off, but it seemed a good day for it what with someone being in here to talk to. There's some as can't get on with their work when they're talking, but I've never been one of them." Maxine began moving plants in pots along the shelves with her left hand while spraying the panes of glass with her right. A vigorous rubbing with one of her dusters followed. "Now the Reverend Hussain as I was supposed to call her, though it always sounded funny, her being a woman and Hussain being one of them Asian names. Talking didn't suit her, she used to come straight out with it, tell me to my face to be quiet. D'you know what she said to me once? There was this prime minister, she said, or archbishop or some such, and he went to get his hair cut and the hairdresser said to him like they do, 'How would you like it done, sir?' and this prime minister said, 'In silence.' How about that?"

Snatching an opportunity that wasn't likely to come again, Wexford laughed, but forbore to say he'd heard it before.

"Well, I said to her, I said it to her face, I'd never heard such rudeness. But there it is. She used to come out with things like that, she called them anec-somethings. Anecdents? Anecments? Never mind. I thought she was sending me up, that's what it looked like. Not right, is it, in a person who's supposed to be religious?" Maxine was moving along the shelves, polishing the glass while she talked. "Not that there was much sign of religion in that house. Many a time I've seen her sit down to a meal with that Clarissa and no one never said grace. And language too. She lost her mobile one day, ran about the house saying, 'Where's my bloody phone?' I was shocked, I can tell you, and the F-word once. I said to her to call the phone number and then she'd know where it was, and she did and it was down under the cushions on the settee. Well, that's where they always are, aren't they? She didn't know. 'You're an angel, Maxine,' she said, and I just wondered what my old dad would have thought to that. Taking the name of the Lord in vain, he'd have said."

The glass brightly polished, Maxine, carrying the glass spray and a clean duster, climbed with surprising agility onto a low shelf and then onto a higher one. Wexford resisted telling her to mind or to be careful as window cleaners know this already or else long ago decided they led charmed lives. "She christened my Jason's Isabella. When he told me she was going to do it—well, it shocked me, it really did. I'd got to know her by then, thought she was a decent enough woman in spite of the language, and she was kindness itself, always giving me little presents and once or twice she kissed me, but a woman christening a baby? Now I don't go to church, never have, except for weddings and funerals and suchlike, but I know what's right and what's wrong. And I couldn't get my head round a woman doing a christening. And I wasn't alone, I can tell you. There was those in this place who couldn't stomach her being coloured, and there was those who took against her for being a woman. The anonominal letters used to come, there was no end to them. I knew they was anonimal on account of her name printed on the envelope. Anyway, I read some of them.

"You needn't look like that. People who leave letters lying about are just asking you to read them, is what I say. I can see you want to know what was in them. Well, it was mostly bad language, the F-word and the S-word and even the W-word, though that was a funny one to send to her. 'Call yourself a woman of God?' was in a lot of them, and 'Go back to India.' One day she asked me if I'd ever been married. I thought that was a bit of a cheek considering she knew I'd got four kids. I said no, I hadn't, and had she? I could tell she didn't like it but if she could ask me, why shouldn't I ask her? 'Yes, I was,' she says. 'He died.' 'When was that then?' I said, thinking that Clarissa was no more than seventeen, and d'you know what she said? 'Long ago,' she said. 'Long long ago.' And I don't know how to put it, but there was like *agony* in her face. Well, she went up to the study to write her sermon. And the opportunism like never arose again.

"My Jason never liked his mum working in a place where they got anonible letters. He kept on at me about it. Ever since Isabella was born, he's got ever so responsible like he never was before, telling me what I ought to do and telling his sisters things, like not to go with boys before they was sixteen. That don't go down a treat, I can tell you. The eldest one, that's Kelli with an *i*, she went to church one Sunday—never been before or since, needless to say—on purpose to speak to the Reverend Hussain about her brother. Would you credit it? 'You tell him he ought to get married to that Nicky,' she says, 'and them with a baby. You're the vicar,' she says, 'and you want to teach them what's right.'"

Unable to resist, Wexford intervened. "What did she say?"

"The rev? She just laughed, Kelli said, and then she said something about first casting something out of her own eye, but Kelli didn't know where she was at and nor don't I."

If Wexford had a pretty good idea what Sarah Hussain had been getting at, he gave no explanation to Maxine. He had an appointment to talk to Dennis Cuthbert and he was very nearly late. The vicar's warden lived in a four-storey Victorian villa, tall and narrow, red and yellow brick, incongruously steep-roofed and without quite enough windows.

A widower, Dennis Cuthbert lived in darkness or near enough. There were, of course, overhead lights, both in the hall and the living room Cuthbert took Wexford into, but no table lamps, no standard lamp, and the bulbs were of low wattage. Opposite the fireplace, half-covering the wall, hung a greyish-pinkish folk weave bedspread, intended perhaps to look like a tapestry. The impression in this almost bookless room, with no plants and with ornaments of the kind you could pick up in seaside resorts half a century ago, was of almost total indifference on the part of its occupant to his surroundings. One book there was, *The Book of Common Prayer*, a worn black-leather-and-gilt copy, lying facedown on the low piecrust table. Wexford was ushered to an armchair covered in brown corduroy in front of an old-fashioned heater, the kind once called an electric fire, in a black-marble fireplace in which lay a few ashes and numerous cigarette stubs that had evidently been there a long time.

But Dennis Cuthbert himself wasn't old. He might have seemed so to Clarissa, but not to Wexford. Not much more than fifty perhaps. Sitting down himself, Cuthbert rather ostentatiously picked up the prayer book, marked his place with a ribbon bookmark attached to its spine, and laid it on the table in a position where Wexford could hardly fail to see what it was. Cuthbert then switched on the heater, lighting up one bar of the three, and a faint breath of warmth came into the icy room. If Wexford hadn't been able to see him but only to hear his high voice and old-fashioned accent, a perfection of what was once called BBC English, he would have supposed him a small, thin, elderly man, but Dennis Cuthbert was quite unlike the impression these things conveyed, being at least as tall as Wexford with heavy shoulders and thick neck, a muscular body and big hands. His hair, still thick and dark, was untouched by grey. He was also, again unexpectedly, a smoker. Wexford had thought the smell of cigarettes and the stubs in the grate must have been left behind by some other visitor, but that illusion was soon dispelled by Cuthbert's lighting up as soon as they sat down. His yellow-stained hand shook a little.

"You don't object if I smoke, do you?"

Wexford smiled and shook his head. "It's your home." Then: "I've got some questions for you, but I have to tell you that you don't have to answer them. I was once a policeman but I'm one no longer. It's entirely up to you."

Unexpectedly nasty, Cuthbert said, "Maybe, but we both know what you and your *real* policemen colleagues would think if I didn't answer, don't we?"

Best to act as if he hadn't spoken. Making what turned out to be an inspired guess, he said, "You've a copy of *The Book of Common Prayer* on the table here and I think you'd been reading it when I came."

"I often read it."

"And like it, I imagine. What did you think of

the Reverend Ms. Hussain using the *Alternative Service Book?*"

"I hate it. But I'm used to it. It's been in use for forty years. Her predecessor used it and his predecessor. She *loved* it. She said now people could understand what God meant. I'd hoped things might change when we had a change of incumbent, revert to what they used to be, I mean." He drew deeply on his cigarette. "I may as well tell you that I nearly gave up this job when I was told we were to have a woman. In the Church of England! I didn't believe it at first."

"Women have been priests for quite a long time now. There are a good many of them and they've been around since you were young. Like the *Alternative Service Book*, come to that. You can't have been much more than a child."

"I'm sixty-three. I know I don't look it." The shaking was no longer confined to one hand. Cuthbert's whole body was trembling. "Age makes no difference. There are some things you never accept. You never get used to them. I've no objection to women doctors or lawyers or bankers, don't mind any of that. Women priests are a blasphemy."

He was on his third cigarette since Wexford's arrival. "She had no morals, had a boyfriend who used to wait outside in a car. She used bad language and in the daughter's hearing. One of her sermons—if you could call them sermons—was about what a good idea it was to give unmarried mothers a flat to live in with their babies. And she contrasted it with the old ways when such a woman would have been ostracised. The congregation didn't like that, I can tell you, especially the ones that are on the council's housing list."

"Are you pleased the Reverend Ms. Hussain is gone now and can't come back, Mr. Cuthbert?"

"I'm not answering that. I'll tell you something, though. I went into the vicarage one day to talk to her, I wanted to ask if the rumour I'd heard was true, that she was going to get a rock band playing at matins instead of the organist. D'you know what she said, what she did? 'Don't worry, Dennis,' she said. 'It'll be fine. They're very good musicians and they worship our Lord with every note.' I hadn't told her she could address me by my Christian name and I didn't much care for it. Then, as I was just leaving, she came up to me and *kissed* me."

He got up and blew storm clouds of smoke almost into Wexford's face. Wexford retreated a little. "Did the rock band come?"

"It would have. She died." Cuthbert inhaled on his cigarette, strangely seeming to Wexford not so much like a smoker as a heavy drinker who might need a strong draught of whatever his poison might be. "She'd already got rid of a lot of the old hymns. 'O God, Our Help in Ages Past' was the latest to go. She brought in a hymn written by a schoolgirl. A schoolgirl, I ask you! 'Jesus shall reign where'er the sun doth his successive journeys run' was going to be next. D'you know why? D'you know what she said? That everyone has known for hundreds of years that the earth goes round the sun, so the words are nonsense. What do you think of that?"

Instead of replying, Wexford commented on the one framed photograph in the bleak room. It was of a teenage boy in school uniform.

"Your son?" Wexford guessed.

The boy didn't look in the least like Cuthbert apart from being large and dark. Having controlled his shaking by what was perhaps a gargantuan effort, Cuthbert nodded, said strangely, "Are you acquainted with the parable of the Prodigal Son?"

"I am, yes."

"I haven't yet killed the fatted calf for him but I hope to one day."

And what was the point of that? Wexford wondered as he walked home.

In describing Maxine to people who didn't know her, describing that is her voice, her speech, and her malapropisms, as he was doing now to Burden's wife, Jenny, he had noticed they always assumed she was a fat, blowsy, lumbering woman with brassy, home-dyed blond hair who wore low-cut tops and high-heeled boots. In truth

Maxine was tall and slender, her hair its natural light brown and worn in a chignon, and her clothes invariably jeans that were well fitting but not tight with a black or blue sweater in the winter and in summer a plain T-shirt.

"I never assumed that," Jenny said. "Her Jason was in primary school with Mark, and I used to see her picking him up at the school gates. It's not a thing one ought to say, but you could usually pick out the middle-class mums from the working-class ones simply by the latter's appearance, their size, their hair, and those ubiquitous boots. Maxine Sams was the exception. You'd have taken her for a doctor's wife. There, isn't that an outrageous thing to say?"

"Until she opened her mouth," said Burden. "What's she been regaling you two with today?"

They were round at the Wexfords' partaking or due to partake of an Indian meal about to be brought to the door by a man on a bike from a take-away purveyor called the Bombay Bicycle Club.

"Not me," said Dora. "I wisely got out before she arrived."

"Well, you've heard about Dennis Cuthbert, who told me nothing useful but a lot about his character. Maxine gave me a lot of useful stuff about Sarah Hussain. They may not be new to you, Mike, but I made notes of them after she'd gone in case they help."

Dora was making a face and on the point of banning shop when the doorbell rang, announcing the arrival of their food.

"I don't think it's shop," Burden said, "but since we were on the subject of Jason Sams, once well-known to the Mid-Sussex Constabulary but now a reformed character, I don't suppose either of you have picked up anything about the rent he pays in these sessions you have with his mum?"

"He lives in a council house, doesn't he?"

"Well, yes, Dora, he does. But it's not his council house; that is, it was never allocated to him or to his grandfather or grandmother or to anyone who could legitimately have passed it on to him."

"What are you saying, Mike? That his landlord or landlady is a council tenant and letting his rented house off to Jason Sams? That's illegal, isn't it?"

"It's against the council's rules. If you get found out doing it, you can get evicted and of course your tenant too. And then the only roof over your head is a B and B. No doubt there are some who run an extra scam and are tenants of a council house that the council pays for as housing benefit and still rent it out while living elsewhere."

"Suppose you own the house under the right-to-buy provisions?" Wexford asked.

"In that case you can let it to whoever you like. Of course you can. It's a free country."

"What are you going to do about it?" said Dora.

"Nothing. What can I do? It's a matter for the council's housing department."

"I suppose," said Wexford, "that he, whoever he is, could charge any rent he likes if the tenant is prepared to pay. Is it known who he is?"

"'He,'" said Burden, "is a woman called Diane Stow. She lives on the Costa del Sol with a man who's made himself rich by dealing in prescription drugs. It's him I'm interested in. She is quite comfortable enough not to need the rent from a Kingsmarkham council house."

"Right," said Wexford, "but how does she come to be, as I assume she is, the legitimate tenant of this council house?"

"I don't know." Burden spoke in the indifferent tone of one who no more cares than he knows. "She once lived in it, I suppose."

After that they ate their second course, which was Dora's homemade crème brûlée, and talked about their grandchildren, Burden's daughter having just become the mother of a baby girl. But Wexford, five times a grandfather and getting rather blasé about it, let his thoughts wander to Sarah Hussain. The answer to the question which was starting to perplex him was probably that Clarissa's father was a man Sarah had simply had an affair with. What else? Her husband had died, she had met someone she might have considered marrying, and as time went on, she realized that if she wanted a child, there was no time to waste. The engagement or whatever it was didn't work out, there was no marriage, but she had her daughter. It seemed reasonable enough and a lot of women did it, but it didn't quite fit in with Sarah's apparently fervent commitment to Christianity, to the Church in fact. Yet she was only thirty-one when the child was born, not exactly the last knockings of fertility . . .

"Reg, you haven't gone to sleep, have you?"

Wexford came out of his reverie. "If I had, I wouldn't be able to answer that."

"Well, Mike and Jenny are going."

"They'll forgive me," said Wexford, kissing Jenny and, rather to the surprise of both of them, shaking hands with Burden. "Anyway, I was thinking about the case. About the Reverend Sarah Hussain. I'll give you the notes I made."

5

If we consider the purity of the Christian religion, the sanctity of its moral precepts, and the innocent as well as austere lives of the greater number of those who during the first ages embraced the faith of the Gospel, we should naturally suppose that so benevolent a doctrine would have been received with due reverence even by the unbelieving world. . . .

Wexford briefly set Gibbon aside to marvel at this commentary and to wonder that he had never thought of it before. It struck him that Sarah Hussain had tried to make a benevolent doctrine of Christianity. In her view it was kindly, loving, modern, and progressive. What a relief that today wasn't one of Maxine's days. He had undisturbed peace and quiet. It *was* odd that so much cruelty and violence was meted out to these "innocent disciples." No doubt Gibbon would provide an explanation in the next few pages, and he picked up *The Decline and Fall* once more.

An hour or so had passed when Dora came into the room and asked him if he remembered they were due to have lunch with Sylvia, whose day off from work it was. Now that his daughter lived within Kingsmarkham, the Old Rectory at Great Thatto having been sold, they could walk there, Dora said. Wexford agreed. Not that he much wanted to, but it was good for him. His love of walking was mainly confined to London. He looked around for a bookmark and in doing so remembered the letter he had taken out of Sarah Hussain's copy of Newman's autobiography. That he should certainly not have taken out. . . .

It was possibly one of those letters Maxine called "anonimable," foul and at the same time dull and illiterate—but, no, Sarah wouldn't have used such a thing as a bookmark. He put on his raincoat and felt for the letter in the right-hand pocket. It wasn't any of those things but apparently from a friend. He read it while Dora was upstairs getting ready.

The address at the top was 21 Miramar Close, Reading, with a postcode, the date three months ago in the middle of July.

Dear Sarah,

It is such a long time since we worked here together and shared a home that I wonder if you have forgotten me but I don't think you can have. I think you have moved several times since you lived here and Clarissa with you. She is my goddaughter and I would have liked to remember her on birthdays but I had lost touch and didn't know where you were. Then I saw that paragraph in the *Times* that said you were now an ordained priest (you see I remember the correct terminology) with a living in Kingsmarkham. You know, I wasn't altogether surprised. This, I thought, was what you always ought to have been.

I am married now but still living in Reading not far from where we had our flat nineteen years ago. My husband preferred me not to work and to tell you the truth I was glad to give up. I have taken my husband's name but I am still the old Thora Watson who was, I think, your best friend. You and I were so close like the sisters we neither of us ever had. Do let me hear from you.

With love,
Thora (Kilmartin)

So this was the Reading woman Georgina Bray had mentioned when she corrected her claim to have been Sarah's only friend. This woman was a lapsed friend but might be the one to tell them something about Sarah Hussain that others wouldn't or couldn't. Had Sarah replied to the letter? You don't keep a letter as a bookmark,

Wexford decided as he and Dora walked along York Street, unless you've answered it or intend to answer it. It would be a permanent reminder to you and make you feel guilty. Talking of which, though he wasn't . . .

"You're very silent," Dora said. "Gibbon on your mind?"

"I was thinking of Sarah Hussain. You went to church most Sundays. What kind of sermons did she preach?"

"The controversial kind. There was one about her idea that royal-family members shouldn't wear military uniforms. I told you about it."

"Dennis Cuthbert told me about one in support of single parents, and wasn't there one advocating gay marriage?"

"That's right," said Dora. "Her idea was that—well, in everything, not only gay marriage—the important thing was love. That was a central tenet of Christianity, she said. 'Little children, love one another,' which of course comes from the New Testament, and there's nothing about only heterosexuals loving one another. If the Church held on to that, she said, the Church and clerics, there wouldn't be any banning of men marrying men and women women provided they loved each other."

"I don't suppose her bishop was overjoyed at that."

"No, I gather she got a dressing down."

Sylvia had cooked one of her father's favourite dishes for lunch, a fish pie, and her elder son was at home to help him eat it. Always interested in the way families behave, the patterns they follow, Wexford had often noticed that a grown-up child, in his or her early twenties, say, will make a point of being present when grandparents come, make conversation with them and eat with them, but depart pretty fast after the meal is over, leaving mother to explain the pressing business that has taken him or her away. So it was in Robin's case, though he explained the business himself while Wexford listened politely. When his grandson had left and Dora gone upstairs to be shown a dress Sylvia had bought for someone's wedding, he reflected that while Robin was obviously totally bored by Wexford's pursuits, so was he by Robin's. Gibbon held no more interest for the grandson than recording the latest production of a local rock group did for the grandfather. It must always be so. "Crabbed age and youth cannot live together," only he didn't think he was crabbed—but what elderly person did think that of himself?

But he did wonder if the rock group was the same one that Sarah Hussain had hoped would perform in St. Peter's Church, and then his thoughts went back to Thora Kilmartin's letter. Not so much to the letter as to his abstracting it without a word to Burden or any police officer, abstracting it moreover from a crime scene. Guilt wasn't a feeling with which he was very familiar, but he recognised it when he had it. It wasn't just the guilt that troubled him but the necessity of confessing his offence to Burden. It was necessary, he had to do it, but he could hardly think of anything he wanted to do less. In the past Burden had confessed his mistakes and lapses to *him,* he was the appropriate person, the superior officer. Now their roles were reversed or almost. There was no way out. To ignore it, to forget the letter, was unthinkable. Not only should Burden and his team meet Thora Kilmartin and talk to her, *want* to meet her and talk to her, but to withhold that letter and pretend it didn't exist was the kind of act that made him feel—in a phrase he had always despised when others used it—unable to live with himself.

Dora and Sylvia came downstairs, announced that tea would soon be coming, and looked at him as if they had expected him to be asleep.

Most of the time Jeremy Legg watched television. Fiona would put up with it in the morning for the news and weather forecast but always turned it off when she left for work in her Aztec-gold Prius. Jeremy switched it on again, playing about with various channels but mostly just sitting and gazing in a relaxed sort of way at ITV1 or, as the morning wore away to lunchtime, Sky Movies Premiere. He was a househusband but he performed few tasks. Seldom bored, he preferred his own company to anyone else's, and if he wanted a change of scene, he got in his car, a battered-about Nissan, for Jeremy wasn't a careful driver, and went for what he called (and his grandfather had called) "a spin." This took him up Ladysmith Road to have a look at the house which had been his mother's and was now rented to Mr. and Mrs. Patel.

He liked to sit outside in his car and build up his ego thinking that he was a landlord and this just one of his lucrative properties. A house farther up the road similar to this one was for sale. It was going for two hundred thousand, cheap in an area considered within commuting distance to London. If he could get Fiona interested, she might pay the deposit and he could pay the mortgage out of his rents. She might help there as well. He moved off towards the Muriel Campden Estate and Peck Road, parking opposite but a few yards away from his house. Strictly speaking, Diane was the tenant, but so long as the rent got paid, the council didn't pay much attention to where it came from.

After a little while, the time it took to smoke a cigarette—Fiona didn't know he smoked or so he fondly believed—Jason Sams's woman came out with the baby in one of those enormous buggies, as big as an adult's wheelchair and much more lushly upholstered. A child would never learn to walk if it could ride in one of those. Jeremy almost envied that baby girl, all dressed up in a fleecy jumpsuit and enthroned in sheepskin cushions. When Fiona had a baby, they would have one of those and he would push it round the Stringfield lanes. He wondered how he would get on. Would he *like* it?

Would they ever have a baby? "Make a baby," as Fiona put it. He supposed he knew how that was done: have sex without using or swallowing anything, he supposed, and a baby would come. Only they did and it didn't. Was he doing it right? He'd never had a baby with Diane, and they'd been together years and years. Thinking about it, he felt himself lapse into one of those dream states of his when a stillness took hold of him and his mind emptied. He called it a fugue because somewhere he had read that's what it was. He remained sufficiently aware to know not to drive while in this condition. It would pass, he would come back to life and be as he was before.

After about a quarter of an hour he returned to full consciousness, waking, so to speak, to where he had broken off: making a baby, Fiona looking after a baby, looking after the baby himself. Maybe he could go to a class where they taught you baby-caring. Jeremy had been to many classes and joined many courses in his adult life—exercise, elocution, tai chi, Spanish, country dancing, woodwork, even origami—but had completed none of them. Of the tai chi and the Spanish he had attended only a single session. But would Fiona have a baby? They didn't have a lot of sex. He had never been keen on it, believing Fiona was keen enough for both of them. Making an effort was called for if he was to get her pregnant and persuade her to buy that house. But maybe she was pregnant already and, being still in doubt, hadn't said.

He sat in Peck Road for a long time and then drove home to Stringfield, at so slow a pace as to arouse the ire of other motorists, who hooted at him and shouted abuse.

Considering Wexford had no intention—not for a moment—of failing to confess to Burden, wouldn't have dreamt of it, it was strange that this was exactly what he did, he dreamt of it. He wasn't at home in Kingsmarkham but in the kitchen in the Hampstead coach house, quite alone, holding Thora Kilmartin's letter in his hand. The letter was still folded up as it had been when it served as a bookmark. He opened it and tried to read it again, but the handwriting was unreadable and all that he could see was a grey blur. Nevertheless, he interpreted it as horribly condemnatory of himself, as a denunciation of his whole life, exposing his career as dishonourable, his marriage as a fake, his efforts at parenthood as ludicrous, and his preference for classical music and such literature as Gibbon as a pretentious sham. Out of a drawer in the cabinet he took that object so seldom used these days, a box of matches, dropped the letter into a saucer, and, intending to burn it, struck a match. The sound, the flash, the sudden brightness, woke him, and he sat up to ask Dora why she had put the light on.

"You were thrashing about and moaning. Are you all right?"

"I am now."

It had been one of those dreams whose absolute horror is exorcised by the relief of knowing it's not true. Its content never happened. In the morning, as soon as he felt he decently could, he phoned Burden and asked if he could come and see him. It was important—well, it was to him.

"Sure," said Burden. "You ought to know you don't have to ask. I'm usually here."

It was a case, Burden said, of who shall have custody of the custodian. Duncan Crisp, the negative witness, had seemed a valuable custodian, working in the Dragonsdene garden at the time, all the possible time, someone was murdering Sarah Hussain next door. He had been exhaustively interviewed, but had now phoned in to say he had a confession to make. When talking to DS Karen Malahyde, he had said he had been in the garden for three hours without a break. Now he remembered he had gone into the house called Dragonsdene for a cup of tea at two thirty and stayed there to put a washer on a tap because no one else was around to do it. Karen had gone back to Dragonsdene to talk to him, Burden told Wexford.

It was a bit strange, wasn't it, forgetting something that must have taken, if you included the tea drinking, half an hour?

"It seems he'd been going in there every day he worked there—only a few weeks, though—and he always went there at two thirty."

"And Mrs. Morgan and Miss Green—is that what they're called?—do they remember?"

"No, they don't. Only that when he started there, they'd asked him in for tea. Apparently they did this for their previous gardener and so they carried on the custom with Crisp."

"What are you saying? That he missed seeing the perpetrator come or that he's the perpetrator himself? For what reason? Because he nursed some sort of grudge against her?"

"You know that finding a motive is never our principal concern. He may not have been in the garden or he may have been there up until three. Mavrikiev is positive now that she died between two and four, nearer to three."

Wexford liked that *our* but wondered if he would ever hear it again in that context after he had said what he had come to say. "Mike, I'd like to get it over if you don't mind."

"You what? Oh, yes, this confession of yours."

"You may not make so light of it when you know what it is." Wexford drew a deep but silent breath and laid the letter on Burden's desk. "You remember we all went into Sarah Hussain's bedroom, you and I and Lynn, and looked around a bit. There was a book she'd been reading on the bedside table. It was Newman's *Apologia*. Well, she'd been using this letter as a bookmark. I took it out and put it in my pocket, I just took it without saying anything to you. I didn't ask, I just took it."

"I know. I saw you. What's the problem?"

"You *saw* me?"

"Sure I did. I meant to say something to you about it, like it couldn't have anything to do with her murder, it was useless to us, but something came up and I forgot. Why, do you think it's worth following up?"

Wexford was almost stunned by relief. He could hardly speak but he managed to mutter that he did think that, and maybe Thora Kilmartin should be contacted.

"OK, I'll get Lynn to call her, shall I? Maybe you and she could see the woman. Are you all right, Reg? You've gone white."

"I'm fine. Now I've made my own apologia, I'll go. Thank you."

"What for?" said the puzzled Burden.

Out in the street, going home, Wexford thought not so much about guilt and confessions as about how we magnify a small fault into an enormous transgression with no real basis for doing so. He ought to have known Burden better, he ought to have realized that the worst that could have happened was his old friend, the new detective superintendent, saying, "Well, that wasn't like you" or "You must have been having an amnesia moment." But even that hadn't taken place. Burden had *seen* him take it and hadn't cared. If we weave a tangled web when we practise to deceive, isn't it equally true that we dig a pit of horror for ourselves when we pay the price of having a conscience?

He felt so happy and serene that for once his heart failed to sink when the voice of Maxine greeted him before he even saw her. "You know something, I thought you was reading your travel book in the greenhouse and I've been talking to you like a fool for the past ten minutes, well, maybe not as much, but talking I was, and then when I never got an answer, I heard the front door and I saw my mistake or heard I should say. What a fool. My Jason says I talk too much, but I don't know. What do you think?"

Called upon to answer because now she was standing in front of him, Wexford said, remembering how hard it was to find a good cleaner, "I wouldn't like to say."

"You can. I won't take offence." Greatly to his relief, she gave him no chance to reply but charged ahead on one of her tangents. "Mind you, them two, Jason and that Nicky, they never talk. To each other, is what I mean. It's the telly as has done it. Why talk when it talks for you? And the same applies to the Internet. I call it the minitelly. Jason says Isabella is an early talker, and I don't like to correct him there. Well, you don't, do you? Not when it's his kid. But as for early, his sister Kelli with an *i,* she was talking at ten months, and the one we call Barb, though Barbaretta's her name, she was reading the *Sun* at two."

Seated in the nearest armchair, Wexford had fallen asleep.

6

Though Burden clung to his theory that whoever had killed Sarah Hussain had figured significantly in her past, he still felt that Duncan Crisp might join his sparse list of suspects. After all, the man had lied or had suffered a lapse of memory so great as to make all his behaviour suspicious. He was either guilty himself or else he had seen someone else come across the vicarage garden during the afternoon and enter the house by the back door.

When questioned by DI Barry Vine in his own home, a flat on the Deepvale Estate, Crisp had begun by being truculent, then aggressive. By a rather unfortunate chance he had attended the same primary school as Vine's father, some half century before, when Crisp senior had been a form captain or monitor.

"I was your superior then," he said to the sergeant, "and as far as I'm concerned, I am still.

Your DS letters don't cut no ice with me. I'm not saying no more."

So Vine took him in, Crisp's feeble resisting arrest doing him no good.

"I want a lawyer," said Crisp to Burden in the interview room.

"Later," said Burden. "Now Mrs. Morgan of Dragonsdene House says you spent half an hour in her kitchen having tea with her housekeeper and herself on Thursday afternoon from approximately two thirty p.m. to just before half past three. You also replaced a washer on a tap. And the housekeeper, Linda Green, confirms this. Your story is that you were outside in the garden all that time. You weren't though, were you?"

"I forgot. I can't remember every time I have a cup of tea—more like dishwater it was—with a couple of old hens. I went in there and had tea like I do every bloody day I work there. What time it was I don't know and I don't care. I want a lawyer."

"Later," said Burden. "How well did you know the Reverend Hussain?" Wexford would have winced or cringed at this usage but he wasn't there to hear it. "Speak to her, did you? Pass the time of day?"

"I never did. My old mum what passed away last year, Lord rest her, didn't hold with females in pulpits, that's what she called them, females in pulpits, and no more do I. I wouldn't have spoke

73

to her if she'd spoke to me, but she never did."

"Have you ever been in the vicarage?"

"No, I never. What for would I go in there? Two women living there, two Asiatics? Asians they call them now, but Asiatics is what they are. Coloured and got black hair, dressed-up like in fancy dress. Now can I have a lawyer? How many times do I have to ask?"

"Not any more," said Burden. "What do you want one for? I'm not going to arrest you. You can go. But," he added in a magisterial tone, "we shall talk again in the not-too-far-distant future."

Meanwhile, Lynn had spoken to Thora Kilmartin on the phone and been told that she was coming to Kingsmarkham in two days' time to meet Clarissa at Georgina Bray's. She had met Georgina in the past, and Georgina had been in touch with her. Reading between the lines or between the sentences, Lynn got the impression that Georgina was anxious that Clarissa should continue to stay with her.

"But Clarissa's still at school. She's at school now. And with her A-levels next summer it would be very wrong for her to miss classes."

Lynn had just terminated the call when another came in, from Wexford. Did Lynn know about the Congolese community living in Stowerton, members of which had apparently attended St. Peter's Church services? Lynn did. She had heard from another source.

"Wouldn't you to have expected them to go to the Catholic Church?"

Lynn said in an apologetic tone that she didn't know much about religion. "I don't know anything about religion in Congo," Wexford said, "or the Democratic Republic of Congo, as I suppose I should say. A misnomer if ever there was one. But since it was once—notoriously—a Belgian colony, I thought they'd be Catholic and French-speaking."

"There's a woman in Oval Road I interviewed a few months back. Her name is Nardelie Mukamba—not the kind of name you'd forget, is it? She witnessed a burglary. I could talk to her. Would you like to come with me?"

"I would."

The area had always been poor, the little houses, ranged in terraces, originally built in the late nineteenth century, to accommodate workers in the chalk quarries and their families. Now it was run-down, the small front gardens repositories of bicycles, a couple of worn-out motorbikes, no-longer-habitable rabbit hutches and a birdcage, and the local-authority-issue bins for recyclable paper and cardboard, glass and metal, and a larger one for general rubbish. A woman in a tall turban and an elaborately pleated red-and-pink dress was dropping a couple of lager cans into the appropriate bin.

Leaving Wexford in the car, Lynn went up to

her. "Mrs. Mukamba, do you remember me? I talked to you about a break-in at number thirty."

Nardelie Mukamba looked in her midtwenties. Wexford saw that she was beautiful, her skin a deep, smooth bronze, her eyes obsidian black. He got out of the car. Lynn didn't introduce him but included him in her explanation. "We are enquiring about the murder of the vicar, Ms. Hussain. Did you ever go to her church? Did you ever go to St. Peter's, Kingsmarkham?"

Her reply came in fluent English with that accent which most British people recognise as African, as distinct from Caribbean.

"Me and my children went there most Sundays."

"Did you ever speak to the Reverend Hussain."

"I shook hands with her. Everyone did. When you'd been two, three times she kissed you. She said, 'Welcome to God's house.' She made you feel you were a guest in the home of the Lord, and that was nice. My boy Jean-Jacques and my boy Aristide, they loved her. She let them run around the church during the service and there was a woman who complained. Sarah—she asked us to call her that—she said, 'We must all love the little children because our Lord told us to.' " Nardelie looked at Wexford and smiled, a divine smile, he thought it was, warm, wide, and showing those glorious teeth it had become an unwelcome cliché to remark on.

For a few minutes he and Lynn sat in the car

outside Nardelie's house, waiting for what he didn't know, if they were waiting. A couple who looked as if they were Congolese came along and went into the house next door, and then a tall white man, quite young, but who reminded Wexford of someone much older. He too went up to the front door of Nardelie's and stood there, apparently searching for his key. He was wearing gloves but took the right one off to feel in his pocket, exposing a dark-blue-and-red tattoo covering the back of his hand. Wexford could just make out a female figure in a robe, but he saw the man hastily put the glove back on once he had got the door open.

"Yes, I saw him here before," Lynn said. "He lives in Nardelie's place."

"Her husband? Partner? Boyfriend?"

"I don't know, but somehow I think he's just a tenant of the top floor. What do you think of tattoos, sir?"

Wexford laughed. "I don't like them. But you could have guessed that, Lynn, without asking."

He had to refuse her invitation to come back with her that afternoon, reminding her that one of them was due to meet Thora Kilmartin.

"Would you do that, Reg?" she asked, making a real effort.

It was the first time she had obeyed him and called him by what Sarah Hussain would no doubt have called his Christian name.

"Of course. And I'll record our conversation—if she'll let me."

Two women of comparable age and education, both middle-class and belonging to the same ethnic group, could scarcely have looked more disparate. Haggard, with the kind of thinness that is due to stress, Georgina Bray looked no older than her midforties, but an unhealthy midforties, strained and tired. But she had made a sartorial effort for these guests with what Wexford would once have known as an afternoon dress, burgundy-coloured and too short, and high-heeled court shoes her fidgeting feet told Wexford she would like to shed. Thora Kilmartin, on the other hand, was fat. No two ways about it, she wasn't overweight or plump or any of the other euphemisms. She was uncompromisingly fat and apparently happy to be so. He had seldom seen a woman who looked so pleasantly contented. She was appropriately dressed in a tweed skirt, beige jumper, and dark brown cardigan, no jewellery but her wedding ring, brown, lace-up brogues, her sole frivolity lacy but thick, brown tights.

It was Clarissa's half-term break and she was out with a friend. She would soon be back but they wouldn't wait tea for her. Now Wexford was here she would make coffee.

"Or would you prefer tea?"

He had lately noticed that, with the advance of age, people often assumed that tea would be his drink, the pensioner's beverage of choice. "Coffee will be fine."

Much as he had hoped to get Thora Kilmartin alone, he realised that the time Mrs. Bray took to bring in the coffee, even if she had to grind the beans before brewing the drink, would be inadequate for his purposes. In his position, as the rather absurdly named crime solutions adviser (unpaid), he could hardly banish Georgina from her own living room. The question he most wanted to ask, but not in front of Clarissa or, come to that, Mrs. Bray, might have to be put on hold until another time.

Thora was waiting, smiling as she looked round the room, evidently admiring her surroundings. "Lovely house, isn't it?"

"Very nice, yes." It was the same vintage as his own, one of a number of houses, detached, four-bedroomed, which had been built soon after the Second World War. "Mrs. Kilmartin, I have to tell you I have read the letter you wrote to Ms. Hussain last July."

"She kept it then?"

"As a bookmark in the book she was reading at the time of her death. I think that shows it meant a lot to her."

"Perhaps."

"Did she reply?"

79

"To my letter? Oh, yes, she did. We lived rather too far apart to drop in on each other. I invited her to come and stay in the summer holidays, but she said it would be too hard for her to get a locum—or whatever they call them in the church. She invited me but my husband wasn't keen. He has an idea of a female clergyperson as a formidable woman." She laughed and Wexford did too, though Mr. Kilmartin's view wasn't far from his own. A lot of people had disapproved of poor Sarah Hussain, and all of them men. "Still, we talked on the phone and made definite plans to meet. I was anxious to see Clarissa. She was a baby when I last saw her."

Here was his opportunity to ask the awkward or intrusive question, but Georgina Bray chose the moment to return with the coffee.

"Clarissa will be here at any moment," she said, "so I brought a cup for her. Do go on talking. I promise I won't listen. I'll be deep in my book."

But as she opened *Pride and Prejudice* at a point halfway through, fiction recently become as popular as contemporary chick lit, he heard the front door close and Clarissa came in. In the current culture, she was too old for school uniform and wore a knee-length grey skirt, white blouse, and grey-and-burgundy blazer. Thora got up, said how glad she was to meet her at last, and they shook hands. Thora looked as if she would have liked to kiss the girl and even leant a little towards her, but there must have been something in Clarissa's eyes or an almost imperceptible flinching which told her not to touch. The kind of small talk which Wexford could have himself composed word for word ensued.

After a few minutes of this Georgina got up and said, "Come along, Clarissa. I've got something upstairs I want to show you."

"What sort of something?"

Wexford was reminded of a scene from the very book Georgina had been reading where Mrs. Bennet takes her daughters away to allow a visitor privacy to propose to the daughter who remains. The daughters react much as Clarissa had done, and Mrs. Bray much as Mrs. Bennet.

"You'll soon see. Come along now."

The girl went with her, and Wexford thought it just as well the Bray children were grown-up and gone or she would have been shepherding a flock to some nonexistent treat. Thora Kilmartin looked as if she shared his amusement, but her face with its perpetual half smile suddenly saddened as he said he wanted to ask her something about Sarah Hussain's life when they lived together.

"You know you don't have to talk to me, Mrs. Kilmartin. I'm no longer a police officer."

She nodded. "I know that. But there are things I'd like to tell you about Sarah, and I think I can be pretty sure nothing I tell you will be made public."

"It will not," Wexford said firmly. He felt a little surge of excitement at the prospect of something interesting or out of the ordinary at last. "I was going to ask you if I might record this conversation, but I've changed my mind. Even at my age I've got a pretty good memory."

That made her smile. "Thank you."

"First, tell me if I've got these facts right. Sarah's husband died in a car crash. They hadn't been married very long so Sarah and perhaps both of them were very young?"

"That's right. Sarah had come down from university with, incidentally, a very good honours degree. Her husband, Leo, was a couple of years older. I didn't know her then of course. They lived in Basingstoke and were married in church there. She got herself a qualification in teaching English to foreign students and found herself some private pupils. She was bilingual, you know, Urdu was as much her first language as English was. Leo was a landscape architect. It sounds quite grand but she told me he didn't earn very much, though he would have done if he'd lived, apparently. But he didn't live."

"What happened?"

"He was driving his father's car on some motorway. His father was sitting beside him. They had been to a football match. It was foggy and there was one of those sudden pileups. Leo had been the end of the queue, and a lorry came up behind him going much too fast. It crashed into the back of their car, destroying the entire back and forcing the front seats so far into the car in front that it came out the other end. Apparently Leo and his father were killed instantly. Leo was only twenty-eight, Sarah a widow at just twenty-six."

Wexford didn't interrupt. He let her continue, soon realising that Burden's version of Sarah's life had got things out of order.

"Left alone, she went to India—Darjeeling, it was—to live with her grandmother, her father's mother. There was an uncle and an aunt and several cousins already living there. Grandmother was quite well-off and it was a large, comfortable compound."

"That was before Clarissa was born?"

It was a slightly different story from the one Burden had. "Oh, yes." Thora's tone had become weary, almost grim. "Sarah had gone to India originally with an aid agency, but she couldn't stand some of the sights she saw, the poverty, the disease. She had some sort of breakdown and took refuge with the grandmother. She stayed there for two years. After that Sarah said she felt she needed to earn her own living, she couldn't go on living on the grandmother's charity, though the old lady was perfectly willing to support her, would have done so, I gathered, for the rest of her life."

Wexford calculated that Sarah Hussain must by this time have been twenty-eight or twenty-nine. "She came back here?"

"She got a job teaching at Bridgwell Comprehensive. I was teaching history there, we got to know each other, became friends, and shared a flat. Sarah met a man she liked, the first man in her life since her husband died. I suppose you'll want to know his name?"

"He was Clarissa's father?"

"Oh, no. Unfortunately, no. Sarah was—well, not prudish or strict, but let's say she wouldn't have lived with a man without marriage."

"Then, how . . ."

Thora said almost brutally, "She was raped. Clarissa is the result of rape."

At this point Georgina Bray put her head round the door and said in a curiously coquettish tone, "Have you finished with all your secrets? Can Clarissa and I come back now?"

7

Wexford was wondering how and where he could prolong this interview when Thora Kilmartin came to his rescue. "Oh, Georgina, I think I told you earlier that I haven't yet looked in at the Olive and Dove hotel where I'm staying tonight. I wonder if Mr. Wexford would be kind enough to give me a lift there? I think it may be on his way."

Wexford said, of course, it would be a pleasure. "And since you and Clarissa will be having dinner with me tonight, perhaps you'll meet me there at seven?"

At the wheel, he didn't speak. He was sure she would if he kept silent for a moment or two and he was right.

"We were talking about the awful thing that happened to Sarah."

"Did she report it to the police?"

"When she told me, I wanted her to but she wouldn't. She said she couldn't face the questions and the—well, the doctor examining her. And if it came to court, that would be impossible. I think she thought she could forget it, just put it out of her head. But she couldn't because she found she was pregnant. I tell you frankly I wanted her to have an abortion. It was the obvious thing to do, but she wouldn't. She wouldn't take a life, she said. The man she was going out with left her. He refused to believe her story, said she'd invented the rape when she found she was pregnant. I think she was well rid of him.

"Then she said a funny thing. She was crying, she cried a lot at the time, she said the rapist was young and quite good-looking and an *Asian*. I asked her what difference that made, and she said, at least it might be a beautiful baby. And it was."

"Poor woman," Wexford said, a comment he wouldn't have made in these circumstances when he was a policeman. He drove onto the forecourt of the Olive and Dove, parked in the last marked space. "And that was Clarissa. Why the name?" Another remark he wouldn't have made.

"Oh, because she spent a good deal of the pregnancy reading Richardson's *Clarissa*. She loved it. In a way it's about rape, I suppose. It's the most boring novel I've ever read."

Wexford had enjoyed it but he said nothing. "What happened next?"

"Well, of course, she loved the child. She adored her. They were with me until Clarissa was about four. Sarah supported herself and the child by teaching English to foreign students and translating Urdu and Hindi into English for non-English-speaking immigrants. People from India and Pakistan may be able to talk to their neighbours but can't read forms and instruction books and so on. You'd be surprised."

"No, I wouldn't. There can't be much money in it."

"There isn't. Most of the time, anyway, she wouldn't let them pay her. She had to go back to teaching and she did once Clarissa was old enough to go to school. By then she had moved away, and the last address I had for her was somewhere in Essex. She had a teaching job there."

Wexford said, "I don't want to keep you but there are a few more details I'd like to have."

"You aren't keeping me. I've nothing else to do but hang about here waiting for Georgina and Clarissa to come at seven. Why don't you come in and let me give you tea?"

For all the years he had worked in Kings-markham, Wexford had been a habitué of the Olive and Dove. He had seen it change from a typical English country hotel where people, driving through on their way to the south coast, could stop without booking ahead and eat in a sunlit dining room a heavy lunch of soup, roast lamb, lemon-meringue pie, and cheese and biscuits, to what it was today: smart, four-starred, every bedroom with an en suite bathroom, TV, a computer, and a basket of exotic fruits. Over the years the public bar had gone, the "snug" had gone, and the all-pervading cigarette smoke had gone. Food was available almost round the clock, and wine from New Zealand had to a great extent replaced beer and spirits. But as with so many public buildings today, from shops to cathedrals, deconstruction and construction work was going on. The hallway they passed through was apparently about to lose its lift, with a new one to replace it. Much of the area was boarded off, but as he passed, Wexford caught a glimpse of the discarded lift waiting, it seemed, to be taken away to the dump or landfill. The manufacturer's name on it was one he had recently come across in another context: Cuthbert and Son.

As a waitress was bringing the tea things to their table, Wexford reflected that though he had probably drunk gallons of wine, beer, and (once) whisky in this place, he had never before drunk tea here. Regretfully, he declined one of the pink, blue, and purple meringues or the chocolate marzipan slices. Thora Kilmartin, overweight though she was, didn't hesitate but helped herself to a blue meringue.

"If you're happy to go on talking about Sarah," Wexford began, "I'll ask you if you can remember the name of her boyfriend, the man who left when she found she was pregnant."

"It so happens that I can. It was the same as

mine. Oh, not Kilmartin, nowhere near as distinguished. My maiden name, Watson. His name was Gerald Watson, known as Gerry."

"I know it would be too much to ask if you know what the rapist was called?"

"It would be. He wasn't someone Sarah knew. But she had seen him before and she knew where he lived. It was in a flat in a newish, rather expensive block called Quercum Court, quite near where my husband and I live now. But that was all, and I think he moved away very soon after the rape. Maybe he suspected that Sarah would go to the police, I don't know, but he disappeared, and of course I was glad for Sarah's sake. Imagine having him around when she knew he was the father of her child."

Wexford tried to imagine it but found this too difficult a feat. "And Gerald Watson? Do you know his whereabouts?"

"He was younger than Sarah," Thora said ruminatively, as if she were probing her recollections. "About five years younger. He lived at home with his parents. A great mistake, I always think, if you're over twenty. He used to come to the flat to take Sarah out. The evening of the rape they were going out together, they were going to a concert. But he phoned and said he couldn't come, he had to stay at home with his mother, who was upset over the death of a neighbour who had been killed in a road accident. I know. Can you imagine? That's what comes of staying tied to your mother's apron strings. Sarah went alone."

"And that was when she was raped?"

"As you say. That was when she was raped."

"What did he do for a living?"

"He was a solicitor."

"How close was the relationship? I suppose he stayed in your flat over weekends and he and Sarah went away on holiday together?"

"Oh, no, you're wrong there. Sarah wouldn't have had that. I can see I haven't made it plain to you how deeply *moral* Sarah was. Absolutely out-of-date, more like someone living sixty years ago than in the present. She wouldn't have had—well, sexual relations with a man until she was married to him. I don't even know if she and Gerry Watson intended to marry." Thora helped herself to a chocolate marzipan slice. "I wish you'd eat something."

Wexford shook his head. "You said in your letter to her that you weren't surprised when you heard she'd been ordained. You expected it?"

"Not exactly that. It was more that she was always religious and she had high principles. In that way you could say that the rapist, the *handsome Asian,* picked on the most vulnerable and innocent woman he could have. No, perhaps not innocent but very vulnerable. She always saw the best in people but she knew about the worst. I would like to have heard one of her sermons, and it's too late now."

"Would you be surprised to hear she had a boyfriend? Strange word for a middle-aged man but that's what I was told."

"I'd be surprised to hear they had a sexual relationship."

Burden sounded very much more interested in Gerald Watson than Wexford had been. He must be found. He might be that significant figure from Sarah Hussain's past that they were all looking for. It was a phone conversation and Burden had seized upon Gerald Watson before Wexford had reached the rape.

"No, we'll find him," Burden said with that confidence not only in the Internet but in Kingsmarkham Crime Management team's ability to carry out the search. The confidence was common to people twenty or even ten years younger than Wexford. He, for his part, was just about able to get hold of Google and somewhat shakily direct it to produce information.

"You're thinking an ex-boyfriend would bear a grudge like that over eighteen years? Enough to have killed her?"

"I just want to talk to him, get the picture. According to Dennis Cuthbert there was a current boyfriend. If so, where is he? Why has no one else mentioned him? We must meet."

They fixed on two days later for lunch, Wexford reserving the rest of Sarah and Clarissa's story till Wednesday. He returned to Gibbon and the martyrdom of St. Cyprian. *It is not easy to extract any distinct ideas from the vague though eloquent declamations of the Fathers, or to ascertain the degree of immortal glory and happiness which they confidently promised to those who were so fortunate as to shed their blood in the cause of religion. They inculcated with becoming diligence that the fire of martyrdom supplied every defect and expiated every sin; that while the souls of ordinary Christians were obliged to pass through a slow and painful purification, the triumphant sufferers entered into the immediate fruition of eternal bliss. . . .*

"Thirty grand?" said Fiona. "You have to be kidding me."

"You've got it. You told me. You've got more than that invested."

"And that's where it stays, invested."

"It'd still be invested," said Jeremy, "invested in property everyone knows can't lose. It's a nice little house, I looked over it this morning and I reckon I could ask five hundred a week rent."

"*You* could? Who's going to pay the mortgage? Me?"

"I could pay it out of the rent."

"I'm not going to let you have it, Jeremy, I'm just not. It's no good asking me anymore. We do all right as we are, we don't need another property. What's the matter now? Why that face?"

Jeremy's face had fallen into gloomy lines and his lips protruded. "I've heard from Diane."

"So?"

"It's not the best of news."

"What is it?"

"She's split up from Brett and she wants to come home to live. It was all in this e-mail came this morning."

Fiona sat down. "I don't see why that's bad news. So she's split up with Brett. She's not your wife, Jeremy, she hasn't been your wife for ages. What's it to you?"

"That place in Peck Road is hers. That house where Jason Sams lives, she's the tenant, not me. She'll want to live in it."

"Oh, come on. Ever since she left you for that Brett, she's been living in the lap of luxury. Why would she want to live on a council estate?"

"It's not what she wants, Fi, it's what she can get. It's a house and she's the tenant. We lived there, her and me, until she left." He added, "But you know all that," as if claiming virtue for telling Fiona the truth, perhaps a rare occurrence.

Fiona considered what he'd said. "Good thing you've got me to support you, isn't it? What about the other place where you lived with your mum? Maybe that really belongs to Mr. and Mrs. Patel, does it?"

Jeremy didn't answer. There was no need to. He

knew it was one of those questions that weren't meant to be answered, that were meant to be clever. Maybe Fiona would give him the money if she got pregnant. She'd be so happy that she'd do anything for him. Or that was his theory. But when would that be? Possibly months or even years, and meanwhile someone else would buy that house in Ladysmith Road. Another worry was the house in Peck Road. If he told Diane that he'd been letting her house, the chances are she would tell him to get rid of those tenants, who should never have been there in the first place. And she would tell him in no uncertain terms. Why did he always have to get involved with domineering women? The reason was obvious, even to him, so he didn't dwell on it.

On the other hand she might take on the tenants herself. What Fiona said was probably true: after what she'd been used to, Diane wouldn't want to live on a council estate and would rent somewhere else for herself. He would have to find out what her plans were. Jeremy was not skilled with the computer, but he could just about reply to an e-mail or send a new one. Replying was the easier way. *Hi Diane,* he keyed in. *What do you want done re Peck Rd?* Telling her he had let her house wasn't going to be easy at all. Maybe instead he could say he was living there. One of the best things about e-mails was that the recipient couldn't tell where they came from. He had never told her about Fiona or the cottage or even his mother's death. He continued, *Let me know when you arrive in UK. I could meet you at Gatwick.* It was the nearest London airport to Kingsmarkham, and flights came in from Spain all the time. He didn't want to have to go there, he never really wanted to go anywhere, but anything was preferable to having her turn up in Peck Road in a taxi. He didn't end with *love* or even *yours* but simply *Jeremy,* put his finger onto SEND, and pressed.

It seemed to him, though he could hardly have said why, that it would be careless of him just to ignore the house in Peck Road until he heard from Diane. He ought to be keeping an eye on it. He ought to go there even if he did nothing more than look. Jeremy's life was generally calm and uneventful. His wants were catered for by Fiona, he was fed, his limited sexual needs were satisfied, no one interfered with his television watching or expected him to get up early or wear a tie or get his hair cut. He had never been a drinker, he didn't like the taste, but when something happened to disturb the equilibrium of his existence, he took a couple of swigs of strong spirits, brandy sometimes or, a recent discovery, grappa. That rare something had happened now and he swallowed a gulp or two of brandy straight from the bottle, shuddering afterwards at the taste.

Fiona had gone to work in her car. Jeremy got

into his, not deterred by having drunk what amounted to a wineglassful of brandy. It cheered him up and that was all that mattered. It moved him from a state of mild anxiety to something not far from one of his fugues. He sat in the driving seat, feeling calm and a bit sleepy, but that passed after a few minutes and he was more than capable of driving over to the Muriel Campden Estate. Parked a short way down Peck Road, he had a clear view of Diane's house. For some unknown reason, he had expected to find it changed by what had happened, as if its appearance might have been altered by her decision or as if it might not even be there anymore. But it was just the same; even that cracked windowpane was still covered up in cardboard and sticky tape.

There was no sign of Jason Sams or his wife, girlfriend, whatever she was, but the front door opened, and Jason Sams's mother came out with the little girl in a pushchair. How fast they grew, Jeremy thought rather gloomily. Last time he'd seen her she'd been a baby. Perhaps if Diane made them move out, they would go and live with Mrs. Sams. It would be cheaper. He drifted into a half fugue, half dream, in which Diane was handing over a cheque for a thousand pounds to Jason Sams to persuade him to leave and, inexplicably, thirty thousand to him, Jeremy, to put down a deposit on that house in Ladysmith Road.

A pounding on the car window brought him to

full consciousness. "You're on residents' parking," said an angry voice belonging to a bull-necked man with a shaven head. "Get off outa here."

Jason obeyed in silence.

It was one of their less successful lunches. For one thing, it was in a Japanese restaurant, and while Burden loved Japanese cuisine, Wexford, who had only had it once before, hated it, especially sushi. Burden, who had never been like this in the past, Wexford thought, once or twice told him how good for him it was.

"I don't believe anything you don't like can be good for you."

Burden made no reply. After taking apart a square of sushi that looked to Wexford like a liquorice allsort, white and black with a green blob at its centre, Burden said that their visit to the Congolese people in Stowerton had been "a waste of time."

"Oh, I don't know. I had a talk with Nardelie and I thought of going back there."

"Don't bother. Lynn went back and no one could tell her anything. Several of them had been to St. Peter's, but apart from shaking hands with her when the service was over, they had no contact."

Wexford had already given Burden a condensed account of his conversation with Thora Kilmartin but had left out the rape and its consequence. It wasn't that he didn't trust his friend or think him anything but an excellent officer; still, he suspected Burden might be one of those policemen who would say of a woman who had been sexually assaulted that she had been asking for it or that, talking as she did, dressing as she did, she got what she deserved. Wexford was wrong.

A dark flush reddened Burden's face. "My God, and Clarissa was the result? Why on earth did she keep the child? Now that women can more or less have abortions on demand and especially in rape cases, what possessed her?"

"I suppose she wanted a child," Wexford said mildly.

"We've found Gerald Watson, or we've found where he is. Vine's going to see him tomorrow. You can go with him if you like. No sign of the current boyfriend. But rape—it's appalling. Why didn't she come to us? But, no, I know why. Eighteen years ago police officers were still very sexist, still blaming rape victims. Sarah Hussain doesn't strike me as the sort of woman who could have willingly stood up in court and described what had happened to her."

"I doubt if any woman would like it."

"Did you gather she knew her rapist?"

"Thora Kilmartin says Sarah told her he was Asian and very good-looking. She also knew where he lived in Reading. In a block of flats called Quercum Court Thora described as newish and rather expensive, but he moved from there soon after. But, Mike, are you really thinking of him as a suspect? Why would a rapist who hadn't been charged or appeared in court or even been caught want to kill his victim?"

Burden said nothing but pushed his half-empty plate away. "It's not like me, but it's made me feel sick, this rape thing." He drank some water. "What we don't know is if she ever met him again, if, for instance, they got to know each other. Does Clarissa know the circumstances of her conception and birth? Does she know who her father is?" Burden picked up the menu, looked at it with something near distaste. "Do you want any more to eat?"

"I don't think so. Mike, would you feel like broaching this subject with Clarissa? I certainly don't. Do you think Lynn could or Karen?"

"You mean, find out how much her mother told her and take it from there?"

"I suppose so," said Wexford.

"We might be able to find him without troubling the girl. There can't have been many Asians in Reading—not *then*—living in an expensive block of flats, and we do know the name of the block."

"I know how you feel, Mike," Wexford said rather sadly, "but you know yourself you can't really proceed with this line of enquiry without talking to the girl first." He hazarded a small, not very successful joke. "If I wasn't retired, I'd be minded to charge you with wasting police time."

8

Like most women of her age, Fiona Morrison was unwilling to face that the cessation of her periods, two of them absent now, might mean the onset of the menopause. She did face it reluctantly for a couple of days, and then she bought a pregnancy test. It was still a surprise and a welcome one to discover that she was expecting a baby in less than seven months' time. She was, as she put it when telling Jeremy the good news, on the crest of a wave. Though aware that most women in her situation don't find it necessary to reward the begetter, Fiona felt an enormous and unexpected gratitude to Jeremy. She had begun to feel in the previous weeks that her partner was a useless kind of man, not much good for anything except rather shady property deals and rent collecting. Now she saw that he could be a progenitor and she decided to reward him. After all, she would benefit as well. After the crest of a wave had given place to cloud nine and she had given Jeremy a good many hugs and kisses, she told him he could have the thirty thousand for the house in Ladysmith Road.

Before he knew of his good fortune—by which he meant the money rather than the coming child —Jeremy had visited the estate agent and been to look over the house. It was in better condition than he had expected, with a new kitchen and a quite respectable bathroom. He could easily and cheaply get a bunch of local cowboys to paint the place inside. He told the estate agent he would think about it and went home, where another e-mail from Diane awaited him. She was postponing her return as she'd been invited to spend a month in the Algarve, but she would be back—she had already booked a flight from Faro on November 30. There would be no need for him to meet her as she had arranged with a friend to pick her up at Gatwick and drive her to Peck Road.

Jeremy always appreciated postponements. When something was put off, some event and possibly a good one often intervened to change things pleasantly. November 30 was a long way off. Having called the estate agent back to offer ten thousand below the asking price, he sat on the sofa in front of a recording of *The X Factor* to await the outcome.

Gerald Watson was a notary public as well as a solicitor, and when Barry Vine and Wexford arrived at his office in Stevenage, his client was swearing to the facts set out in a film contract. This was far more interesting than his usual line of work, as he explained when excusing himself for keeping them waiting. His affability declined sharply when Vine told him that while he was a detective inspector, Wexford no longer held any rank, was retired, and accompanied him only in his capacity as an adviser.

"I wouldn't have thought a DI needed an adviser," Watson said in a cold tone. "Not that I know what this visit is about. I hope the local police know and permit it."

Wexford said in as pleasant a tone as he could manage that they did.

"Something was said on the phone about the murder of a vicar. What connection I can have with that I really don't know."

"You don't read newspapers or watch television, Mr. Watson?"

"I'm far too busy." Belatedly, Watson asked them to sit down. "I don't suppose I've read a newspaper for ten years."

"The vicar in question was the Reverend Sarah Hussain," said Vine, "incumbent of St. Peter's, Kingsmarkham."

Wexford had expected an astonished reaction. There was nothing, no change of colour to that bland, smooth face, no sudden frown, no gasp. Gerald Watson said slowly, as if making an effort to recall, "I once knew a Sarah Hussain, perhaps eighteen or nineteen years ago. I was living in Reading at the time. It can't be the same one, this woman was a teacher. You say the woman who was killed was a *vicar?*"

Vine glanced at Wexford, but Wexford shook his head, leaving it to the policeman to speak. It was better that way. "That's right, sir. Miss Hussain took holy orders about five years ago. She was living in Kingsmarkham with her daughter, Clarissa, aged seventeen."

Now Watson reacted. He got to his feet, stood in silence staring at Vine, and then sat down again. Sat down heavily, said, "I don't hold with women clergy. They'll be having women bishops next."

Vine ignored this. But Wexford registered silently, another one. "So you had had no contact with the Reverend Sarah Hussain since you last saw her eighteen years ago in Reading?"

"I've told you so."

In fact, he hadn't. Now Wexford did speak, but again in a courteous tone. "Was your parting from Miss Hussain eighteen years ago amicable, sir?"

Watson's look seemed to say that since Wexford wasn't a police officer, he had no business asking questions. He turned his small, grey eyes on Vine and said, "A daughter, did you say?"

"A daughter aged seventeen called Clarissa. You didn't know?"

"Seeing I haven't seen Sarah Hussain for eighteen years, obviously not. And whether our parting was amicable is irrelevant. It was and is private."

"This is a murder enquiry, sir. In such an investigation nothing can be called private."

"For God's sake, I haven't seen the woman for nearly twenty years." In twenty years the human voice doesn't change much, Wexford thought. If it was grating and harsh with a tinny undertone now, so it would have been then. The grey eyes had turned on him, and their expression seemed to show that Watson was reading his thoughts. We shall be getting grumbles to the Police Complaints Commission or I'm a chief constable. "Is that all?"

"Not quite, sir," said Vine. "Perhaps you won't mind telling us where you were during the afternoon of Thursday, October the eleventh."

"I would mind very much," said Watson. "And now I refuse to answer any more questions."

He would probably have adhered to this resolve if his silence when Vine asked him if he had ever visited Kingsmarkham was anything to go by. He spoke once more to say, "That's enough."

When they were outside with the prospect of a long drive from Stevenage to Kingsmarkham before them, Vine said, "I don't believe he didn't know Sarah Hussain was murdered or that she was a vicar, do you?"

"Certainly not," said Wexford. "He knew. But why pretend?"

"He's a lawyer," Vine said gloomily. "I hate having to question lawyers. They're always too bloody clever by half."

"He wasn't."

"No, but he thought he was. Would you mind if I played some bits from *The Daughter of the Regiment* on the way back?" Vine was well-known to be passionately fond of Donizetti.

"Mind? I'd love it."

"There's some dodgy things goes on when it comes to property," said Maxine in her conversational-rather-confrontational style, leaning on her mop handle in the fashion of a maid in a Noël Coward comedy. "Now it turns out that that man Legg never had no right to rent that place in Peck Road to my Jason. It don't belong to him, it don't even belong to his wife, it's council property, and it's a well-known fact you can't rent out what you're renting yourself. Jason never knew. Why would he? Now the wife as was—they was divorced—is coming back from Spain and wants to live there. In Jason's place in Peck Road, I mean. 'Don't think you and Nicky and Isabella can move in with me,' I said to him, 'not while I've got your three sisters at home.' But he said it wouldn't come to that as Legg had plans for another place they could go into. 'And where might that be?' I said. 'Ladysmith Road,' he said. 'It's not ready yet,' he said, 'but it soon will be, and if you go in there, you'll see it's a hundred times better than Peck Road.' Anyway, there's bound to be a drawback somewhere, I said. There's always a fly in the ointment. 'Yes, well, there is, Mum,' he says. 'The rent's a lot higher. But there's three bedrooms,' he says, 'and if Nicky has another one, we're going to need them.' . . ."

Dora had come into the room by this time. Her husband appeared stupefied, his head sinking against the arm of the sofa and his eyes closing. She spoke in her clearest, briskest voice, "Well, that seems to be having a happy outcome, then. Perhaps you'd like to do the dining-room windows before you go."

"All right, I'm going to. No problem. I just wanted to pass all that on to Mr. Wexford. It's sort of in his line, isn't it? I mean, there's fraud in it somewhere and cheating the council and all sorts of things what shouldn't go on. I thought he'd see his way to doing something about it or telling those as can. . . ."

Wexford woke up, sat up, resisted saying that he wasn't asleep but had heard everything Maxine said. Rather wildly as he made his escape, he called out that he was on his way to passing it all on to those who could do something about it. Out in the street, getting into his car, he saw that he was almost late. He had just seven minutes to get to this conference Burden was calling to survey what progress was being made in the Sarah

Hussain investigation. There would be little attention paid to Jason Sams's problems.

A greatly enlarged photograph of Sarah was pinned to the notice board, and with Karen Malahyde seated at the computer, a clearer and more recent one appeared on the screen. The rather gaunt face and the deep-set eyes that lay in hollows of shadow expressed a powerful intelligence. Wexford, as a committed atheist, had long ago passed through that phase of pondering on the anomaly—for it had seemed an anomaly to him—of brilliant intellectuals finding it possible, indeed imperative, to believe in God. Notable figures, the pope, the archbishop of Canterbury, theologians, this woman. He had long come to accept it. They saw or understood or grasped what was denied him. Nor did they ever seem to be turned away from their religious faith when bad things happened to them but rather to see it as strengthened. Sarah Hussain had suffered from the sight of poverty in what was her country as well as England was, had lost a man she had presumably loved, had been raped, had given birth to a child who was the result of that rape, and had, still committed to God, been murdered. No doubt, she had died sending her soul to God.

He realised that he had missed a lot of what was being said. Still, he had heard it all before, knew that Burden still had a sneaking hankering after Duncan Crisp, the gardener, his suspicions wandering sometimes to Dennis Cuthbert, the vicar's warden, but was more firmly fixed on those two men who had played known and dramatic parts in Sarah Hussain's life of eighteen years before.

"We are not going to identify any recognisable sort of motive here," Burden was saying. "And searching for a motive, such as jealousy or envy or gain, is only going to hinder any progress we're making. You, Lynn, suggested that you couldn't see what possible motive Gerald Watson, for instance, could have had." Burden paused and the picture on the screen changed from Sarah to a head-and-shoulders image of Watson. Where on earth did that come from? Wexford asked himself, almost immediately answering that, these days, by means of technology, you could get hold of pictures of almost anyone you wanted to. "Well, I'm saying is that it doesn't matter," Burden went on. "Human nature is so strange and the human mind so diverse that although a perpetrator will have a motive, it may be so obscure as to be totally hidden from us, buried deep, so to speak, in his psyche." Wexford, having never heard Burden speak in these terms before, was impressed but still dubious as to where this might be leading.

"This, I believe, is the case with Watson. Barry will have something to say about this shortly.

Before that, I'd just add that our prime goal today and maybe for days is to find the Asian man, last seen in Reading eighteen years ago, who raped Sarah Hussain and is the father of Clarissa Hussain. But there again, when we find him, we are not looking for motive or speculating what that motive might be."

Burden sat down. In that coffee-coloured suit and coffee-and-silver tie, he really was, Wexford thought, "the glass wherein the noble youth did dress themselves." Or should have been if this scruffy lot lounging at desks had ever thought of following his example. Barry was one of the worst, the pockets of his imitation-leather jacket swollen and split from carrying too many Donizetti CDs about. And I'm as bad, he reflected, in my twenty-year-old suit and open-necked shirt.

Barry was speaking now, airing a theory he had said nothing about on their way back from Stevenage. Watson, he believed, had been obsessed with Sarah Hussain all those years, nursing a bitter resentment. Such an obsession, fuelled with hatred, could easily have culminated in a determination to kill her. Vine, Wexford thought, seemed to have forgotten all about Burden's instruction to his team to forget about motive. The image on the screen changed to a kind of chart with Sarah Hussain's name and photograph in the middle of it and various arrows radiating out from it to the names of Georgina

109

Bray, Thora Kilmartin, Duncan Crisp, Dennis Cuthbert, Gerald Watson, and, to use Burden's soubriquet for him, Ahmed X. Clarissa's name was absent, but when the chart disappeared her face, so beautiful and film-star-ish, filled the screen.

Burden turned to Wexford and asked him if he had anything to contribute. "Not now," Wexford said, and when he found himself alone with his friend, "I see the apologetic racism is still going strong and not so apologetic."

"What on earth do you mean?"

"Ahmed X."

"Are you saying I'm to be deferential to a rapist who was probably an illegal immigrant?"

Wexford's smile turned into a burst of laughter. "Is there any coffee going in this place?"

"Come upstairs with me and we'll send for some."

Burden sulked for a while, said when the coffee came, "There's no pleasing you," and stirred two lumps of sugar into his cup. "Lynn's talking to Clarissa now."

"Still half term, is it?"

"I suppose so. She's going to ask her about her father. Ask her if she knows who he is. Lynn's the best person for the job. I'm glad I haven't got to do it."

"Me too," said Wexford, reestablishing their amicable relationship.

9

Diane Stow's homecoming was no longer such a long way off. Fiona wanted to know what had happened to the furniture and equipment which had been in the house in Peck Road when Diane moved out. Or, more to the point, when Jeremy moved out about a year later and in with her.

"We've got some of it here." Jeremy found the whole business profoundly boring. "That table over there, and wasn't there a microwave?"

"There was," said Fiona, "but you put a tin plate in it and buggered the thing up."

"I left a lot there for Jason and what's her name."

"Only they'll take stuff with them, and what happens when Diane comes home and finds she hasn't got a bed to sleep in?"

"I'll think about it. Hush up a minute, will you? I'm watching *The Voice*."

Relations between Clarissa Hussain and Georgina Bray were far from good. Clarissa would stay until Christmas, or maybe until Christmas was over, she told Lynn Fancourt, but after that . . .

"I'm supposed to go to Mrs. Kilmartin, but how can I go to school from where she lives? I've got to go to school, I've got my A-levels next summer. Why can't I live on my own? I can, I'm over sixteen and in January I'll be over eighteen. Why can't I?"

Lynn was nonplussed. This wasn't at all what she had anticipated when she had agreed to meet Clarissa in the café called Twice because it was situated at 200 Kingsmarkham High Street. In law, at her age, Clarissa could live on her own and where she liked, but Lynn sensed that she would be laying up trouble for herself (not to mention the girl) if she agreed with this proposition.

"Well, I suppose you could, but where?"

"In the vicarage. Why not? It's empty, no one's there. Why shouldn't I live there?"

Lynn was on firm ground there. It was a question to which she very well knew the answer. "Because the Church of England wouldn't allow it. The vicarage belongs to them, and when anything happens to the—well, the incumbent, I'm afraid they take it back. If it's a widow and child, like in your mum's case, three months, I think, they allow, but I'd have to check that."

"That's so unfair!"

Clarissa sounded—and looked, flushing deeply —so young. It wasn't unfair, of course it wasn't; it was, Lynn thought philosophically, just the way of the world. She hoped their coffee wouldn't be long in coming. This encounter wasn't going at all the way she had hoped. She had to get on to Clarissa's antecedents, but she couldn't just leave things there. "You'll be going to university next autumn, and that means you'll have somewhere to live. Meanwhile"—she knew she was ducking the issue—"we'll have to find a place for you." She retrieved things. "I'll see what I can do. I'll ask around."

Simultaneously, with the arrival of the coffee and pastries of a standard Lynn would hardly have thought Twice capable of, Clarissa burst into tears. "Why did Mum have to die?" she sobbed. "Why?"

Lynn wanted to get on, but she had to make some sort of answer, and she could only say that this was something no one knew. To Clarissa's rejoinder that God should have stopped it only God didn't exist, Lynn could only shrug and shake her head. Clarissa grabbed a handful of paper napkins and scrubbed at her eyes.

"I'll be all right now. It's just that I liked the vicarage, I *loved* it, even though Mum died there. But now I know I'll never live there with Mum again, it—well, it breaks my heart."

"I can imagine," Lynn said, though she couldn't.

She watched Clarissa reach for consolation in the shape of a chocolate éclair, then said, "I'm sorry to have to talk to you about this, but I assure you it's necessary. Do you ever see your father?"

At any rate, she hadn't shocked or even astonished the girl. "I don't know who he is."

Lynn said nothing, just continued to look enquiringly at Clarissa.

"I'll tell you everything I know, but that's not much. I think he's still alive, he may not be any older than Mum was. She said she'd tell me when I, like, got to be eighteen. That's in January, January twentieth." Clarissa turned away from Lynn, stared at the café window. A sob caught at her throat. "But I'll never get there, will I? Not for Mum." The tears came fast after and she sobbed into her hands.

Lynn gave her a tissue, then the whole packet. She would have liked to hug her, but of course she couldn't. Unreasonably perhaps, she felt suddenly angry with Sarah Hussain. Keeping the girl in the kind of suspense that might now never end. Clarissa scrubbed at her face with handfuls of tissues, took a deep breath, then gave a long sigh. Crying had made her face swell without disfiguring it.

"Go on. I'll be OK now."

Lynn thought the next question that came to mind was worth a try, though fairly hopeless. She was to be surprised.

"Gerry Watson? He was always turning up, like a stalker, I suppose you'd say."

"The solicitor? The one who lives in Stevenage? Are we talking about the same man?"

"Got a smooth, flat face and a very little mouth. Pompous."

Lynn had never seen him. "He came here? He knew who your mother was and what she did?"

"Sure."

"Tell me about him," said Lynn.

"A lot has happened since yesterday."

Those were Burden's words when he phoned Wexford and invited him to come to the police station. Wexford wanted to say sarcastically, "Not another conference?" but he restrained himself. No doubt discoveries had been made, perhaps the identity of Clarissa's father. Even if it had, what good could that be to Burden? Imagining alien motives and mind-sets, Wexford tried to picture a rapist who would kill his victim. During or immediately after the attack, yes, that was common, his motive to prevent the woman's identifying him, but eighteen years later? Because perhaps he had asked to see his daughter? Why wait all those years? A distant father or putative father might make that request when his child was a baby of two or three years old, but when she had become a woman? There might be an explanation for such behaviour (apart from paranoid

115

schizophrenia), but he couldn't think of one.

Crossing the police station forecourt, a car swept past him, stopped by a flight of steps leading to the basement, and two officers got out, followed by a handcuffed man of about twenty-five. Wexford didn't recognise him, noting only the preponderance of tattoos on exposed parts of his body: neck, upper chest, arms, and the ankles revealed by short, loose jeans. A plethora of metal was anchored to his nostrils, eyebrows, ears, and lower lip. As Wexford had often thought before, such ironmongery must be uncomfortable, and what would happen when you tried to kiss someone? Did you take it off first or was it perhaps sexually attractive? The two policemen hustled the man down the steps to the door at the foot. Behind that door were interview rooms and Kingsmarkham's two cells, for one of which the detainee was no doubt destined. The local youth, particularly the Stowerton gangs, hinted darkly that it was behind this door that the torture of suspects was carried out.

"Sometimes," he quoted to himself, "these cogitations still amaze the troubled midnight and the noon's repose." Well, it should be the noon's repose now, a pleasant after-lunch rest with Gibbon. He confessed to himself that he was quite interested in learning what Burden had found out, or what Lynn and maybe Barry had found out for him.

Burden was in his office that had once been

116

Wexford's own office, the room unchanged but for the absence of padded chairs and the rosewood desk, which was his own and which he had removed on retirement. In its place was a horror (Wexford kept this description strictly to himself) of stainless steel and expensive black plastic. More chairs than would ever be needed hung about the room, and these, also of some slippery black substance, had narrow seats and high backs with cutouts in the shape of dotless question marks. In one of these Lynn was sitting.

"Now Mr. Wexford is here," said Burden in a mildly scathing tone, "perhaps you'd like to start again, Lynn."

Wexford wasn't late. He knew he wasn't. "She calls me Reg."

Burden said nothing. His expression said for him, "She's not going to call me Mike."

"Right." Lynn looked from one to the other, as a patient mother might to her two little boys. "I didn't record the conversation I had with Clarissa Hussain. I couldn't, we were in a café. The first part of it is in my report, that's the stuff about the rapist, the man who we think may be her father. The second part—Mr. Burden said you'd like to hear it."

"Especially because you and Barry met the man, Reg." Burden seemed to have forgotten his previous irritability.

"Yes, well, I asked her if she knew a man called Watson, Gerald Watson. Frankly, I expected her to say she'd never heard of him. But she actually knew him—well, she knew him by sight. She described him to me, said he had a sort of flat face and very small eyes. She said he was pompous. Is that right?"

"Exactly right," Wexford said.

"He'd been stalking her mother or something very like it. For about six months before she died. Clarissa said he never came to the vicarage, or as far as she knew, he never did, though once he came into the garden through the back lane. She said he drove here. From Stevenage would be quite a long way. I asked her what her mother's reaction was to these visits, but she didn't really know. Was she frightened? Clarissa said no. They had once been what she called 'good friends.' Why she never invited him to the vicarage Clarissa didn't know and apparently never asked. I suppose when you're seventeen you're not interested in the friend-ships or relationships of your parents. Perhaps she did invite him, perhaps he came and Clarissa never knew. She told me her mother didn't seem in the least troubled by Watson's turning up every couple of weeks, just walking past and waving to her or sitting outside in his car till she came out and calling to her, engaging her in conversation, and that was all. It didn't worry Sarah, and because it didn't, Clarissa wasn't worried either. 'I once called him "your stalker," ' she said, 'and Mum was quite annoyed, said that was an awful thing to say about a perfectly innocent man.'"

"Do we know where he was at the relevant time?" Burden asked.

"Of the murder, sir? It's in the report."

Burden had it in front of him. "He refused to say? We shall have to see him again. Your talk with Clarissa puts things in a very different light. Perhaps he'll respond better to you, Lynn."

"You could have him in here."

"I could try. If he said no, there's nothing I could do. I think I'll go and see him myself and you could come with me. He knows you."

"Yes, and it's quite within the bounds of probability that when he sees me, he won't speak a word."

In the end they all went, but in two cars in case it was necessary to bring Gerald Watson back with them.

"Donaldson will drive us," Burden said in the tone a fond father uses when promising his small son a visit to a theme park. Donaldson had once been Wexford's own driver, and Wexford acknowledged that he would be pleased to see him. For the first time in their fifteen-year-long association they shook hands, and Wexford said he would sit in the front. It amused him, but not in an unkind way, to see that Burden was put out.

In Wexford's opinion it was a big entourage to undertake such a mission, the questioning of a man who had done no more than tell a face-saving lie to the police. Burden, of course, was convincing himself that Watson had done more than that. He had a particular hatred of stalkers, and he had cast Watson in that role without much evidence for it. Surely the definition of a stalker was one whose attentions annoyed or frightened his victim, but Sarah Hussain seemed to have been on friendly terms with Watson.

It was a long drive. Lynn with Barry Vine got there just ahead of them. They all encountered each other outside the storm-cloud-grey tower where Watson's office was. Wexford said he would stay in the car, have a chat with Donaldson about times gone by. The look on Burden's face showed he had plenty to say about that, but Wexford knew he wouldn't in front of the driver. He and Lynn went inside the heavy revolving door, and Donaldson began the tedious search for somewhere to park in case they needed to leave the car. The only possibility was underground, which made Wexford wonder what it must be like these days to be a claustrophobe. They sat in the car amid concrete pillars, facing a concrete wall, and Wexford asked Donaldson about his wife and children and the clever one who had started at his Oxford college a month before and his mother-in-law's recovery from cancer and they talked until Burden came on the phone to say Barry and Lynn had already left while he was ready to be picked up and would be bringing Watson with him.

10

Dora was out somewhere. It wasn't one of Maxine's days. Wexford made himself a cheese-and-tomato sandwich and settled down with Gibbon, the only interruption a phone call from Sylvia to ask him his opinion of her plan to let a room in her house now only she and two of her children were living there.

"You don't want my opinion," he said. "You want me to say I think it's a good idea."

"Well, do you?"

"I don't think letting part of your house is ever a good idea unless you need the money."

After he had ended the call, he remembered Clarissa Hussain and Lynn's half promise to help her find somewhere to live. Then he thought of Georgina Bray and Thora Kilmartin and asked himself, why stir it? More Gibbon, then a phone call from Burden.

"Watson's gone back to Stevenage. Well, I

questioned him for a time, and then I had him taken back. He cried."

"He what?"

"You heard. I mean, he wept, shed tears. When I got him onto his feelings for Sarah Hussain."

"Come round and have a drink."

Burden arrived looking gloomy and morose. "When we were in his office, he blustered a bit more. Then he suddenly said, 'Oh, what's the use?' and admitted to being deeply depressed ever since his wife died about a year ago. Well, I knew all about that as you can imagine, but somehow I didn't feel much sympathy."

Wexford remembered the death of Burden's first wife and his grief. "You said 'admitted.' You have to *admit* to depression?"

"His word, not mine. 'I admit I was very depressed,' he said."

"*Admit,* I suppose, because to be depressed is seen as weakness." Wexford offered him red or white wine or whisky.

"Better not. I'm driving. That was when I brought him back here. Anyway, he said that Sarah Hussain was the only girlfriend he had ever had before he met his wife, and he began thinking of her, wondering where she was, what had happened to her and so forth. Well, he googled her and what he got was St. Peter's website. I was amazed. I didn't know St. Peter's had a website, did you?"

"No, but I wouldn't."

"That was when the stalking started, if you can call it that. I don't know. He came down here and sat about in his car outside the church and outside the vicarage until he saw her."

"Why not write to her or phone her, come to that?"

"He says he was afraid of a rebuff."

"Considering the way he'd treated her, I'm not surprised. But eventually he didn't get a rebuff, is that right?"

"So he says. And so Clarissa says. Sarah spotted him and came up to his car and spoke to him, and apparently he asked her if he could take her out. To dinner or something. She said no. Then he asked if she minded if he sometimes came here just to see her. He told her he was in love with her and always had been. 'Have pity on me' was what he says he said."

Wexford laughed. "Contrary to what the poets tell us, that one never goes down well with women."

"When he told me that, he started to cry. Lynn fetched him a glass of water. He put his head down on the desk and sobbed. I told him this wouldn't do and to pull himself together. The result of that was an outpouring of his feelings about Sarah Hussain. On one occasion, he said, she invited him into the vicarage. They talked and she said his following her and waiting outside to see her must stop, but he told her he couldn't live without her even if that meant just an occasional sight of her. When he left, he encountered Clarissa coming home from school and was introduced, but he didn't know and doesn't know now that she was the result of the rape. He thought Sarah must have had an affair with someone."

Wexford fetched himself a glass of red wine. "You must have decided not to charge him with anything?"

"I asked him if he would mind our taking fingerprints and he said no, that was all right. After that he said his life was over when he heard she'd been killed. It didn't occur to him that he might be a suspect or so he says."

"D'you believe that? The man's a solicitor, for God's sake."

"I don't know, Reg. I really don't know."

Wexford told him about Sylvia's proposal to let a room in her house. "If she decides to do this and I think she will, would it be out of order for me to suggest Clarissa Hussain as a tenant?"

"Clarissa's living with Georgina Bray, isn't she?"

"Yes, but she doesn't like it. She wants to be on her own."

"I daresay," said Burden. "Don't they all? Why shouldn't you suggest Clarissa? It wouldn't do if it was my Pat wanted to let a room to her, but you're—well, a private citizen."

"Well, yes, I suppose I am."

Still, he would wait a while. Be sure of Sylvia's intention first and then check that Clarissa hadn't changed her mind. Sylvia phoned just after Burden left and Wexford heard Dora talking to her. The subject of their conversation was clear from Dora's remarks: "You surely don't need the money" and "Will you bring yourself to evict him or her if they wreck your home?"

Wexford said, "Let me talk to her when you're done."

Dora handed him the phone. Rather angrily, Sylvia, who often had spats with her mother, launched into a tirade against Dora for her "interference" and treating her "like a child." But Sylvia's intention remained.

"Leave it to me, will you, before you advertise?"

Dora wanted to know what he was up to and said to him in a gloomy tone that he would land himself in a lot of trouble. Ignoring this advice, he wrote a note to Clarissa care of Georgina Bray giving her Sylvia's phone number. "I have a mobile number for Clarissa," he said, and continued rather humbly, "You can send texts to mobile numbers, can't you? Would you show me how to send a text?"

"No, I don't think I would, Reg. It would be teaching her to do a rude and underhand thing to a woman who's shown her hospitality."

"But I've written her a letter. It comes to the same thing, it only takes a little longer."

"Yes, but that's nothing to do with me."

"I think that's why I've loved you all these years," said Wexford. "Your undiminished and sometimes absurd integrity."

Next day an ecstatic phone call came from Clarissa, a satisfied phone call from Sylvia, and a visit from a furious Georgina Bray. Dealing with all this, Wexford postponed reading his newspaper until the afternoon. He sat with Gibbon in the conservatory, but not reading, going instead over the events of the past few hours, two of them pleasant, the third anything but. It is always nice to know you have pleased your child, and Sylvia sounded very pleased at the idea—if not yet the actual presence—of her new tenant. Because her father had recommended her, she thought she could waive a deposit on the room, and the girl seemed quite willing to pay the rent Sylvia asked. Clarissa had phoned two hours later to tell him she had been interviewed by Sylvia and seen the room. It was a bit small and the rent, she thought, a bit high, but she had liked Sylvia and hoped Sylvia had liked her, and it was all due to him, Wexford, so thank you very, very much.

Georgina Bray's visit was unexpected. Dora was out, Maxine had left, and Wexford had just picked up Gibbon. The doorbell rang and the knocker banged, but the bell was ringing as if a finger was held on it, kept on it, and pressed hard while the knocker crashed simultaneously again and again. Whoever was on the doorstep must have been using both hands. The phone was also ringing but Wexford let it ring while he answered the door before the noise aroused the neighbours.

The woman looked as if she was about to spit in his face. He stepped back. This gave her the chance to burst in and kick the door shut behind her.

"How dare you, how dare you, how dare you," she shouted. "I can have you charged with abduction. I can have you charged with false imprisonment." A string of imprecations followed, including expressions referred to in print by so-called family newspapers with a letter succeeded by a string of asterisks. Wexford was reminded of descriptions in novels he had read of sophisticated men being amazed by the language used by respectable and proper women in moments of extreme stress. "I wouldn't have believed she knew such words," they were supposed to have said. He knew better than to have supposed that and waited patiently until she finished with a "You fucking bastard!"

"Let's not stand here," he said mildly as both his landline phone and mobile began to ring. "Come in here. It's warmer."

She had started to cry, a frequent consequence of outbursts such as hers, but followed him into the living room. Burden would have told her to pull herself together, but Wexford's reaction, after handing her that old-fashioned solace, a clean handkerchief, was to ask her if she'd like a drink. He would have one if she would, in spite of its being three o'clock in the afternoon. She nodded miserably, said if he had any whisky that was what she would like. When he came back with the two glasses, she launched into a diatribe against her husband. It was as if this onslaught was as much the purpose of her visit as to attack Wexford for his interference.

It all came out, the man's ill-tempered criticism, his sarcasm, his protracted silences, what she called his verbal abuse. Clarissa had been a companion for her, a comfort, and now she was going. Knowing he was being biased and judgmental, Wexford thought how unattractive she was, how grating her voice, how bitter her expression. He wanted to say that living with her and Mr. Bray—if her name was his name—must have been an experience miserable enough to drive Clarissa away, but of course he couldn't. The poor woman was to be pitied.

She emptied her glass but he didn't offer her any more. Her home was in easy walking distance, but he saw that a second drink would lead to a third and then most probably to her falling asleep on his sofa.

"I'll walk you home," he said, and thought up a reason for accompanying her. "I have to go to the corner shop."

His mobile started up again as they were leaving the house. Instead of answering it Wexford turned it off. "I can never bring myself to let a phone ring," she said conversationally. It was as if there had been no outburst of rage, no stream of abuse.

He saw her to the end of Orchard Road. "Thank you for the drink," she said, and trotted off rapidly up the street. Wexford went into Mr. Mahmood's shop and bought a small wholemeal loaf and a half-pint (or whatever you called it these days) of semiskimmed milk.

Three messages were on answer. Just as he marvelled at the behaviour of those people who contemplate a sealed envelope, speculating as to who the sender might be, so now he had no intention of doing the equivalent with a "sealed-up" phone message. All three were from Burden, and all were much the same, recommending that he read that morning's newspaper.

He read it, a single paragraph under the heading "Death of Lawyer." Why didn't journalists accept that while *lawyer* was correct American English, British English called them *solicitors?* Maybe it was a question of the number of letters.

Gerald Watson, 43, a partner in the law firm of Newman, Watson, Kerensky, was found dead in his home in Cleland Avenue,

Stevenage, this morning. His body was found by Mrs. Maureen Jones, a cleaner. Foul play is not suspected.

"How about that?" said Burden on the phone. "Where have you been, anyway?"

"Having a row with Georgina Bray."

"I suppose Clarissa's told her she's moving in with Sylvia, and Georgina took exception."

"Something like that. What are you going to do about poor old Watson?"

There was a pause. "I've got a meeting in about twenty minutes with a DI Stewart of Herts Constabulary. Shall I come in on my way back?"

The first thing Burden did when he walked in was hand Wexford a letter. "It's for you. Left for you by Gerald Watson."

"I didn't know him. I only spoke to him once."

"You'd better read it."

There was no *Dear* nor that irritating *Hallo* or *Hi there.* Watson had begun with Wexford's name, underlined.

You seem a decent man, which is more than I can say for most policemen I have known. If I wrote to you, I thought you might not scoff or mock me, though I do not expect sympathy. I was in love with Sarah Hussain and had been for more than twenty years but pride and vanity prevented me from getting in touch with her after her child was born. When I tried again years later I could not find her. That was before the days of easy discovery of a person's whereabouts. By that time I was married. I had always been a solitary and, I suppose, inhibited repressed sort of man, and my wife was a companion if nothing else.

She died and though I felt considerable guilt, I am disgusted with myself when I say there was relief too. Her death meant I could begin looking for Sarah once more. When I found her, and in such extraordinary circumstances, I began to feel happy for the first time since I deserted her when most she needed me. I was not stalking her, I want to make that finally clear. By coming to Kingsmarkham as often as I could, as often as I *dared,* I got to see her, to understand her life, observe her daughter (who might if things had been different have been mine), and she never rejected me. She was too kind for that. One day, I think, I truly believe, she would have really responded to me. She would have agreed to marry me. She had already asked me into the house, given me tea, and talked to me about those past eighteen years. I could talk to her then about the real reason for my desertion of her, my mother's opposition to the marriage we contemplated. Perhaps it is needless to say that she objected to Sarah's race and I lacked the strength of will to defy her.

All that is past now and my mother has passed away. When I read in the newspaper about Sarah's death I felt that my life was over. Everything I had hoped for was gone for the second time. I haven't much experience of making someone else happy but I had thought I had found the secret. It was too late and that very day I decided to kill myself. Thank you for reading this.

Gerald Watson

"Poor devil," said Wexford.

He said no more but maintained for a moment or two the minute's silence requisite for an untimely death.

Fiona believed Jeremy to be a teetotaller. She never saw him drink. She was the drinker, though more abstemious now the baby was coming, and knew nothing of the brandy flask and the vodka flask from which he took fortifying sips while out of the house.

The purchase of 123 Ladysmith Road was to be completed in a week's time, and Jeremy felt all had gone well. He called at the house in Peck Road and asked Jason for a deposit of three months' rent. Confident and using a slightly bullying tone, he had made a mistake there. Jason knew that whatever Jeremy might say, Jason had the upper hand. He wanted somewhere to live, yes, but not at any price. Any threatening and two could play at that game, such as an anonymous letter to the Housing Department.

"You must be joking," said Jason.

"You'll get it back when you leave the place."

"I'm not planning on leaving."

"Not for about twenty years," said Nicky.

"Why don't I drive you round there," said Jeremy ingratiatingly, "show you over the place? I know you're going to love it."

"We'll go under our own steam, thanks. You can let me have a key."

This went against the grain with Jeremy. He suggested they leave it "a day or two" and reminded Jason he had asked for a deposit. Maxine was arriving as he departed. For some reason she had stopped speaking to him altogether, and this unnerved him even further. She turned her head pointedly away. Jeremy got into his car, sat at the wheel without moving until she had gone into the house, and, when the street was empty, took a small swig of vodka.

Maxine told Wexford all about it next day. "You ever heard of such a thing, and them paying him rent all these years. He's too honest, my Jason, that's his trouble, while that fellow

Legg, he'd sell his grandmother for fifty pee."

"He couldn't do that," said Wexford. "His grandmother's been in Meadowbank for the past ten years."

"You know what I mean." She stamped on the vacuum cleaner switch but talked all the same. Her strident voice rose above the roar. "He's having the place painted white all the way through. Got a bunch of East Europeans to do it. You know why white, don't you? Its cheaper than colours. I was passing and one of them Poles called me in to look. Looks bigger from outside than it does in, he said, and he never spoke a truer word. That fellow Legg he told them only to put two coats of paint on, keep the cost down."

"I'm going down the road to post a letter," said Wexford.

"Now you're the first person I've heard say that for a good couple of years. Letters are all them e-mails these days, aren't they? And texts. E-mails and texts, and there's even some as has faxes still, though they're sort of fading out. Got a stamp, have you? The price they are, I'd rather not write . . ."

But while her back was turned, Wexford had slipped out. He had thought of little but Gerald Watson's letter since Burden had put it into his hands, and now, try as he would, he couldn't get the man's misery out of his head. Every line of that letter was pervaded by inhibition and distorted by repression. He felt too how much pain might have been avoided if Watson had been with Sarah that night rather than staying at home with his mother. For Sarah would never have been attacked if Watson had been with her, Clarissa would never have been born. All of Sarah's life would have been different. Perhaps instead of eventually being ordained, she would have become a headteacher herself, perhaps married Watson, had other children, gone to live in Hertfordshire, not been murdered, and Watson not shot himself.

Jason and Nicky hadn't much furniture. Most of the contents of 11 Peck Road belonged to Jeremy Legg and had to be left behind. Maxine was giving them what she called "some bits and pieces" from her own home, and Nicky had bought some from Marks and Spencer in Kingsmarkham. All this amounted to more than could be squeezed into Jason's ancient Land Rover. He decided to hire a van, which he would pick up after work on November 29, Nicky and Isabella having been taken to Ladysmith Road in Jason's car earlier in the day.

Nothing seemed likely to go wrong with this plan. Jason and Nicky with Isabella in the pushchair had walked down to Ladysmith Road the previous Saturday, where Jeremy was waiting for them with the key. He was still unwilling to surrender the key but promised to hand it over to Nicky on the day she and the baby were brought there. This peculiar behaviour put Jason in a bad temper. He said it still wasn't too late for the Sams family to remain where they were and Jeremy need not think Jason didn't know what game his landlord had been playing at.

Nicky was delighted with the house and ran about the rooms taking photographs with her mobile phone. Isabella got out of her pushchair and took her first real steps without anyone's holding on to her. Nicky said it was an omen and meant they were bound to be happy in the house. But still Jeremy didn't hand over the key. He gave no explanation for this refusal. In fact he didn't really know why retaining it for a few days meant so much to him. Perhaps it was only that it gave some amount of power over Jason Sams, and driving home to Stringfield, Jeremy told himself several times that once given that key, the man would take over the house at once and very likely take half a dozen pals in as tenants. The thought of this was quite upsetting, and he pulled into a lay-by after three or four miles and took a swig of brandy from his flask.

Back at home he told Fiona that he had carried out a successful showing over of the house and by the end of the week the whole business would be off his hands. On the morning of the twentieth the plan fell apart. Not an e-mail but an old-fashioned letter, handwritten and altogether rather formal, arrived from Diane. It appeared that more plans had changed.

Dear Jeremy,
 I doubt if it will affect you much if at all but I am coming back a few days early and I don't want to have to go to a hotel. As I have a house in Kingsmarkham and you have been keeping an eye on it, it will be best for me to go straight there from Gatwick. My fiancé will be coming with me. I don't suppose you will meet but if you do his name is Johann Heinemann, he is German and a property developer in Barcelona. My flight gets in at 15:25 on November 23rd. Unless the lock has been changed on the front door I can let myself in as I have kept the key I took with me when I left.
 Yours,
 Diane

Fiona had picked up the letter from the doormat and brought it up to him in bed. Jeremy didn't particularly want to tell her what it was about, but if she didn't recognise the handwriting, she knew the Spanish postmark.

"Fiancé," Jeremy muttered, and handed her the letter.

"He can't be much of a property developer if

she's going to take him to live in Peck Road."

"I don't suppose they'll stop long," said Jeremy, too worried to care.

No phoning for him and not much thinking either. He got up and dressed, got into his car, and took a sip of vodka on an empty stomach. It took immediate effect, which was what, of course, he wanted, though he would have preferred it not to have felt as if he'd been kicked in the stomach. He drove more carefully than usual for the traffic was heavy on the little country lanes that variously led from the villages to the town centre, the big roundabout, and Kingsmarkham station. What happened when he got to 11 Peck Road he could have done without. The front door was opened to him by Maxine Sams, who greeted him with "What brings you here?"

"I'd like to see Mr. Sams."

"Well, you can't. He's gone to business." This antediluvian phrase, dating from long before Maxine was born and previously unheard of by Jeremy, had been dredged up from her memory as used by her grandfather when she was a small child. Why she uttered it she couldn't have said except as having something to do with the dignity and prestige of her son's job.

"Mrs. Sams, then. Nicky, I should say. She hasn't gone to business, has she?"

"Don't you be cheeky with me." Maxine turned her head and yelled at the top of her voice,

"Nicky! Here's that fellow Legg wants to see you."

They didn't ask him in. Nicky and Maxine were seldom united but now they were. They listened in grim unison as Jeremy explained what had happened. Now able to walk with expertise, Isabella emerged from the room at the back and, immediately taking a dislike to their visitor, clutched at her mother's jeans and screamed.

"Well, I'm sure I don't know," said Nicky. "You'd best take yourself like down to Questo and see him yourself. He won't be pleased, that's for sure."

Both women began naming at the tops of their voices all the tasks they would have to perform, packing all the furniture and "bits and pieces" the Samses would be taking with them, how long it would take, how it could never be done in time. Jeremy retreated, got back into his car, and drove back to Kingsmarkham and the Questo on the outskirts of the town. Half a mile outside he stopped and had recourse to his flask.

As he moved into a vacant space in the car park, the man he knew as Chief Inspector Wexford drew up alongside him. Jeremy watched Wexford get out and walk across the car park to the cash dispenser in the wall by the entrance. The chief inspector or whatever he now was turned round, looked without much interest in Jeremy's direction, and went into the store. Jeremy sneaked another sip and then another out of his flask. It gave him a surge of confidence, making him feel ready to face Jason Sams.

But when he got out of the car and stood between it and Wexford's Audi, he found himself shaky on his feet. He grabbed hold of the Audi's driver's door handle and immediately snatched it away lest Wexford should return just at that moment and see him trying to break into his car. Taking a few deep breaths, he made his way slowly and carefully to the entrance. His heart was now beating rapidly.

But once inside the store he began to feel more confident, found a door marked PRIVATE: STORE MANAGER, pushed it open, and banged it shut behind him. None of the shoppers reacted to his appearance or departure into Jason's office until the row erupted: shouts, abuse, and the sound of one, then another, heavy metal object apparently hurled to the ground. A woman lifting a king-size bag of muesli from a top shelf was so startled that she let it fall to the floor, where it burst and leaked grains and nuts all over the floor. Two babies in a twin pram began to scream. Other shoppers stopped what they were doing and stood still, hoping for the trouble, whatever it was, to erupt beyond the confines of the office. Knowing he would no longer have to intervene, whatever happened, Wexford looked in the direction of the continuing noise with interest, then helped himself to the pack of eight Cumberland sausages Dora refused to buy him on health grounds but which he wanted to fry for his lunch and took it to the checkout. The minute his back was turned, Jeremy Legg issued from the office, not running but walking fast.

Wexford was leaving for his car when Jason emerged, hailed him with a halfhearted wave, and set off in pursuit of Jeremy, who was by now edging his car out of its slot next to Wexford's. By this time both men appeared to have calmed down a little. It seemed that Jeremy, his head stuck out of the car window, was making some sort of request of Jason, and this was now being grudgingly granted. Wexford knew neither man to speak to but, as he approached Jeremy, said to him ingratiatingly, "So sorry, not hemming you in, am I?"

Jeremy's voice was thick and the words not clear so Wexford had to bend towards him to make sure he heard when Jeremy repeated them. "No, no, it's fine," he said, and Wexford stepped back to escape the vodka fumes. Jason had also received a blast, and Wexford could see Jason was one of those people who believe every policeman or ex-policeman, no matter how high ranking in the CID, is also a traffic cop intent on breathalysing the public. But Jason said nothing on this subject, only terminating his altercation with Jeremy with "OK, if I must. You take Nicky and Issy round there on Friday afternoon, and I pick up the van with the bits and pieces after I finish here at six." Jason ended on a rougher note. "Give me the key then."

Jeremy put a hand, curled into a fist, through the open car window. Wexford, intent on watching and on appearing indifferent as he lifted his boot lid, saw the fist pulled back teasingly. "It has to be Thursday, not Friday. Thursday evening. I'll take your family in the afternoon, and you move the furniture in the evening. That's best."

"What's the deal on Friday then?" Jason said in an aggressive way.

Jeremy didn't even want to mention Diane's name. An increasing nightmare was for Jason and Diane to meet. "Tomorrow," Jeremy said. "I'll get the key to you later. I'll bring it round. No worries. You go tomorrow and bill me for the removers taking the furniture in the evening. There's an offer you can't refuse."

Jason had gone red in the face. "I'm not taking no man's charity. I'll do it myself Friday morning. You can take Nicky and Issy and I'll follow. Never mind I lose a morning's wages."

Wexford drove home to decide how many fried sausages could be eaten for lunch without detriment to his figure.

Detective Superintendent Burden was holding yet another team conference. Wexford was not invited. He had criticised, and not very politely, Burden's fondness for such gatherings, calling them a waste of time and, in a currently favoured phrase rather with his tongue in his cheek, a misuse of the hardworking taxpayers' money. Why repeatedly collect the team together when they are in the building already, take statements and reports from them, and the whole group together examine yet again the evidence for this man's or that man's being the rapist who was Clarissa's father, and looking once more at the behaviour of a gardener and a churchwarden? Wexford had suggested that instead of holding any more such conferences Thora Kilmartin should be visited and questioned more comprehensively because she of all the people associated with Sarah Hussain had known her best at a crucial time in her life.

"What, spare a couple of people from my team for that?" had been Burden's response, followed by a defence of the conference policy, and in due course his rather pointedly not inviting Wexford to attend "as an observer" the newest gathering of police officers who saw each other every day anyway.

Wexford went to Reading. A journey by train would be too awkward, so he drove, having asked Thora Kilmartin if he could come and having been invited to lunch. Before he left, he found himself landed with Maxine's company.

Dora had gone out shopping, leaving the house with many whispered apologies for deserting him. Wexford told her not to worry as he would soon be leaving himself, but he hadn't allowed for Maxine's being fresh and stimulated after the three days' holiday she had taken for herself and bubbling over with things to talk about.

The house looked perfectly clean to him, but Maxine announced that everywhere was "grubby" and would need "turning out." Because the Wexfords didn't possess one, she had brought with her a handheld vacuum cleaner, which when applied to upholstery made a high-pitched whine rather like the cry of a seagull. She talked over the top of it.

"My Jason's moving tomorrow. I don't know what's come over that Jeremy Legg, taking that Nicky and Isabella to the new place himself, but that's what he's doing so Jason can pick up the bits and pieces I'm giving them from my place and collect the three-piece suite they've bought. Kelli with an *i* will be there to let him in. Mind you, he's having to take the morning off work to do it. He told Legg he'd lose a morning's salary, but that was a bit of a porky. Jason's in too high a position for that.

"Legg offered to pay for removals but Jason wouldn't have that. 'I don't take no man's charity,' he said, and it's true, he wouldn't." The nozzle of the vacuum cleaner, appropriately beak-shaped, thrust down between sofa cushions, emitted a louder than usual squawk, and Maxine screamed over the top of it, "They wasn't supposed to move till the twenty-fifth, then tomorrow came out of the blue. I wonder what's behind it. Must be something. That Legg never does nothing open and aboveboard. . . ."

"I'm going out," Wexford shouted. "See you later."

He had for years used this phrase to mean he would see whoever it was in the next few hours, but everyone now—his grandchildren and their parents and friends—used it to mean see you anytime in the weeks, months, or years to come. It is so easy to pick up these habits and, really, why not? That was how the language grew or, at any rate, changed.

She introduced him to her husband, a thin and weedy man, as spare as she was fat. His greeting to Wexford was cold, a limp handshake and a few muttered words. They had lunch, a much larger meal than Wexford had expected, soup, roasted ham with mashed potatoes and peas, a baked Alaska and cheese and biscuits. Thora Kilmartin wore a rather-too-tight, green wool dress and the same sort of lacy stockings or tights she had had on last time he saw her. She ate well, while Tony Kilmartin ate sparingly. They talked about the planned refurbishment and extension of their bungalow, she enthusiastically, he in a more restrained way. Wexford had the impression, though nothing was said, that no reference was to be made to Sarah Hussain in Tony Kilmartin's presence. Perhaps he was imagining it. But once the meal was over, Thora got up and said to Wexford that she would like to show him round the neighbourhood a little. They could go out for "a bit of a walk." It was as if he were a prospective house-buyer.

No one spoke for a few minutes once they were outside. It was mild for the time of year, the sun going down in a brilliant display of red and gold streaked with strips of black cloud. The walk they were to take led only as far as a garage on the other side of the street, and Wexford was shown into the passenger seat of the car inside. They were almost at the end of Thora's road before an explanation was forthcoming and then not much of one.

"I want to show you where Sarah and I were living at the time." She left it to him to deduce at the time of what. "And where the man who raped her was living at the time. Quercum Court. It's at the bottom of this street, and we lived over there in the lower half of that house."

It was one of a row of small Victorian houses called Jameson Villas. The flat must have been tiny; two small rooms, a shower room, and a kitchen, Wexford guessed. It looked from where they sat as if a single apartment would fill the lower half of the little house. The sun was already setting and a late-autumn dusk coming. Lights were coming on everywhere. Thora parked the car outside Quercum Court, a large block of flats with bay windows on the ground floor and balconies above.

"I begged her to go to the police or at least to see a doctor. It was the time when everyone was very anxious about AIDS and drugs for it weren't as effective as they are now. She did go to an AIDS clinic and get herself tested. She was all right."

"So nothing more was done?"

"Nothing more was done by Sarah so far as I know. There was something I did. I went round to Quercum Court a few weeks later, a month later maybe, and I looked at the mailboxes in the hallway. There was no one with an Asian name of any kind there. A porter came up to me and asked me if he could help me, but when I asked, he said he wasn't allowed to divulge the names of residents."

Asians don't necessarily have Asian-sounding names, Wexford thought. And surely she would have known a porter wouldn't make a guess of that kind. It would be more than his job was worth. But Wexford let it pass. He wanted to ask her about her husband. Had he disliked Sarah Hussain or disbelieved her? Wexford couldn't. He was no longer a policeman.

"This was all before you were married, Mrs. Kilmartin?"

"Oh, yes. We knew each other. We were friends. I didn't feel I could leave Sarah, and I didn't until after Clarissa was born and she'd moved away herself. I got married soon after. I may as well tell you that my husband never cared much for Sarah. He doesn't care to talk about her. I honestly don't know why, and as he prefers not to talk about her, I don't attempt it."

By now it was getting dark. Only ten to four but dusk was closing in. Thora began the drive back. "I don't know whether the Asian man had moved or never lived there. Sarah could simply have got that part of it wrong. It was down there the rape took place, more or less between where he lived and she lived."

The alleyway, a lane between back gardens, was overhung by trees, now leafless. Lamps were alight at intervals along the lane, which was perhaps a hundred yards long. Had Sarah entered it from the south, heading for Jameson Villas, and the rapist followed her into the lane?

"There weren't any lights down there then." The pause that followed seemed to throb with unspoken words. Then Thora said, "Would you mind not mentioning Sarah's name to my husband?"

Wexford answered her question with another. "Why does he think I'm here?"

He would never normally have asked this; it was an intervention between husband and wife. Maybe she would say no more. She didn't reply to it but, pulling to the kerb and turning off the engine, volunteered a lot he would never have asked for.

"I first met Tony while Sarah and I were living here. We were friends but not close friends. He never liked her nor she him, and when the—well, the rape happened, there was a sort of breach between us. He didn't believe me when I told him she'd been raped. He said no woman would have that done to her and either not have an abortion or not go to the police. We quarrelled, and I didn't see him again for years. Then when we met again—by chance incidentally—we—well, we fell in love.

"By the time we married, Sarah and I—well, we weren't estranged but we'd just sort of moved apart, the way friends sometimes do without any sort of quarrel. Tony never mentioned her; I sometimes thought about her. Then I read in the paper that she'd been ordained. It was a story, you know, because of her being what they call 'mixed race' and a single parent. On an impulse I wrote to her. I didn't tell Tony, though perhaps I should have. I'd never told him about Clarissa and that she was my godchild, but I have now."

"He realised it was Sarah who had been murdered?"

"Oh, yes. He was—well, how can I put it? Not like the man I fell in love with, a different man, I thought. He said—not that she deserved all she got, but that women who lived like she had generally paid a heavy price."

Thora put her head in her hands for a moment. "Tony thinks you've come here to talk about Clarissa's future. He doesn't really know who you are or what you do."

"I do nothing now."

This rather lugubrious response she ignored. "Would you mind terribly if I don't take you back to the house? I mean, if I drop you where your car's parked?"

It would be a relief, he thought. To have to deceive a man at his wife's request and in his wife's presence didn't appeal to him. Still it was an odd request and seemed out of character. Was this the woman who had been so gracious when they were in Kingsmarkham? "Not at all," he said rather coldly.

She had left him with plenty to think about. Were all Sarah Hussain's women friends married to difficult men? It came back to him how Georgina Bray had hinted at what she called verbal abuse from her husband. There was a mystery here but perhaps a minor one.

11

Driving away from the house in Peck Road on Friday morning in the van he had picked up the night before, Jason left Nicky still in bed and Isabella snuggled up beside her. Nicky muttered something about getting up soon and expecting Jeremy to pick her and Isabella up at nine. Jeremy had never appeared with the key, but Jason calculated that he would be following Jason, Nicky, and Isabella to Ladysmith Road. The rush hour was still a long way off, and Jason drove through almost-empty streets to his mother's house on the Pomfret side of Kingsmarkham. His sister Clodella let him in, but his mother almost immediately appeared, talking (as she put it) nineteen to the dozen about the weather, what Mrs. Crocker said to her yesterday, the paper fastener she had found inside a Cornish pasty, and Kingsmarkham Borough Council withdrawing their garden-waste recycling service on economy grounds.

"Let's get on with moving the bits and pieces," said Jason.

The three of them shifted into the van a kitchen stool, a grandfather clock once the property of Maxine's own grandfather, a broken table lamp that could perhaps be mended, a china donkey with laden panniers with A PRESENT FROM MARBELLA on its base, and a cardboard box full of kitchen utensils. Maxine asked him if he had had any breakfast and, when he said he didn't want any, made him drink a cup of tea "to keep your strength up." Jason got away just as the High Street shops were opening, the same time as traffic wardens started on the prowl. The furniture they had ordered and paid for was difficult to locate, its being apparently still in the warehouse at the back of the shop, still bandaged in brown paper. Jason was offered a cup of coffee while he waited and got angrier and angrier. But eventually the two burgundy-coloured armchairs and a sofa were fetched out and unwrapped. Unusually patient for her kind, the traffic warden had waited quite a long while but eventually gave him a ticket, which he doubted he could foist on the van-hire company. He was growing angrier and angrier because he still had no key. Jeremy's promise to pass it on to him before this had come to nothing. Presumably he had decided to give it to Nicky. Having started early that morning, Jason drove off late, reaching 123 Ladysmith Road just before ten.

Jeremy must already have come and gone with Nicky and Isabella. It seemed unlike him to be punctual and prompt, but Jason admitted that he didn't know Jeremy well. There appeared to be no one in the house. He rang the doorbell, then pounded on the knocker, calling through the letterbox, "Nicky?" and "Where's my sweetheart?" No answer. No one was in the house. He called Nicky's mobile and got nothing, not even her voice mail. Emerging on the pavement in a thin rain which had begun to fall, he stood looking helplessly about him as if his missing family were likely to appear, smiling and gleeful from down the road or the house next door.

Jeremy had promised to borrow a car seat from Fiona's sister. But he left too late and when he got to her place in Stowerton, she had already gone to work. It didn't seem important. He had a vague idea that a baby or small child was not allowed to sit in the front in the passenger seat, so showed Nicky and Isabella into the back, where the child could sit on her mother's lap. Nicky complained about that and about the state of the car and the uncomfortable conditions on the backseat. She went back into the house and fetched the four rather shabby pillows she and Jason had deemed unworthy to go to the new house and which would anyway be replaced by new bedding. These she arranged to make a kind of nest for Isabella between herself and the nearside rear door.

It was as well she did.

Her efforts at making his car more comfortable, accompanied by little snorts of exasperation and pursing of lips, were making Jeremy increasingly nervous. The second time she went back into the house he took a surreptitious swig from his flask, this time containing grappa. He got the flask tucked away just in time. She stuck her head through the driver's window.

"I don't know why we're messing about with all this. Me and Isabella could easily have walked."

"Oh, I couldn't have had that," said Jeremy with a wild laugh.

The swig of spirits seldom made him feel cautious, but this one did. Perhaps it was the presence of a woman and child in the car—well, of anyone in the car. Usually, travelling in any car but his own meant being driven by Fiona in hers. He was cutting it too fine, that was the trouble. Today was the twenty-third, and this afternoon Diane and this Heinemann guy would be arriving. But now he was wary, and this unusual feeling made him avoid the bypass and take the network of small roads that culminated in the long, straight Kingsbrook Street that led down into Ladysmith Lane and then Ladysmith Road.

On that sharp corner, a junction—for the Sewingbury traffic came along from the right—

the accident happened. But cars from that direction were infrequent, and Jeremy, when he took the turn, had got into the habit of not looking to his right. He did in any case rely on other drivers in his vicinity to do the looking for him. He began to turn. The driver of the large, green van coming at fairly high speed from the right swerved to avoid him and smashed head-on into the Mini approaching also quite fast from the left. Meanwhile Jeremy screeched to a stop, and the Lexus behind him ran into his rear. This wasn't the end of it as a large, black Mercedes estate, the kind of car that Wexford said looked like an old-time hearse, slid into the green van–Mini pileup.

The police were there quickly because the vehicle following the Lexus, though some fifty yards behind, was a police patrol car. Its driver was on the phone for help before he reached the corner and the accident site. PC David Rouse got out of the car and walked into the chaos, surveying the damage and the single fatality. This was the driver of the Mini, a young woman from Stowerton on her way to work in Pomfret. The policeman could see she was dead, could not in any case have moved the crushed and hemmed-in body. The driver of the van, covered in powdered glass but otherwise unhurt, was pacing up and down moaning that it wasn't his fault, he had swerved to avoid something like this happening.

The nest of pillows had saved Isabella Sams. She had been squeezed between her mother and the back of the front seats, a well-padded crushing, and it seemed that her only injury was bruising. She had banged her head, and if she lost consciousness for a moment or two, no one noticed except that she was briefly silent. Nicky was screaming even louder than her daughter but from indignation and rage rather than pain. As for Jeremy, he did what he always did in a crisis— though he had never before been in one as bad as this. He went back to the womb—in other words, curled up, drew his knees up under his chin, and tucked his head in his arms. PC Rouse found him like this. By this time ambulances had arrived, and Nicky and Isabella were taken away to the Princess Diana Memorial Hospital, but Jeremy was apparently not seriously injured. The accident, strictly speaking, wasn't his fault, for the green van and the Mini drivers had both been exceeding the sixty-mile-an-hour speed limit. However, the interior of Jeremy's car reeked of grappa (or "seriously strong liquor," as PC Rouse put it to PC Evans) as they got him to his feet and breathalysed him.

"There was so much alcohol in his blood," David Rouse later said to his wife, "it was a wonder there was any room left for haemo-globin."

12

Jason had unloaded the new furniture and the "bits and pieces" into 123 Ladysmith Road but been obliged to leave the sofa in the van until help came. He phoned his mother. When things went wrong, he usually phoned his mother, and this time what had gone wrong was that Nicky and his precious Isabella had apparently disappeared. Maxine was "turning out" the Wexfords' bedroom and was in the middle of changing the bed linen, but she dropped everything and ran downstairs to tell Wexford what had happened.

He was sitting in the room Dora called his study, though he had never studied anything there apart from what he happened to be reading at the moment. Gibbon stimulated thought, and that morning Wexford was thinking, or trying to imagine, what it must have been like, literally, to fall on your sword, or get your devoted slave to hold the sword for you to fall on, when Maxine burst in. She was not supposed to come into the study at all, not even when he wasn't there, but she had never taken any notice of this injunction and he was tired of telling her. He looked up and resigned himself to listening as she began on this tale of a vanishing mother and child.

"I always said he was bonkers, that Jeremy Legg. Out of his tree he is. Do you reckon he's kidnapped them and he's going to ask for a ransom? It could be. Stranger things have happened. Well, he'll be lucky. Every penny my Jason's got has gone on new furniture, and it'll be no good coming to me or his sisters."

"Has Jason called the police or the hospital?"

As Wexford uttered those words, the Princess Diana Hospital was calling Jason to tell him his partner and daughter had been brought into the emergency department and the hospital would call him when they had further news. Jason jumped in his van, the cumbersome sofa still in the back, and drove as fast as he dared to Stowerton and the Princess Diana.

That he found his daughter fit and well, running about the Prince William children's ward, did something to allay Jason's anxiety, but nothing to cool his anger. Nor did the sight of Isabella's bruises soften it when she proudly held up her arm to the purple patches on the smooth, white skin. Nicky had a tale to tell, an exaggerated version of the truth, naming Jeremy Legg as "blind drunk" and "hardly able to stand up." Jason, of course, wanted to know why she had even got into the car, why she hadn't called him, putting his daughter in serious danger. And look what had happened! The hospital refused to tell him the whereabouts of Jeremy Legg. However, he was able finally to get the key, Jeremy having at last handed it to Nicky just before the crash.

Jeremy was, in fact, in the same hospital, cut and bruised and suffering from a hangover. At 1:30 p.m. he had received a furious call on his mobile from Diane, who, accompanied by Johann Heinemann, had taken an earlier flight, this one from Barcelona, and on arriving at the Muriel Campden Estate found that the lock on the house in Peck Road had indeed been changed and her key failed to open the front door. This being the least of his troubles, Jeremy sent her to 123 Ladysmith Road, beyond caring by this time if the extent of his duplicity came out. He remembered now, very late in the day, that the lock had been changed when Jason and Nicky moved in.

All these details were relayed to Wexford or to Dora and/or the Crockers by Maxine; they pooled their knowledge over a drink, and at first the whole story was a source of amusement, pronounced "hilarious" or "absurd." Exasperated or bored by Maxine, Wexford had always found her anecdotes or longer stories funny, especially in retrospect, but the humour vanished from this one as events took a different turn. First he heard that Jeremy had been charged with causing death by dangerous driving and driving with over the prescribed limit of alcohol in his blood. It wasn't an item of news to be imparted to Maxine. In fact he never imparted anything to her, founding their relationship on her talking and he more or less listening. Whether Maxine's son knew about this Wexford had no idea. After all, the fatality was the driver of the Mini and no connection to Jason Sams.

When the news came that made the comedy into something like a tragedy, Wexford was in Burden's office drinking coffee and being told that Duncan Crisp, the gardener, had finally been arrested and charged with the murder of Sarah Hussain.

"You're sure about this?"

"Well, yes, Reg, I am. His alibi doesn't stand up and in each account he's given us the times differ. He has a history of violence against women, if no convictions, but when he was kicking his wife around—twenty years ago, she's dead now, poor woman—we weren't treating domestic violence very seriously. He's known around here as being what I could reasonably call a militant racist and is a member of the BNP. He doesn't attempt to deny it."

"But he does deny any hand in Sarah Hussain's death?"

"Yes, but that may well change. He was in

court yesterday morning, pleaded not guilty, of course, and was committed for trial."

A woman PC brought them tea, and Burden talked about the evidence he had against Duncan Crisp. As soon as a news item about his arrest had appeared in the *Evening Standard*, the people's warden at St. Peter's, a woman called Jennifer Lomax, had come to the police station asking to see Burden. Now she had read about the arrest, she thought it was time she told the police about a quarrel she had overheard between Crisp and Sarah Hussain, carried out over the garden fence. Crisp called Ms. Hussain a "coolie playing at being a memsahib" and "a blackie," and she had told him he should be more careful about the racist things he said, saying that the names he called her many people would have passed on to the police as they were against the law. Ms. Lomax, who had had a prearranged meeting at the vicarage, had felt embarrassed about what she'd overheard but the vicar had smiled and said she felt sorry for Mr. Crisp, who was an unhappy man. But Ms. Hussain had never told the police, Burden said. Could they have prevented a murder if she had?

"Are you saying he killed her to stop her telling us—I mean, the police—what he had called her? Bit thin, isn't it?"

"You know I'm not interested in motive. It's enough that he hated her. A 'coolie' as he called her, living in that big house, being an important figure in the public eye. He admits calling her that, it's not just Ms. Lomax's word. There is other evidence. A pair of cloth gloves, gardening gloves they are, apparently, found in his home and worn it seems just once. A gardener—he calls himself a professional gardener—never wears gloves, but he had these, says they were a gift from a friend, and he put them on only in the presence of the giver when the gift was made."

"But you think they were worn when he went into the vicarage to kill Sarah Hussain."

"I do."

"So he went into the house carrying a pair of cloth gloves with the intention of wearing them once he'd found a weapon? Or did he carry them on him all the time just in case?"

"When he was inside, he was wearing them. He left no prints, never did find a weapon, of course, his hands were his weapon," said Burden crossly. "The way I see it, he went into the house for some reason we don't yet know, and Sarah Hussain was there alone dressed in those trousers and tunic—salwar kameez, is it called. It was more than he could stand. Perhaps he shouted at her. Perhaps he told her to go upstairs and change into something an Englishwoman—or a white woman—would wear. Did she laugh? Did she tell him not to be absurd?"

"She would never have been rude or unkind," Wexford said. "We know enough about her to understand that."

"Whatever it was, it maddened him. He threw himself at her and strangled her with his bare hands. No weapon, no need for gloves."

"He put them on to avoid leaving prints." Wexford said nothing about Burden's having no evidence that Crisp had ever been in the house, but his doubts likely showed in his face.

"All these details will be cleared up before Crisp comes to trial," said Burden firmly.

Wexford's walk homewards took him past Sylvia's house, and at the gate he paused. Dropping in uninvited on a daughter was something he had nearly always avoided doing. With Sheila it had been impossible. She had always lived in London and occasionally abroad. Sylvia too, ever since she'd left her parents' home to marry Neil Fairfax (that marriage long dissolved), had invariably lived too far away, at the other end of Kingsmarkham or in one of the villages, to make a casual call impossible. But now . . . she would be home from work by now and unlikely to be busy. He opened the gate and went up the path to the front door.

Hers had always been a difficult temperament, warm and generous enough except when she had a grievance, sometimes imaginary. She bore grudges too. Her "Oh, hallo, Dad" carried an aggrieved note, discernible perhaps only to a parent. But after a small hesitation she asked him if he'd like a cup of tea.

"Yes, please."

She appeared to be alone in the house, even her small daughter, Mary, out somewhere.

"I've taken her to a birthday party, which I could have stayed at along with a bunch of other mums. But there are limits."

A large mug of tea was rather heavily plonked down in front of him. He made what turned out to be an intelligent guess. "How are you getting on with Clarissa?"

"I thought you'd never ask, but maybe you know already."

"I know nothing."

"Clarissa is out. With Robin. For the third time this week. And no doubt they'll be off somewhere for the weekend. I heard him introduce her to someone as his girlfriend."

"So what's wrong with that?"

"Can you ask? Yes, well, maybe you can. You brought her here, after all. A mother who was murdered, very dubious antecedents, mixed race—not that that matters—"

"I should bloody hope not." Wexford had had enough racism for one day.

"I said it doesn't matter. She says she doesn't know who her father is, and that shows the kind of background she comes from. Do you realise she could *marry* him?"

Little as Wexford felt like laughing, he suddenly did. "Are you serious? Their combined ages don't add up to forty. That's the age people get married at these days—if they get married at all."

She was glaring at him. He didn't drink the tea she had brought him either but got up, shook his head, and, managing a small wave, walked out of the house.

Only Jason was at home when Diane Stow and Johann Heinemann called at 123 Ladysmith Road for the key to the Peck Road house. Nicky and Isabella were still at the hospital and likely to stay there overnight, Isabella for observation and Nicky to be there because her daughter was. Jason intended to join them, was indeed about to leave the house for that purpose, when Diane arrived, she and Johann in a rented car.

If Jason had been inclined to be rude or even abusive to any connection of Jeremy Legg's, he changed his tune when Diane, usually a fairly placid woman, expressed her opinion of her ex-husband even before Jason admitted them to the house. Suddenly hospitable, he made tea. Diane, backed up by Johann, who had never met her ex-husband, began taking Jeremy's character apart. Not only was he idle, had never had a job, was unfaithful to her with anyone who would have him, but was a secret drinker, too much of a hypocrite to have a drink in a pub or bar like any honest person but a user of a hip flask he covertly filled with spirits.

"You know like most people don't have a drink or maybe just one before they drive," she said. "Well, he drinks before he drives. You want to know why? Because he's frightened. He's scared stiff of everything like anything new. You can bet your life if you see him at the wheel of a car, he'll have been drinking."

At this last Johann Heinemann let out a loud peal of laughter.

"They'll have got him this time," said Diane. "Breathalysed him at the site, you want to bet?"

All this was known to the police but not until that moment to Jason. He thanked her, gave her the key to her own house, and, once they had left, set off for the Princess Diana Memorial Hospital.

Next day Isabella was pronounced perfectly well and Jason and Nicky were told she could go home. Maxine, coming round to Ladysmith Road later, remarked that of course they sent her home. It was Saturday, wasn't it? Hospitals always got rid of patients at the weekend, as everyone knew. Nicky remembered later in the day how Isabella had screamed when Jeremy's car crashed but been briefly silent, for certainly no more than a few seconds, then started screaming again. Nicky said nothing about it. What would have been the point? The hospital had said she was OK and that should have been good enough. Besides, Nicky wasn't going to say anything with Jason's mum there. She'd have been bound to make a big production of it.

13

All this formed the principal part of Maxine's narrative to Wexford on the Monday. Without apology, she interrupted Gibbon to tell him about 123 Ladysmith Road, Jason's anxiety over Isabella, and the dramas of Diane Stow's arrival. Wexford had been reading about "two fierce and enormous bears," named Innocence and Mica Aurea, pets of the Emperor Valentinian's. *The cages of those trusty guards were always placed near the bedchamber of Valentinian, who frequently amused his eyes with the grateful spectacle of seeing them tear and devour the bleeding limbs of the malefactors who were abandoned to their rage. Their diet and exercises were carefully inspected by the Roman Emperor: and when Innocence had earned her discharge by a long course of meritorious service, the faithful animal was again restored to the freedom of her native woods.*

He laid volume two down and listened to Maxine. A kind of foreboding had taken hold of him—highly unusual with him—that all might not be well with Isabella Sams, that beautiful blond child with her one-word vocabulary. As he had thought before, this might not be a laughing matter. Perhaps Maxine's son might not be an overanxious parent. Perhaps there was real need to be alarmed about Isabella's condition.

He seldom spoke seriously to Maxine about the Sams family, he seldom spoke at all, but now he did. "What is Jason worried about?"

"He reckons the Princess Diana didn't do enough tests, scans, whatever you call them. They sent her home too soon. It's like I said, hospitals never want to keep you in over the weekend."

"He should take her back there if he's worried."

Maxine reacted not as he would have expected her to, aggressively, militantly, but as her own parents might have done or her farm-labourer grandfather, with the onetime working-class awe of doctors and hospitals. "Well, you don't like to, do you? It's like they know better than what you do. Jason said the same."

Wasn't it most likely that the Princess Diana Hospital did know better than Jason Sams and his mother? Of course it was. What did Maxine and her son know about scans and tests? Less than nothing, he thought, and went back to Gibbon and wondering what made a man enjoy seeing wild animals tear a prisoner to pieces, a man otherwise merciful enough to give that wild animal its freedom rather than kill it. People were strange, then and now.

He saw nothing of Burden all the week. There was nothing to say. December came in with a snowstorm, and phenomenally large flakes clogged the train lines, making the London-to-Eastbourne train seven hours late. The lead story in Wexford's newspaper on Friday morning was the release of Duncan Crisp, with a photograph of the gardener outside his own front door in Greenwood Court.

"Why did you let him off the hook?" Wexford asked in Burden's office, where he, Burden, and DI Vine sat having coffee.

"It was your buddy Jason Sams who unhooked him," Burden said.

"No buddy of mine. What had he to do with it?"

"He's the manager of Questo, and in that job, wandering round the store at all hours, he gets to know his customers, at any rate by sight."

Vine took up the story. "He particularly knew Duncan Crisp because Crisp had complained about one of his staff, a woman on the checkout. He said she'd called him 'elderly' and he wanted to see the manager. This was at two fifty on October eleventh. All complaints have to be noted and logged, apparently. Crisp was told at first that he couldn't see the manager, Mr. Sams was busy. Crisp, who was sort of in his rights, I'd say, refused to move and just stood there, refusing to pay for his shopping until he got what he called justice. Well, after about ten minutes a supervisor appeared and said she'd take him to Mr. Sams. He said the checkout woman had to come too, so she did, causing a great deal of disruption in the store."

"More complaints ensued," said Burden, "from the people in that particular checkout's queue. Anyway, Crisp and the checkout woman, Mrs. Louise Wilson, and the supervisor, Mrs. Amina Khan, all went to see Jason Sams, and Louise Wilson said that what she'd said to Crisp was that they usually packed the goods into bags for elderly people and would he like the service? That was the cause of it all. By this time it was twenty past three, and Crisp was pacified by having his stuff packed and a free lift home in the car belonging to the supervisor whose shift had just ended."

"We've talked to all these people, sir," said Vine. This time Wexford didn't bother to correct him. "Louise Wilson and Amina Khan all corroborate Jason Sams's story. There's no doubt Crisp was in the store from some twenty to three until three thirty, and then in the car with Amina Khan until she dropped him off at his flat in Greenwood Court."

"Never mind the gloves," said Burden. "Never mind the faulty memories of those women at Dragonsdene House. You might ask why Crisp never mentioned this Questo business before."

"I was just going to," said Wexford.

"Well, he says he didn't forget, he just thought it would show him up in a bad light as a trouble-maker."

"OK, I can believe it. As a matter of fact Jason's mother told me the story weeks ago, but without the names." Wexford met the astonished eyes of the two officers. "People are strange," he said, and thought of the Emperor Valentinian and Innocence, the bear.

14

When next she came to Wexford's house, Jason's mother began telling him the story all over again, albeit in a slightly different version. Jason was now a hero. He had mended his ways when his daughter was born, but only now had he made a positive move to ally himself with the law. Or "work with the police," as Maxine put it.

"I wouldn't be surprised if they made him a special constable," she began, "but you'd know more about that than me." This was certainly true, Wexford thought, laying aside Gibbon for politeness' sake. "He went to Mr. Burden of his own accord, you know, went to volunteer what he knew would be vital information. Out of the goodness of his heart it was, no one told him he ought to do it, nothing like that. What's more, that fella Crisp had caused him a load of trouble, bringing the whole store to a standstill. Anyone else wouldn't have stood up for Crisp the way

172

Jason did, they'd have left him to stew in his own juice.

"Now he'll have to take the stand in court and give a testimonial, but Jason will do it. There's many as would flinch but not Jason. He's a tough nut."

Wexford was aware that he ought to set Maxine right. There was no prospect of Jason's going into a witness box and giving evidence either for or against Duncan Crisp. Crisp hadn't done it, Crisp was innocent and free (like the bear), but Wexford couldn't face telling all that to Maxine, couldn't face the argument that would ensue. He had never yet argued with Maxine and didn't want to start now. Besides, he had an appointment with Georgina Bray.

He walked to her house, noting that Christmas decorations were already going up inside houses and one of his neighbours had a Christmas tree, as yet undecorated. Mrs. Bray too had put up a few dispirited paper chains, the old-fashioned kind that people used to make themselves out of coloured paper strips. Wexford, taking a seat under one such chain, remembered making one for his children years ago, licking the end of the strip and linking it with the previous.

"I think it's a pity to buy everything ready-made, don't you?" said Georgina. "The things you make yourself are unique, after all, and much prettier."

Wexford couldn't agree and again didn't want to start an argument. Any Christmas decorations he made would be a disaster, he thought. Still, it was a relief to be able to talk to this woman without being sworn at or begged for forgiveness.

"My husband says it's ridiculous putting up decorations when you're not religious, but I like to do it for old times' sake."

Having no idea what she meant, Wexford only smiled. "You were a close friend of Sarah Hussain's but you're not a churchgoer yourself?"

"None of us are, not me, not my husband or the children. Sarah didn't seem to care. She and my husband had long talks about theology. They were quite close—too close, I sometimes thought, though there was nothing in it." She gave a shrill laugh. "He said he liked talking to an intelligent woman for a change."

Was this the verbal abuse she had mentioned? Perhaps. "Mrs. Bray—or do you prefer *Ms.?*"

"Oh, call me what you like. So long as you don't call me too late for breakfast, as my father used to say."

He was rather taken aback, wondering why on earth Sarah Hussain had chosen this woman for a friend. Loneliness? Any port in a storm, as *his* father used to say? "Mrs. Bray, would you tell me what you know of Sarah's family? And her husband's family. And what Clarissa knows—if in fact you know that."

"What a lot of *knows,*" said Georgina with a giggle. "If you want a family tree, I can't do that. Anyway, when people get into third cousins once removed and all that stuff, I'm lost."

"So am I. I don't want that sort of thing. How about her husband? I don't even know what he was called apart from Leo."

Georgina was silent for a moment. As her face grew pensive, so she seemed to become more intelligent. When at last she spoke, she sounded like the close friend she had claimed to be. "His father was killed in the crash. His mother was still alive when Sarah came here. He had a twin brother, an identical twin in point of fact. He was called Christian, and when she told me, I thought, with a name like that and being *identical* you'd think she might have taken up with him, but when I suggested it—maybe I shouldn't have—she got really angry.

"She talked about Leo a lot when I first knew her. That was four years ago. She had just come here and she seemed to need a friend. Well, I was that friend. I expect you're thinking we didn't have much in common, her so brainy and me, well, not so brainy." He might well have been thinking along those lines, but he hadn't been. His thoughts were centred briefly on this woman's having once told him that she had met Sarah not four years before but at university. "She had really adored him," Georgina went on.

"But I expect you've heard that already. His name was Leo Steyner. I'll write it down for you because it's got a weird spelling." She fetched a sheet of paper from a desk in the corner of the room and wrote Sarah Hussain's husband's name down in large block letters.

For about five minutes Georgina digressed into a long and repetitive description of Sarah's grief, the poetry she wrote, all for Leo, the diary she had kept throughout her short married life and frequently reread, his parents she kept in touch with, often staying with them—all this coming to an end when Clarissa was born.

"But you didn't know her then, did you?"

"She told me." It seemed to Wexford that Georgina explained herself rather too hastily. "She said she didn't talk about her husband anymore. She thought about him just as much but she no longer talked about him. When I got to know her really well, I asked her how Clarissa had—well, how she came to exist. Leo, her husband, had died years before. She looked me straight in the eye and said she'd prefer not to say. She liked to be open and honest about things, but there were some things that just had to stay private. There were questions I wanted to ask but I couldn't, I just couldn't, I felt too awkward. I'm sure I was blushing all the time."

Wexford thanked her and left. Sylvia had invited him to lunch, it being her day off. The altercation over Robin and Clarissa apparently forgotten, she had been inviting him rather a lot lately, and he thought it was therapy for what she must consider an idle life. Poor old dad, not enough to do, often at a loose end, give him one of his favourite unhealthy dishes, perk him up. It need not happen more than, say, once a fortnight. She mentioned her son and his girlfriend only to say that they had been busying themselves in arranging Sarah Hussain's memorial service.

The dish today was lamb's liver and bacon, mashed potatoes, and peas that had once been frozen but tasted like fresh. Women, he thought, were no longer prepared to sit down with a colander and shell peas. It puzzled him that they had done it for so long. Ever since Georgina had told him about Sarah's insistence on privacy, and how she, Georgina, had blushed as if she detected something to her unmentionable, he had silently been speculating. Now he brought it out into the open.

"Have you ever known anyone who inseminated herself?"

"Who *what?*"

"Come on, Sylvia, you heard. Have you?"

"The thing is to use a turkey baster, I believe, but I'm not really sure what that is. I never needed that kind of thing myself."

"Don't pull your rank."

She laughed. "I heard of someone doing it,

and she chose a gay friend to be the donor. Apparently, he was very good-looking and had a nice personality."

Wexford left it, moving on to another enquiry. He thought he'd better ask even if she bit his head off. "What news on the Robin-Clarissa front?"

"It's still going strong." There was to be no severing of heads. "I wouldn't tell Mother, she'd be shocked, but I bought a whole lot of packets of condoms for Robin. The pharmacist did a double take in case I might be a transvestite, but he sold them to me. Robin was *grateful*."

"So I should think would Clarissa be."

"I wasn't bothered about her," said Sylvia, bringing in the Eve's pudding. "I don't want to be a grandmother just yet."

Happy to be on good terms with his daughter once again, Wexford walked home by a circuitous route, which took him along Ploughman's Lane, Kingsmarkham's millionaires' row, from the heights of which he could have a panoramic view of Cheriton Forest and the downs. Such walks were not so much for his health and his figure as for thought. He had sometimes read of writers and artists giving interviews in which they said how much more fruitful a walk was for thoughts and the working out of problems than sitting at a desk or standing at an easel, where you only fell asleep. Falling asleep was not possible even while taking a break by sitting on the bench at the crown of the hill. The sudden gusts of wind that day would blow you awake if you momentarily dozed off.

No one was on the bench, just as he had met no one while climbing the hill. The citizens of Kingsmarkham were not inclined to walking, especially in December. A good many of them in their cars had gone by.

His thoughts and observations in the past quarter of an hour mainly concerned Georgina Bray, and he concluded that she was a fantasist. Or *fabulist,* which he thought an even better word for it. She invented events but she also embroidered. He was sure about her mentioning the meeting at university. He wouldn't have been mistaken about that. Was the woman's motive to impress her hearer, to make that hearer believe that she was cleverer ("brainier" as she would put it) than might be assumed from her conversation? In that case, why tell him her intelligence was so inferior to Sarah Hussain's? When he had been a working policeman and interrogating a suspect or just a potential witness, he had put probable liars to the test by asking them to repeat the story they had just told him. Such people rarely succeeded in repeating the same narrative in accurate detail. But he could hardly ask Georgina Bray to do that. He was a policeman no longer.

If she was lying—*fantasising* would be the kinder term—this implied that everything she had told him was untrue. No doubt Sarah's husband really was called Leo Steyner and he had really died in a car crash, but had he an identical-twin brother? Was he called Christian? He took out of his pocket the piece of paper on which Georgina Bray had written Leo's name: *Leo Steyner.* Why did he want to know it, anyway? It was of no use. Would there be any point in finding Christian Steyner, a man no doubt long married and probably a father, a man who had by now half forgotten Sarah Hussain?

Perhaps he could put all this to the test by trying it out on Thora Kilmartin. Thora he could trust. She was, of course, lumbered with that difficult husband. But there was a way of circumventing him. One of the advantages of the mobile phone, he sometimes thought, was that the chances were that when you made a call to it, you could be sure of the identity of the woman or man who answered. Possibly one would lend one's phone to someone else, but surely rarely. At any rate, he knew that when he called Thora's number, she would answer and not Tony Kilmartin.

He completed his homeward walk thinking of Jason Sams and his intervention in the case of Duncan Crisp, made no doubt not, as Jason's mother thought, out of public-spiritedness or respect for the law, but just to look well with the police. Laughing at Maxine's tales of Jason and his partner, child, and siblings had been suspended around the time of Jeremy Legg's car accident, but Wexford and Dora could cautiously revive it once danger seemed past. After all, the prospect of another anecdote of Jason's business success, wild estimate of Isabella's future, or comment on Nicky's good fortune in having such a partner mitigated the presence of Maxine in the house.

Thora Kilmartin he called when he got home. Their parting had been friendly in a cold sort of way, but now she seemed genuinely pleased to hear his voice. Of course they must meet again, but she would be coming to Kingsmarkham for Sarah's memorial service. Would he be there? He had forgotten about the memorial service, but now he'd been reminded it was taking place, he would. Perhaps they could talk afterwards. Thora said her husband wouldn't be with her, and from her tone when she mentioned the man's name, he could almost see the distortion of her face and the casting up of eyes.

Wexford and Dora had their shared laughter and their amused mulling over Maxine's narrative of the morning—but just once. Although they didn't know it, the laughter was due to stop. Almost from this moment Jason Sams was no longer funny.

Without exaggeration he could be called a figure of tragedy. For them it began with Maxine's not coming to work and not phoning to explain why not, an almost-unheard-of happening.

"Lost her mobile, I expect," said Dora.

"Hasn't she looked down the back of the sofa?"

Maxine hadn't lost her phone. She was not thinking about phones except as a means of summoning medical help, and this had been done within two minutes of Jason's going into his daughter's bedroom at seven thirty in the morning. In spite of Nicky's telling him to leave her alone, be thankful for a bit of peace, he had been surprised by no sound coming from Isabella's room, no crying or shouting and no sudden appearance of the child calling out for Daddy. She was still in her cot and was jerking up and down, her whole body making violent rhythmic movements. Jason called, "Isabella!"

All her attention seemed concentrated on these dreadful jerks. She was voiceless, not crying, showing no pain or fear, simply caught up in what her father could recognise, though he had never before seen one, as a fit. Standing there, aghast, sick with terror, he pulled his mobile from his pocket and dialled first 999 and then his mother. Then he shouted out to Nicky. She came in, the words of reproach for his calling her from sleep stilled on her lips. She ran to Isabella and would have lifted her up but for Jason's shouting at her to leave the child alone, help was coming, an ambulance was coming.

Maxine arrived a minute before the paramedics. She had seen a baby "fitting" before, her own brother when she was five and he was nearly one, and she had never forgotten it. But what had caused it she couldn't remember if she had ever known. He had grown out of it, and while she was telling Jason that Isabella would surely grow out of it, the ambulance arrived, the paramedics were let in by Nicky and came upstairs. They called Isabella's condition a seizure, which sounded worse than *fit* to Jason. The jerks had now stopped, she was still, her lips were blue, and she seemed to have fallen asleep.

"Maybe it's in the family," said Maxine.

"Not in mine," shouted Nicky.

"Never," said Jason grimly. "I know what's caused it. I know."

But no one was interested in Jason's diagnosis. Isabella was taken to the Princess Diana Memorial Hospital, and her parents and grandmother went with her. There the doctor told them that seizures were quite common in infants, the cause often unknown, they seldom lasted more than a minute and seemed not to cause any permanent harm. They would do some tests, and meanwhile she was sure there was nothing to worry about.

Jason could have gone to work, Isabella was in

no danger, but he said in an ominous tone that he had better things to do and phoned in to say his daughter was seriously ill. They would have the test results in a day or two, but meanwhile—a favourite word with the lady doctor—they should take her home. Jason also returned home and went immediately on the Internet, where he looked up seizures and children and found that such phenomena could be caused, as he already knew, by some accident or trauma to the head. A doctor would have told him how unwise it was to consult the Internet about medical matters. But Jason didn't ask a doctor, and if he had, he would only have interpreted such advice as fear of patients' taking away doctors' jobs. He didn't ask anyone. He jumped into his car and drove straight to Stringfield.

Having been released on police bail, Jeremy Legg was at home. Jason saw him peering out of one of the upstairs windows. Jason parked the car in the lane, close up under the overhanging hedge, which was dripping water from the recent rain. All the way here he had been feeding his rage, reminding himself how Jeremy had insisted on driving Nicky and Isabella the shortish distance to Ladysmith Road, how he had withheld the key until the last possible moment, and, worst of all, how he had been drinking prior to that drive. Jason himself wasn't much of a drinker. He seldom drank because he didn't like the taste.

Therefore, he deeply disapproved of people who drank, particularly those who drank to excess. All these things that he had been thinking about on the way to Stringfield had exacerbated his anger. If he had looked at himself in the car's mirror, he would have seen that his normally whey-coloured face had grown a blotchy dark pink. He could feel a pulse beating in his neck. He clenched his fists and on his way up the path kicked at a tree trunk.

Jeremy was at home alone and expected to be for the next two days. Fiona was going to her mother's in Pomfret after work and intended to stay there, returning home on Sunday. Audrey Morrison was down with flu, and Fiona would be looking after her, doing the shopping, and monitoring her condition as her mother tended to pneumonia. Jeremy was glad to see the back of Fiona for a while. When she was with him, she seemed to talk of nothing but the coming baby, mainly her lecturing him on how to care for infants, what you fed them on, watching them for signs of malaise, and, worst of all, changing their nappies. A new trouble had come upon him. Diane had phoned and followed up her call with one of her handwritten letters, not an e-mail. The house in Peck Road was in "a disgusting state." The carpets were stained with blood and "worse." Someone had papered the walls in the bedrooms, one with a paper patterned in scenes from SpongeBob SquarePants, the other with bunches of red roses and blue ribbons. Her pictures which still hung on the walls when she left for Spain had been taken down and stacked in the cupboard under the stairs, two of them with their glass cracked. She estimated the cost of the damage at eight hundred pounds and expected that sum either from him or "those people who have been illegally squatting in my house." He could have a week in which to pay up or he could deal with her solicitor. There was no mention of the house's being rented and not belonging to her.

Jeremy was rereading this letter and sipping grappa from the bottle when the doorbell rang. Having seen him come, he already knew it must be Jason at the door. Would Jeremy take this opportunity to ask him about Diane's money? His usual course in like situations was to postpone, always to put off till tomorrow what he could do today. He opened the front door, said, "Hi," and stepped aside to let Jason in.

Jason said nothing. He went inside and slammed the door behind him.

Jeremy said in an ingratiating tone, "Come along through. What can I do for you?"

"You've done enough," said Jason, smelling the grappa on Jeremy's breath. Pulling back his right arm, he punched him on the jaw. Jeremy gave a choking cry as his body crumpled, sinking from the waist down, his horrified eyes staring as he fell. But before he touched the ground, Jason had grabbed him by the shoulders and pulled him to his feet. Pushing him against the wall, which Jeremy began feebly to slide down, Jason aimed a second punch at him and, as he fell, groaning, kicked his crumbling shins.

He was still lying there, moaning now, his eyes staring when Jason left, walked out to his car, and drove to the supermarket. At least he could put in half a day's work. Unable to resist telling someone what he had done, he first phoned Nicky, then his mother. Nicky he first asked how was Isabella, was told she was fine, and gave an account of his prowess at Stringfield that morning. Instead of congratulating him, Nicky asked what he wanted to do that for and she hoped there wouldn't be any trouble. His mother was a more gratifying audience. Jeremy Legg had got what he'd been asking for. Driving drunk and with an innocent baby in the car! Could she tell Mr. Wexford what had happened? Would he mind? Tell him what you like, said Jason. I'm in good with the cops, they love me.

Jeremy had promised to call Fiona at her mother's that evening, but this promise, like most that he made, was broken. When it got to nine thirty, she phoned him but got no reply. This wasn't unusual. His mobile phone was stuffed full of unread messages, and as for the landline, he seldom got to it in time. She wasn't worried. Knowing that she might not be in touch with him for forty-eight hours hardly perturbed her. She would see him soon enough. Since she'd discovered her pregnancy, Fiona had almost ceased to think about Jeremy. Her thoughts and inner musings were concentrated on the coming baby. Jeremy she already regarded as a child-minder but one without as yet a child to mind. She tried phoning him again in the morning from the optician's, but after four rings she ended the call, it wasn't worth the trouble.

The weekend came and with it, on the Saturday, Sarah Hussain's memorial service. Dora and Wexford attended it, she because she was a parishioner and a church attender, he in the hope of seeing everyone who knew the murdered vicar gathered together under St. Peter's angel roof. They were among the first arrivals, as were their grandson Robin and Clarissa Hussain, probably the first occasion in their lives, Wexford thought unkindly, that those two had been on time for anything. Both were unsuitably dressed in jeans (in Robin's case, the ragged kind, with holes in the knees), T-shirts with pictures on them of endangered species, and distressed-leather jackets. Stepping out of an ancient Jaguar just outside the church gate and on a double yellow line was an old woman in an equally ancient fur coat holding the arm of a man in his early fifties, a tall, handsome man whose once-golden hair had faded to straw, his light complexion reddened and his blue eyes paled to silver, as often happens with very fair men. He reminded Wexford of someone, not his colouring but his classical features, but who it was Wexford couldn't remember. Left behind in the old Jaguar, seated at the wheel, was a dark-haired man of much the same age, good-looking in a surly way, who looked as if he intended to remain there for he had taken a book from the glove compartment and was reading it. Had he stayed where he was in case some assiduous traffic warden told him to move? Was he waiting for the fair man and the old woman to return at the end of the service?

Wexford and Dora went into the church and were presented with an order of service. Just ahead of them was Dennis Cuthbert, holding on to the arm of a man in his thirties who looked rather like him and was even taller. Dora nodded to both of them, smiling in the decorous way that is correct at such functions. Nardelie Mukamba, the Congolese woman from Oval Road, Stowerton, was a surprise attender, though Wexford reproved himself with racism for thinking that way. The organist was playing a voluntary. Handel, Wexford recognised, but which Handel he couldn't tell, only that it wasn't the "Dead March" from *Saul*. They took their seats more or less in the middle and found themselves one row in front of Dennis Cuthbert, who was now seated next to a woman Dora whispered was the president of the Young Wives' Group. Cuthbert could be heard speaking scornfully about the "modern" hymns Clarissa had chosen, scoffing at the folksinger she had chosen to sing "She Moved Through the Fair" and pontificating in outraged tones about the *Alternative Service Book.* The people who had been in the Jaguar were in the front row as if they were family, which Wexford doubted they could be.

Georgina Bray arrived with her husband, a mild-looking man, though appearances of course were deceptive, and behind them Thora Kilmartin. A host of parishioners followed, many of whom Wexford knew by sight, and rather to his surprise, Mike Burden. The detective superintendent came to sit beside him.

"What brings you here?"

"When you had my job," said Burden, "didn't you always attend things like this?"

"I suppose I did."

As the organist moved on to some Handel Wexford did recognise, the overture to *Scipione,* Mrs. Morgan of Dragonsdene and her housekeeper, Miss Green, arrived. Clarissa walked up to the communion rail and then into the chancel, unaccompanied this time by Robin, who came down to sit beside Dora. Clarissa was so beautiful,

Wexford thought, her loveliness transcending those hideous garments she wore, that the sight of her made him wonder why comely women bothered to spend so much on clothes and so much time choosing them when their own good looks were enough. An old proverb came back to him: good wine needs no bush. She spoke about her mother, how good she had been, a true Christian, a perfect mother, one who, if she had been spared, would have brought many errant souls back to this church. Wexford listened, but all the time he was watching the pale, faded man in the front row—whose profile he could see from where he sat and whose eyes were fixed on the speaker—who leant forward and lifted his head the better to devour with his eyes everything about the girl who stood and spoke. Who could he be? Sarah Hussain had had so few men in her life. A cousin? A onetime boyfriend no one knew about? Wexford would ask him, but ask as a private person, not a former police officer.

Clarissa went up into the pulpit and read a poem by George Herbert. The last lines Wexford thought might have applied to Sarah, they were well chosen.

I envy no man's nightingale or spring;
Nor let them punish me with loss of rhyme,
Who plainly say, my God, my King.

Dennis Cuthbert looked angry. No doubt he expected and would have preferred a passage from the Authorised Version of the Bible. They sang a hymn Wexford didn't know but Dora did. The rector of the Parish of St. Cyprian, Myringham, spoke a twenty-minute-long tribute, there was a prayer, then another hymn, during which the fair, faded man and old woman in the fur coat left. *Slipped out* would be the phrase, Wexford thought. He attempted to follow them but Dora stopped him. "No, darling, you mustn't, you really mustn't."

When it was over and they were all filing out, the woman in the fur coat and the pale man were getting into their car, the Jaguar driver holding the door open for the old woman. He no longer looked surly but solicitous. Wexford heard him say, "There you are, Victoria. Take your time," as she slowly eased herself into the backseat. Wexford looked for Thora Kilmartin among the departing guests but she had gone.

15

It was Sunday evening when Fiona left Pomfret and drove home. Her mother was much better. The next-door neighbour would look in next morning and do the necessary shopping. Fiona would of course phone as soon as she got home, and if she said she would do it, she would do it. In this respect as in many others she was unlike Jeremy. It was ten minutes to eight when she let herself into the cottage. Jeremy was lying on the hall floor. She dropped to her knees beside him and laid her hand on his forehead. It was ice-cold and she didn't have to feel for a pulse, she knew he was dead. She walked, rather unsteadily, into the living room, where she sat down on the sofa and called 999. He was just dead, she thought, a natural death, he hadn't been strong, he had those sort of fugues and maybe his heart was bad. For a moment she felt a flash of guilt for all the times she had been impatient with him. She was on the phone to her mother, saying she was home, saying nothing about finding Jeremy dead, when an ambulance arrived.

One of the paramedics told her what she already knew, that Jeremy had "passed away," but he added that he didn't like the look of those bruises on his face and the police should be called. That made her feel rather weak, and she had to sit down, fearful she would faint. By this time her pregnancy showed, and the paramedic called the police before making her a cup of tea. Jeremy's body lay where she had found it.

The police came, far more than Fiona expected, photographers, a doctor named Crocker, who was retired but called in as a sort of stopgap until the arrival of the pathologist, someone to measure things, someone to put blue-and-white tape round the front garden, and a woman DS called Karen Malahyde and a DC called Lynn Fancourt. All these women, thought Fiona, what an excellent thing that was. She was feeling better, partly due to the solicitude shown by those two women, both of them anxious for her to take care of herself. Was there anyone they could fetch to be with her?

Fiona said her mother, and once she had got over the shock of hearing that her daughter's partner was dead, Mrs. Morrison, coughing and sneezing and with a raised temperature, arrived in a taxi. Dr. Crocker gave Fiona a sleeping pill, and the two women were eventually left alone.

Next day they had to put up with a police search of the cottage. It was Lynn Fancourt who found Diane Stow's letter, a threatening letter as Burden interpreted it. Had Diane, or more likely Johann Heinemann, caused the injuries that resulted in Jeremy Legg's death? Both of them denied having anything to do with it but since they alibied each other, their denials were considered unsound.

Wexford, at home reading, knew nothing of this. That Jeremy was dead wasn't released to the media until the afternoon. As far as anyone knew, as far as the Sams family knew, and they knew it only from Jason, Jeremy had had a richly deserved beating, which left him a little the worse for wear but in no danger.

"Now no one could deny," said Maxine, "that Isabella would never have had that nasty fit but for her getting a contusion in Legg's car crash. And she could have another one at any time. Caesars, doctors call them." Reminded of the Roman Empire, Wexford laid aside Gibbon, making sure his sigh was silent. "No one could blame my Jason," she went on. "There was a lesson to be learned, as they say, and what he did was to teach him a lesson, make sure he realises what he's done. He went over to Stringfield and gave Legg a sock on the jaw and then another one, just the two, and then he left him there. Let's

195

hope Legg's thinking about what he's done now. Let's hope he's learned that driving with a baby in the car when you're over the limit just isn't on."

"Let's hope so," said Wexford neutrally.

Maxine had been hustled away by Dora and urged to clean the silver, leaving Wexford alone with Gibbon for the remainder of her stay. He seemed to be reading about a kind of tsunami. *In the second year of the reign of Valentinian and Valens, on the morning of the twenty-first day of July, the greatest part of the Roman world was shaken by a violent and destructive earthquake. The impression was communicated to the waters; the shores of the Mediterranean were left dry by the sudden retreat of the sea; great quantities of fish were caught by the hand, large vessels were stranded on the mud; and a curious spectator amused his eye, or rather his fancy, by contemplating the various appearance of valleys and mountains which had never, since the formation of the globe, been exposed to the sun.* He was reading of the tide which rolled in and the enormous flood that succeeded it when his phone began to ring. It was Burden.

"You've heard about Jeremy Legg?"

"Something," said Wexford cautiously. "He's had a beating?"

"He's been killed. It looks like murder, but we're still waiting for Mavrikiev's report. Keep it to yourself of course, but his ex-wife and her boyfriend are in line to be suspects. Can you get down here?"

"Of course."

Maxine had never said that the news she imparted to him and Dora was in confidence. She would certainly have done so if she had known of Legg's death. Wexford had been a policeman, she was well aware of that, but he was one no longer, and as far as she knew, the police never shared their secrets and mysteries with him or he his with them. She had told him of her son's action in ignorance and innocence. But now he knew that Jason Sams was responsible for beating up Jeremy Legg, he was bound to tell Burden, wasn't he? For *killing* Jeremy Legg? Of course he was.

He took his time, not hurrying, thinking, walking quite slowly to the police station. Perhaps he must remember that Maxine had never asked him not to repeat what she told him and he had never promised to keep silent. But he knew it was that ignorance and innocence which led her to confide in him and knew too that she would never have said all those things if she had known he would repeat them to Detective Superintendent Burden. And by the time the police station came in sight, he knew that he must repeat them. He couldn't let Diane Stow and Johann Heinemann continue as suspects.

At his desk, reading a report Wexford guessed

must have come from the pathologist, Burden looked up as Wexford came in and laid the papers aside. "If he'd been found sooner, if he'd not lain there for so long before his girlfriend came back and found him, it looks as if he might be alive now."

"But he died of the beating, didn't he?"

"He died of a heart attack. According to Mavrikiev, and whatever you think of him he's very sound, he had a bad heart, seriously bad. The details are all here. Any trauma—Mavrikiev's word—would have been enough to trigger a heart attack. Mavrikiev even thinks he had a small one as a result of that car crash. This beating he had was just too much. But you can't call it murder. Manslaughter perhaps or unlawful killing."

Wexford was silent. He sat gazing at a horrible calendar Burden had on the wall, a calendar with photographs of police stations across the United Kingdom, one for each month, old, recent, or fairly recent, rustic and urban and one built in the thirties in Hollywood Moderne style. The photograph for December was of a police station in the Yorkshire Wolds thickly covered in snow. He must have turned pale or gone red, something like that, for Burden said, "Are you all right?"

"Oh, yes. I'm fine."

"What is it?"

"You know Jason Sams's mother works for us? She's our cleaner. Well, of course you know. She talks. I mean, she talks all the time and mostly about Jason Sams and his girlfriend, partner, and the baby, Isabella."

"And that's a problem?"

"I don't know if what she told me was in confidence. At any rate, I'm sure she didn't expect me to come running to you. And I don't want to but I must. Of course, I must." Most unwillingly, Wexford told Burden what Maxine had told him, the cause of the trouble between Jason Sams and Jeremy Legg, the beating, the abandonment of Jeremy on the floor in his own home.

"You were quite right to tell me," said Burden, "but of course you know that." He was silent for a moment, but it wasn't Wexford's kind of silence. He was simply pondering and at last he said, "You realise what this does, don't you? I mean you realise the effect of this?"

"Should I?"

"It puts a different complexion on Jason Sams's alibi of Duncan Crisp. He is no longer the trust-worthy, incorruptible store manager whose evidence that Crisp was in the store at the crucial time on the afternoon of October the eleventh is sound. It immediately becomes unsound."

"But those two women, Mike, the checkout woman and the supervisor?"

"I'll bet you anything you like that their evidence will be more than shaken, will be revoked, when they know that Mr. Sams's can't be relied on. They'll both be uncertain of the day. Maybe it was the twelfth or the tenth, they'll say."

"Yes, but wait a minute. Beating up a man out of retribution and being an unreliable witness, a liar in fact, are two completely different offences."

Burden said almost triumphantly, "Try saying that in court. Can't you imagine some lawyer, and not even a very clever lawyer, learning that Duncan Crisp—supposing that he's charged with Sarah Hussain's murder—relies for his alibi principally on the word of a man who savagely beats someone with a heart condition and then leaves him alone to die, a man who by this time would doubtless be in prison."

"All right, Mike. You win."

"In my position, you would have thought just the same."

16

Crises of conscience, if that was the way to put them, had never come his way before, or not to such an extent. He had had all that heart-searching and lying awake at night and bad dreams over taking away Thora Kilmartin's letter, and now it was due to happen all over again. Should he tell Maxine that he had imparted to Burden what she had told him? That she might say she understood he had to do that was out of the question, that she might recognise he had a duty to do that was impossible. Yet he had really had no choice. About that business with the letter he had simply told Burden after a night of agony. Now he had to tell Maxine before the sun went down. Or, more realistically, resolve to tell her in the morning in such a way as to make deviating from this decision impossible. There was only one way to do this.

He found his wife in the conservatory, examining one after another of the tired midwinter plants while outside the window a thin drizzle of snow fell.

"What shall I do?" he said when he had told her of his dilemma, which was almost a dilemma no longer. "If I confess to her that I've told Mike, she'll almost certainly leave. But I must tell her."

"Oh, yes, you must tell her. I shall have to put up with doing without her if that's what happens. But, darling, I do wish you'd found a way of handling her like, for instance, getting up and walking out, saying, 'I don't want to hear,' and putting your hands over your ears. Too late now, though."

His confession in the morning came, unbeknownst to him, after DS Karen Malahyde and DC Stephen Ryan had arrived at 123 Ladysmith Road to question Jason Sams. His mother had dropped in on her way to work and heard some of it. By the time she reached Wexford's house her anger was building up, was simmering, and when he began speaking of how he had been obliged to pass on to the police details of Jason's attack, she exploded in wrath. It was so much worse than he had expected that he even wondered if she was going to jump on him and, screaming in his face, use her long, red nails. He took a step back, saying no more, knowing that anything he said now would make things worse. Her own tears silenced her. First it was noisy sobs, then quiet crying as she sat in a chair, laid her head on its arm, and bathed her face in tears. Dora came in and brought her, not brandy or an aspirin, but a small glass of oloroso sherry.

Calmer after the sedating shot of alcohol, Maxine spoke in tragedy-queen tones. But, as Wexford told himself, she *was* a tragedy queen. Her only son was in dire trouble, and if tragedy is a fate someone has brought on herself, this situation fulfilled the definition perfectly. "I can't go on working here. You've seen the last of me."

"I appreciate that, Maxine," said Dora, "and I appreciate all you've done for us."

"There's nothing you can say to make me change my mind."

As Wexford said later, they didn't even make the attempt. Maxine went home to cry some more and to think of ways she could avoid having to tell Jason how the police had known.

17

Once Jason Sams had appeared in court on a charge of manslaughter, Mrs. Wilson, the check-out assistant, and Mrs. Khan, the supervisor, were interviewed again. With no way to prevent its happening, both had heard about their store manager's court appearance and his alleged offence. It was hard to say if they were affected by this, but both changed their evidence. Mrs. Wilson said she was confused and had only said the date of what she called the "ding-dong" with Duncan Crisp was October 11 because Mr. Sams had said so. A man who would beat up another man for no reason except that he'd been driving a car and had a crash, well, he couldn't be trusted, could he? Mrs. Khan now remembered overhearing the noisy row that had taken place in the store on November 20 between Jason Sams and Jeremy Legg, shouting and swearing, and she'd lost all respect for Mr. Sams since that date. She wouldn't trust him an inch.

Duncan Crisp, who had gone back to work at Dragonsdene, also shouted and swore when the police came to question him again. After calming down, he said he had just remembered seeing a young man through the French windows at the back of the vicarage on October 11. It was the middle of the afternoon and still light, as it would have been until 6:00 p.m. before the clock went back. Why hadn't he remembered before? You couldn't account for what you remembered and what you forgot, Crisp said.

"It's an eleventh-hour or last-ditch try at getting himself off the hook," said Burden when he and Wexford met for lunch at Farewell to the Raj, the Indian restaurant both liked.

"Did he give a description?"

"Of the young man? Yes, the kind of thing that might apply to almost any dark-haired male in his thirties. He added what was plainly an afterthought: 'One of them Asiatics, most likely.' Crisp is a real racist. The whole thing was trumped-up."

"Supposing there was such a man," said Wexford, "could he have seen him from the Dragonsdene garden?"

"Going for his tea with Mrs. Morgan and Miss Green, he could have done or coming back from his tea."

"Where is he now?"

"Crisp? Back home. He's not going anywhere,

so I've left him there. But he killed her, Reg, I'm sure of it. I won't leave him there for long. I never had much faith in that alibi of Jason Sams. All he wanted was to look well with us. He's probably something of a psychologist. He knew that if he said that row happened on October eleventh, those women would agree with him. They'd take it that he knew, and if they disagreed, they must be wrong."

Was it possible, Wexford asked himself, that Crisp had been telling the truth? It was well-known that elderly people's memories often behaved in a peculiar way. They often forgot what had happened yesterday while having clear recall of the events of fifty years before. Was Crisp such a one? "Old men forget," as *Henry V* has it, but some significant things they remember. Wexford could be called elderly himself and was making himself admit it; he was unaware of such things happening to him, but maybe they were imminent. Crisp might recall his school days without even trying, while the sighting of the dark young "Asiatic" man had slipped his mind for weeks, for months. Burden would never be got to believe this. He had been set against Crisp from the start and been disappointed when Jason Sams came up with that alibi.

If the dark man was a fact, a real person who had really appeared to Duncan Crisp at Sarah Hussain's back door (and presumably been admitted), could he possibly be the rapist? As soon as this thought came to Wexford, he realised he was letting his imagination run away with him. Such an idea presupposed that the man was much older than Crisp had said (elderly people generally saw the middle-aged as young), that he had become acquainted with Sarah, that they were on speaking and calling terms. Impossible, he told himself, don't be ridiculous. Mike had always said he had too much imagination, and now he realised it himself. Crisp was a liar, Crisp was old, Crisp had killed Sarah Hussain because he disliked the colour of her skin and the race she came from. It was a crime thousands committed from a motive thousands had.

For the walk homeward, he took the long way round, giving him more time to think. If it was the plain, undeniable truth, he would have to accept it. Passing the end of Sylvia's road, he decided against calling on her. She would almost certainly be at work. As he stood for a moment looking up towards her house, Clarissa Hussain emerged from the front garden and began to walk in his direction. As she approached him, he recalled certain facts about her and her life which, in the past few weeks, had slipped his mind. Her date of birth was one of them.

But the first thing he noticed about her after they had said hallo and she had stopped to talk was the blueness of her eyes. They were dark but still as blue as the sea under a cloudless sky. It was impossible that she should have come from brown-eyed parents.

"How do you like living at Sylvia's?" he asked.

"I love it. It's really nice. I'm so happy I left the Brays and went there." A smile made her even more beautiful. "Most of all because I met Robin."

"That's good." He must ask. Who else would know? "When will you be eighteen, Clarissa?"

"On January twentieth." Then she answered the question he felt he couldn't ask. "Mum was going to tell me about my—well, about my birth when I'm eighteen. I don't care so much about that, but it's incredibly awful Mum not being here to tell me." She hesitated. "I said I was happy and part of me is, but I do miss Mum so much. I'll never get over that."

In most circumstances when young people said they would never get over some pain or loss, he would have told them that in time they would, it was only a matter of time, but it was different here. Clarissa would likely never fully recover from her mother's death. That death and memories of her mother would always be with her, just under the surface of her life, lying beneath but emerging when she was alone, in dreams, in recollections, awakened by objects, by names, and by words once uttered. People who killed others never thought of those others' perpetual remembering, the pain, the sadness, the inability ever to put the crime behind them. Or they didn't care.

"Robin's been marvellous," she said, her face glowing when she thought of him. "I never knew a boy could be so kind. Like thoughtful, you know?"

"I'm glad."

It was always good to hear of one's grand-children's academic success, the passing of exams, the graduation, but surely just as satis-fying to be told of kindness to a girlfriend. Robin in the role of comforter to a bereaved young woman was unexpected and immensely pleasing. Wexford went on his way, feeling more cheerful and content than he had in the past week, feeling that peculiar gratification that only comes from hearing praise of a family member, close to one for the whole of his life.

There was no one at home. Dora was spending the day in London with their younger daughter, Sheila. Dora had picked up the post from the front doormat and put it into the brass plate on the hall table. Mostly it was flyers, brightly coloured advertisements of pizza and curry restaurants and a rather pathetic misspelt offer on lined paper of the services as cleaner (willing also to iron and mend) of a woman called Parveen, describing herself as honest, reliable, and with references. A replacement for Maxine?

He was sure Dora wouldn't want to take this poor woman on.

The only "real" letter in the pile had a Reading postmark. A reply at last to his letter suggesting another meeting with Thora Kilmartin? Probably, but he didn't recognise the handwriting. He took it into the living room, where it was warm, and opened it. The address at the top of the sheet of paper was Miramar Close, but the writer was Tony Kilmartin. Reading only the preliminary *Dear Mr. Wexford,* he thought for a moment the man who had seemed when they met to have disliked him was warning him off writing to his wife. But no. This was quite other and wholly unexpected.

Dear Mr. Wexford,

No doubt you will be surprised to hear from me. Perhaps I should have e-mailed you but I have no e-mail address for you and wasn't willing to ask my wife. I found this address in her address book. Reprehensible, you may say. But there are some cases where the end justifies the means.

The object of this letter is to ask you if we might meet. What I have to say can't easily be said on the phone. I will gladly come to Kingsmarkham if that suits you. Christmas will be upon us in two weeks' time and if possible I would like our meeting to be in advance of that. I suggest Tuesday the 18th or Wednesday the 19th of December. I will drive, so suggest reaching Kingsmarkham in the late morning or early afternoon.

I look forward to hearing from you.

Yours sincerely,

Anthony Kilmartin

Wexford was pleasantly mystified. What on earth could the man have to say to him? His wife had said he disliked Sarah Hussain and had no interest in discussing her or her death, so it couldn't be that. Wexford had not been welcome back in the house, had almost been warned against returning there with her. It began to look as if he was to be warned again, but this time against having further contact with Thora. Could it possibly be jealousy? Like most men, Wexford had a specific taste for a type of woman. There were of course exceptions, but his wife had exemplified that type, dark haired, dark eyed, with handsome, regular features and an hourglass figure. The full bosom, small waist, and good legs were (as the horrid fashionable phrase had it) key, and these attributes Dora had gracefully retained into post–middle age. No fat or over-weight woman would ever have attracted him. Tony Kilmartin didn't of course know this. Wexford had noticed, in private life and as a police officer, that men married to the ugliest of women, those whom to call plain would be charitable, were among the most jealous, the most likely to imagine other men were gazing lust-fully at their wives.

That evening, when she returned from London, he did something he would never have done while a serving police officer. He showed the letter to Dora. She laughed at his theory, then apologised. "Of course you're very attractive to me, darling, but do you think you're likely to appeal to this fat lady?"

"Of course not," he said crossly. "It's just that I can't account for his wanting to meet me."

"If it were jealousy," she said, still laughing, "he'd be more likely to want to fight you."

Next morning he wrote back to suggest December 18 at his home. The man would hardly pick a fight or attack Wexford in his own home and would come off badly if he did, Wexford being about eight inches taller and getting on for twice as heavy.

Christmas was to be spent this year with Sheila, her husband, and their small daughters. Sylvia and Mary would join them, while Ben had elected to stay with his father and stepmother. Robin and Clarissa would be camping in Mallorca. Previous Christmases had entailed weeks of preparation, but this one left Wexford and Dora with almost nothing to do except amass the necessary presents, which Dora had started months before.

Wexford told himself to stop speculating, to dismiss any possible subjects of this meeting with Tony Kilmartin from his mind as unprofitable and probably wrong, but still he couldn't stop sometimes thinking about it. Burden's asking him if he would "sit in on" yet another interview with Duncan Crisp took his mind off Kilmartin and gave him something else to occupy his thoughts. Persuading himself that Jason Sams was an unreliable witness and therefore totally unsound, Burden hadn't yet rearrested Crisp, though this was the fourth time he had had him in for questioning. And probably the third time Burden had asked him about the dark man glimpsed through glass.

This time Burden asked him why he remembered this man, and Crisp replied that he always remembered "one of them Asiatics." They stayed in the mind because they shouldn't be here. Wexford listened, he didn't say anything. Burden asked Crisp, not for the first time, if he had seen the man on entering Dragonsdene for his tea or on leaving the house to return to his gardening.

"When I was coming back," Crisp said.

"You told me before," said Burden, pretending to look at notes, "that it was on your way into the house."

"You can't expect me to remember everything,

not when you put me through this third degree."

Karen Malahyde intervened to ask Crisp how old the man was. Crisp glared at her. He seemed to be a misogynist as well as a racist. "Have I got to answer a lady detective?"

"Yes, you have," said Burden, though not having charged the man, he couldn't enforce anything.

"I don't know how old he was. Young. I said young. He was young to me. How good d'you think you'd be guessing someone's age in a bad light through glass?"

"If you were really seeing this person through glass," said Burden. "If it wasn't an optical illusion or a shadow or the Reverend Hussain herself."

Wexford stayed for a cup of tea and a renewed declaration from Burden that he'd let Crisp get Christmas over and then he'd arrest and charge him. "He's not going anywhere in the next couple of weeks."

Parveen was due to start work after Christmas, not because Dora had high hopes of her but because she was sorry for her. Meanwhile Dora was doing the housework. In theory she and Wexford were sharing it, but as she had known from the start, she was doing almost all of it. It wasn't that he was unwilling, but that he was so bad at it. Like many a woman in her position, she watched him attempting to dust, make a sandwich, clean the oven, and said, "Never mind, darling. I'll do it."

He watched her, lost in admiration, not to say incredulity. How did they do it? How could they bear it, day after day and probably for a lifetime? He'd do the sweeping up outside, he said, he'd clean the windows, but it snowed so much, then rained, that no outdoor cleaning or sweeping was possible. On December 18 there was neither snow nor rain, nothing to stop Kilmartin's driving here. At least, Wexford told himself, he could do the shopping. He bought smoked salmon, quails' eggs, asparagus, white peaches, and black cherries for their lunch, and Dora said if he went on like that, he'd impoverish them.

Out of his own environment, Tony Kilmartin was a changed man. He was still thin, of course, his hair sparse and his back more hunched than it should have been in a man barely in his fifties. But his smile transformed him still further as a smile does with many dour or grim-faced people. Wexford had long ago stopped offering wine or beer to those who had been driving and would soon be driving again. Tony Kilmartin had water and so did Wexford, though it went against the grain, and his visitor's remark as the glass was handed to him, he found astonishing.

"What I'd really like would be a stiff whisky. To prepare me for what I've got to say to you.

But I know I can't have it. I have to drive back."

The wild thought came to Wexford that the man was going to confess to murder. But it *couldn't* be, not unless he was mad. "If it's like that, you'd better get it over before we have lunch."

"Yes, yes." Kilmartin drank some water. "It concerns my wife. My wife, Thora. You may think me disloyal and what I am about to do indefensible. But I have to do it." He hesitated, briefly closed his eyes. Opening them and looking away, he said, "I hope it isn't being rude to you when I say that if you'd still been a police officer, she wouldn't have said what she did. She wouldn't dare. I tell you this in case you think she doesn't know what she's doing, but she does. Oh, she does."

"Knows what, Mr. Kilmartin?"

"*Tony,* please. Here goes, then. My wife is a fantasist. I mean by that, that she invents things, stories, narratives. When I first knew her, I believed them, she is tremendously plausible. Then one after another I found they weren't true. I know a lot about fabulists now, and the first thing to know is that you can't find them out, confront them, and get them to admit what they told you is a lie. They come up with every excuse, every defence.

"Now I know my wife gave you a life history of Sarah Hussain while she was over here after

216

Sarah died. Some of it will have been true, some of it always is, but not the gist of it and not the main points. That's why she didn't want you to see much of me when you came to lunch with us. In case you brought the subject up with me. Did she tell you I disliked Sarah?"

"Yes, she did."

"Not at all. On the few occasions I'd met her I liked her very much. Did she tell you the girl—what's she called? Clarissa?—did she tell you the girl was the result of rape? And that the rapist was a very good-looking young Asian living in a block of flats called Quercum Court?"

"Yes, to all of that."

"And you believed it. Naturally you did. Everyone always believes Thora. She's so plausible, she looks so honest and straightforward. I used to believe it. The effect is of course that I scarcely believe a word she says now. I mean she'll say someone phoned for me and I don't believe it. I don't call them back and they call me and ask if I'm all right. Even so, in the nature of things she'll tell more of the truth than lies. The most accomplished liar does that."

Wexford wanted to ask why Kilmartin put up with it, why he stayed, but of course he couldn't. But his visitor must have seen the question in his eyes. "I love her, you see. And I'm sorry for her."

"Let's go and have lunch."

According to their prior arrangement, Dora had

217

had her lunch and gone out. They ate alone, Wexford disinclined to that expensive luxury food but Kilmartin tucking in enthusiastically.

"I should tell you," he said, "that if my wife wants to meet you again, I will do my best to stop her. Well, I shall stop her. I always do this —I mean, stop her seeing the people she's told her fantasies to. She thinks I'm jealous and of course she rather likes that." He paused. "I'm being very frank with you."

"Yes. You are."

"May I ask if you've passed this tale of Thora's on to anyone else? I mean the police, of course."

"I have," Wexford said unwillingly. But what a blessing it was that Burden had been only mildly interested in the so-called rapist, had never really been able to see this man or anyone connected with him as a possible suspect. "I'm afraid I'll have to pass on some of what you've told me."

"Oh, yes, I know. People always do. Depending of course on how fantastic and dramatic Thora's tales are, they can't resist passing them on to their families and friends. And why not? They believe what she's told them. You believed. I have to undo it as best I can." Tony Kilmartin sighed. He took a long draught of water. "Believe me . . ." Saying that made him laugh. "Believe me, I don't usually tell people my wife is a liar. I try to tone it down a bit. I've told you because—well, I suppose I thought I could trust you and I think I can."

Half an hour later, when Kilmartin was leaving and they had talked about the weather and Christmas and what the traffic would be like on the way back to Reading, he said, "D'you know what I'm really relieved about?"

Wexford waited.

"That she didn't tell this fantasy of hers to the girl." He said in a different tone, "She didn't, did she?"

"No, oh, no. I know she didn't."

Sick of having to confess to Burden, Wexford nevertheless did so that afternoon, walking into the detective superintendent's office as he had been asked to do, with a prior knock but without a prior phone call.

Burden said, "I never really believed it, anyway."

"You put up a good imitation of believing it."

"Well, it was the idea of it rather than its being true. Amazing a woman inventing that."

"Is it?"

"It seems to me like a man's fantasy."

Wexford suddenly felt grateful to Burden. His friend was growing into a better and wiser policeman every day, he thought. What a disaster it would have been if a full-scale hunt for the man, the nonexistent man Burden had once called Ahmed X, had been set in motion. As it was, because of Burden's lukewarm response to Thora

Kilmartin's story, all that had happened was a new DC's spending an hour or two trawling the Internet and another pointless conference.

"Instead," Wexford said, "you've got another dark man glimpsed through glass."

"And that's just as unbelievable as Thora Kilmartin's story. If ever there was a farrago of lies. What's a farrago, anyway? I'm sure you can tell me."

"I looked it up once," said Wexford. "It means 'mixed fodder for cattle.'"

"The things you know," said Burden in a rather scathing tone.

But once again Burden, who might have been severe with Wexford, had been nothing more than indifferent. When I was in his place, he thought, I don't think I would have been as mild and kind with an elderly retired cop. But we are friends too, we are good friends. And he sat down in the conservatory, now decorated all over with Christmas cards, and read Gibbon.

The Huns were ambitious of displaying those riches which were the fruit and evidence of their victories; the trappings of their horses, their swords and even their shoes, were studded with gold and precious stones; and their tables were profusely spread with plates, and goblets, and vases of gold and silver, which had been fashioned by the labour of Grecian artists. The monarch alone assumed the superior pride of still adhering to the simplicity of his Scythian ancestors. The dress of Attila, his arms and the furniture of his horse, were plain, without ornament and of a single colour. The royal table was served in wooden cups and platters, flesh was his only food, and the conqueror of the North never tasted the luxury of bread.

We judge people by ourselves, Wexford thought, and by our own beliefs, customs, and prejudices. How disapproving almost everyone would be these days of a diet composed entirely of meat. It gives you scurvy and bowel cancer was what would be said, and imagine thinking of bread as a luxury. Men and women died before they were fifty, and often they died violent deaths. He caught up with Attila's death some thirty pages later. It wasn't of bowel cancer but in bed on his wedding night (to one of his "innumerable wives") when an artery burst. The men brought to dig his grave were all massacred afterwards. And foolish people, thought Wexford, look back nostalgically and say life was better in former times.

18

On the way to Hampstead on Christmas Eve, Dora picked up on an innocent remark her youngest grandchild, Mary, made about holidays on islands. Why did people like staying on islands? Why were Robin and Clarissa going to an island? Which island was that then? Not only Robin and Clarissa's destination had escaped Dora, but also that they were going together. Wexford, inwardly amused, could tell by the look on his daughter's face that some deliberate deception had occurred.

"Don't you think you're to some extent in loco parentis?" said Dora.

Provokingly Sylvia said, "I *am* Robin's parent."

"You know what I mean, Sylvia. Letting that girl go with him to Mallorca."

"It's not a matter of letting her, Mother. She'll be eighteen in a month's time. If she were sixteen, it still wouldn't be my business. This is the twenty-first century, you know."

"I wonder," said Dora, ignoring this, "what her mother would have said. I knew her, you know, which none of you did. There was no one in her life after her husband died."

If both Wexford and his daughter thought simultaneously that the subject of this admonition must in that case have come into the world by parthenogenesis, neither of them commented. Wexford said quickly that they should change the subject, and Mary asked promptly if she and Sylvia, Robin, Ben, and Clarissa could all go on holiday to the Isle of Wight.

No more was said on the subject, but a phone call came to his mother from Robin on the twenty-fifth, wishing everyone a happy Christmas and sending Clarissa's love. Dora said nothing; she didn't even make a disapproving face. She always knew when she had failed, Wexford thought, and accepted it with a good grace, in this case smiles at both her daughters. He was pleased to have received no socks among his Christmas presents and only one scented candle. The iPod from his grandson Ben he thought a beautiful colour—an iridescent turquoise—but had to ask what it was for. Reading Gibbon or anyone else would be condemned as antisocial, so he thought instead, principally about Clarissa and her eighteenth birthday. Let him get home and the almost two weeks that constituted Christmas in this present day be over. Burden, though, and

Kingsmarkham Crime Management wouldn't take off two weeks. Wexford would be surprised if they weren't back at work for the last three days of the old year. Burden might even spend them at last charging Duncan Crisp with murder.

The detective superintendent waited until after the New Year. Wexford knew Crisp had been arrested and charged only from the newspaper, though Burden apologised next day for not informing Wexford in advance. Burden looked and sounded slightly ashamed. Not so much, Wexford thought, for "forgetting" to tell him as for charging the man at all. Had Burden done it because of continued pressure from the media "to bring the killer to justice in this high-profile murder" and because he couldn't find any other perpetrator?

When Wexford was told, he was sitting in Burden's office, listening to his friend trying to change the subject by describing in a tone of mixed fascination and horror a Christmas present he had been given, a wall clock with a British bird pictured on its face and a few notes from that bird's song sounding at every hour.

"I've seen one of those," Wexford said. "They've got two batteries. Take out the lower one and you won't have any more cuckoos or hoots. But, Mike, back to Crisp. Can you really *see* that man in the role you've assigned to him?

All he was to Sarah Hussain was next door's gardener, an elderly man she may have seen but can barely have noticed. A man deeply prejudiced on his own admission against immigrants from the subcontinent, Africa, and the Caribbean—immi-grants and their children and grand-children—a violent dislike based on nothing but colour of skin, but who had never, again on his own admission, spoken to her. Every afternoon, while he is working there, he goes into the house next door and has tea—a cup of tea and a biscuit—with his employer and her housekeeper. One day, according to your theory, he doesn't go straight back to his gardening—even you aren't suggesting he might have done the deed *on the way to have his cup of tea*—he goes into the vicarage by the back, which is always left unlocked—how did he know that?—puts on a pair of gardening gloves he happens to have with him, and finds Sarah Hussain. He has never spoken to her, but now he does. He confronts her and, accusing her of something even he must know she can't help, the colour of her skin, charges at her and strangles her. . . ."

Burden had held up one hand. "It wasn't like that. I'm not for a moment saying it was like that. You seem to believe everything Crisp says while I believe almost nothing. Of course he had spoken to Sarah Hussain, probably they'd had arguments and quarrels that almost came to blows before. The gardening gloves he had been given by Mrs. Morgan. She had heard you could get tetanus through the soil round here if you had a scratch or scrape on your hand. He never wore them, he refused to, but he had them. He knew the back door was always open because he had gone in that way many times before. His prejudice was far worse than you seem to think. It was paranoia, and in this case it was coupled with his dislike—that's an understatement—of women clergy."

"He never went to church, did he? He had no knowledge on which to base this?"

"They don't need knowledge. It's almost instinct. The way cats feel about dogs."

Wexford laughed. "And what of the dark man inside the vicarage living room that he saw through the glass?"

"You noticed it was a *dark* man. In his book good is fair and bad is dark. My mother once told me that when she was a child, fair-haired children were prized above dark ones. And I'm talking about hair, not skin colour. Black or brown skin would have been beyond the pale in those days —sorry about the pun. Crisp went in there and saw an Indian woman in *Indian dress* and that sent him over the edge."

Wexford had to accept it. He had no choice. But that didn't mean he had to give up looking. In the past few weeks a possibility had been building up in his mind, increasing until it had become a conviction, that whoever had killed Sarah Hussain was closely linked to Sarah's daughter. This certainty had nothing to do with reason, it was some kind of intuition. Yet no one was closely linked to Clarissa. Since her mother's death she had been alone in the world. Her grandmother was dead and she appeared to have no relatives, no aunts or uncles, no cousins. She had a father, that anonymous invisible man. Wexford would ask Lynn if she would search for him, but she would probably have to say no. The case was closed. One could search for family members on websites, but he knew himself incapable of instigating such a search. Robin or Sylvia would do it for him, but both were too near to Clarissa for him to ask them. Could he *ask* Clarissa? It was so simple he hadn't thought of it before.

She was off school at the moment. The new term was about to begin, but with a few days to go. That evening he was thinking about phoning her when the front doorbell rang and there they were, she and Robin, on their way to the cinema.

It amused him, in a fond kind of way, how people of their age always suppose that their company is not just acceptable to their elders but positively sought after. They don't even have to tell Mother and Father, Grandma and Granddad, that they will drop in. They just come and, if not greeted with rapture, are not simply offended but incredulous. Dora, however, had greeted them with the requisite joy—or had greeted Robin that way, Clarissa a tad less warmly—before Wexford even saw them. He performed his effusive-grandfather act, only delighted to see his wife in conversation with the girl. Such a beautiful girl, those blue eyes that seemed to shed an azure light of their own, that skin the colour of a tea-rose petal.

Dora was offering coffee. They looked politely dismissive of this idea and brightened up when Wexford suggested wine. He was opening the bottle and thinking of ways to broach the subject of her family or nonfamily, if need be in the presence of Dora and Robin, when she asked him if he thought it would "be all right" for her to go into the vicarage.

"I mean just have a look round."

He couldn't ask her why. It wasn't for him to do that. "I don't see why not. I can ask for you."

"I've still got a key."

He was sure Burden wouldn't like that. Maybe the Church of England wouldn't like that. She shouldn't have a key. "I'll ask Superintendent Burden, shall I?"

"Please." She drank her wine at a gulp as if it were medicinal and a lifesaver.

"Why does she want to go in there?" Dora

asked after they had gone. "That's a rhetorical question. I quite see you couldn't ask."

"Sentimental reasons, if that's the word. Nostalgia? I would think that would be painful. Just the last time, maybe."

"Or there are papers in there she wants to look at."

Dora turned out to be right.

Burden didn't want her going into the vicarage alone. He gave no reason for this prohibition. "I want someone with her. Lynn, perhaps, or Tim." Tim was the new DC. "Or you. Would you?"

"Sure," said Wexford. "I wouldn't mind taking another look at the place myself."

"Well, don't get any ideas. The case is closed. Crisp did it and Crisp is safely on remand. Oh, and you can take that key from her when you're finished or get her to bring it round here."

Wexford thought she might resent his presence, but she seemed glad of his company. It rather surprised him that she had shed the faded, ragged jeans for a wool dress under a thick winter coat. In his honour? Or out of some kind of respect for the house and the memory of her mother? He asked her, sure she wouldn't mind, if she had any relatives she knew of, any aunts or uncles—he knew she hadn't—or distant cousins. But, no, she hadn't. She was alone in the world and smiled ruefully when she said that. She unlocked the front door and they went inside. It was cold. The heating had been off for nearly three months. A dull, sour smell pervaded the place and cobwebs had appeared, a cluster of them linking the brass chandelier in the hall to a Gothic beam.

"I may as well tell you I'm looking for a letter," Clarissa said, lifting the lid of the desk in the living room. "There may not be one—it would be in an envelope addressed to me—but I had to find out." All that was inside the desk were receipted bills and a couple of notices from the local authority. She opened two drawers in a chest, but if they had once held papers, these had been cleared out. "There's a desk in Mum's bedroom. She told me there was a copy of her will in there, but it wasn't important because the will itself was with her solicitors. But we could look in there." On the way upstairs Clarissa said that probate had been granted and some two thousand pounds, which amounted to her mother's savings, had come to Clarissa as well as a few pieces of jewellery. "It's not very valuable but it has a lot of sentimental value." Her voice broke. "Her wedding ring and engagement ring. She some-times wore them, you know, but like only when she was alone. I once saw them on her finger." On the top stairs Clarissa sat down and sobbed.

If she had been his granddaughter, he could have taken her in his arms and hugged her, but she wasn't and he couldn't. All he could do was hand her his snowy, beautifully folded handker-chief. Thanking him as she took it from him, she looked at it in wonder. In a world of tissues, it was probably the first time she had seen such a thing.

"It doesn't seem right to spoil it with my tears," she said as she dabbed her face.

It seemed that no one had been in to clear the place. Perhaps the Church of England waited until just before the new incumbent arrived. The bedroom was unchanged. There were the portraits, and still on the bedside table Newman's *Apologia Pro Vita Sua*, from which Wexford had taken the letter that had brought him so much anxiety and stress. Thinking of it prompted him to ask if she ever heard from her godmother, Thora Kilmartin.

"I had a Christmas card."

Wexford guessed that in a strict talking to, Tony Kilmartin had warned Thora to back off. Any contact with Clarissa might lead to some fresh farrago (Burden's favoured word) of myths being imparted to her. The bedside-table drawer open, Clarissa had found the copy of the will Sarah had discarded as unimportant and a blank envelope stuffed full. But they were postcards from long ago, sent by school friends from sea-side resorts. "There's one more place to look," Clarissa said.

It was a safe. As in a hotel bedroom, it was in

the bottom of the wardrobe, hidden under the hem of a long, black skirt. Clarissa knew the combination. Presumably, no one else did, which was why the safe was still there and had never been opened. Inside was a packet of letters, all in their envelopes, the lot rather grimly tied with black ribbon.

"They're not for me," Clarissa said, and the tears began again, silently flowing down her cheeks. "They're from her husband. You know he was a landscape architect, and when he had to go away, he wrote to her every day. She kept them all." A tear splashed onto the ribbon. "I don't want to leave them here. What shall I do?"

"Take them with you," said Wexford rashly. This time he would tell Burden at once. "They're no use to anyone else. You take them."

But no letter addressed to Clarissa could be found. It was less cold outside than in, a mild sun shining out of a watery sky. "Come along," he said. "We'll go and have coffee in that little place round the corner."

"Tallulah's, it's called," said Clarissa. "My friend's waitressing there."

The friend, Maeve, was as pretty as Clarissa but a dazzling blonde. Sitting at a table in the window, Wexford ordered black coffee and Clarissa an elaborate variety of cappuccino. While they waited for it to come, she said, "You haven't asked me what would be in the letter that never was."

"I didn't think it was my business."

"I'll tell you anyway." He thought she was going to cry again, but she made a big effort to control herself. "My mother said she was going to tell me about my—well, she didn't say 'my father,' but what my parentage was. She'd tell me when I was eighteen. She can't do that now because she's dead." In a harsh voice Clarissa repeated her last words. "She's dead." She took a little time, a second or two, before going on. "But I thought she might have written it down. I mean, written it in a letter to me and put it in the safe. But why would she? She didn't know she was going to die."

Clarissa put her head in her hands. The coffee came and she lifted her tearstained face. "Will I ever get over it?"

"You'll get used to it." His black coffee tasted more like gravy. Probably it would be improved by milk and sugar, but there was none and he didn't feel like asking for it. "So she didn't give you a hint as to who your father was?"

"Not really. She was like very strict about a lot of things, but I don't think she would have found much wrong with having a relationship with someone. Well, provided he wasn't married. I suppose I think she was going to tell me about this lover she had and maybe he *was* married and he was my father and his wife found out—and, well, I don't know but something like that."

He walked back with her to Sylvia's house, but as Sylvia was at work, he didn't go in. Robin was there, she said. Robin would comfort her, he always did, he was so wonderful. Wexford heard her call out to him as she opened the front door and a distant voice answering. At any rate, the course of true love seemed to be running smooth. Was there no family member to be found that he could talk to? She had said no, but might there not be a family connection? His mind went back to the memorial service, the car with the surly-faced driver at the wheel, the man who had driven the old woman in the fur coat walking into the church with her son. She had known Sarah and known her well while she was married to her other, long-dead son. Sarah had stayed with her after the death of their husbands, and she had cared for her enough to come to her memorial service. She was no relation to Clarissa, but no one was related to Clarissa. Now if I knew her name, he started to say to himself, and then he remembered that he did. Steyner, she was called, and the driver of the Jaguar had called her Victoria. There couldn't be many Victoria Steyners about.

"There are three," Dora told him, coming from the computer. He was always lost in admiration for her when she found something or accomplished something online. Never mind that children of seven did as much and more every day. "You're amazing."

Pleased, she gave him a lovely smile. "One's in Fort William, one's in Mexborough, and the third's in London west eight. Where's west eight?"

"Kensington, I think. That's the most likely. Now for the phone book. Have we got a London directory?"

"I think so, but Victoria Steyner, if she's the one, is very old."

She found a directory for West London dated 1996. It was under a pile of directories and catalogs in the cupboard under the stairs, the sort one never throws away. A V. B. Steyner was listed at a different address from the one Dora had found in the online electoral register. That looked like a flat, while the address in the phone book was probably a house. She moved, Wexford thought, when she grew old and the house was too much for her. It meant the phone number might have changed too. He hesitated. Wait, he thought, think about it, sleep on it. For one thing, she could be the Mexborough Victoria Steyner. He didn't even know where Mexborough was, but it might be a select seaside resort full of comfortably off elderly ladies. Fort William was less likely. At least try Kensington first, he told himself, and think about what you're contemplating doing first. He phoned Burden and told him he'd given Clarissa permission to take her mother's love letters.

"Love letters?"

"Well, letters from her husband. They were in the safe."

"Oh, right." Burden's voice was heavy with boredom. "That's OK. We saw them when we searched. Did you think I'd mind?"

Alone, Wexford shook his head for no one's benefit but his own. Still, you never could tell with Mike and he must be careful. If Wexford was going to set in train an investigation of his own, he must consider what tactics he was going to employ. No deception, that was certain. In talking to people, Mrs. Steyner, her son (obviously not the one who had called her by her given name), the other man, friends of Clarissa's, even the pretty blond waitress, he wouldn't even think of giving a false name or inventing a false role in this murder case. He had once been a police officer, a detective chief inspector, but he was one no longer. People were not obliged to tell him anything, even to talk to him. They could say no and show him the door, always supposing he got past the door in the first place. This he must make clear to them, and when he looked at it from that angle, he couldn't see why anyone would agree to talk to him. If they had anything to say, if they weren't bored by the whole thing and incredulous. At this point he nearly gave up. It wasn't his business, no one else would understand why he was doing it. Why not wake up tomorrow morning a free man, with nothing to do but relax and enjoy himself? It wasn't an inviting prospect.

Dora was watching television. He sat beside her on the sofa, wondering why characters in British television dramas never looked as if they had really punched their adversary in the jaw but that their fist had landed in the air, and why they looked as if they never really smoked a cigarette but reluctantly took the smoke into their mouth and quickly expelled it. It was probably a matter of cost; it always was. Then, as the activity on the screen became wilder and even less convincing, a revelation took shape in front of his eyes: he must do this talking, he must find out more, and before January 20. That date was less than three weeks away. Something would happen on that date. Sarah Hussain could no longer confess or admit or simply tell her daughter about her origin but someone else might. Someone, and he had no idea who, might honour a promise made to Sarah that, in her absence for whatever reason, he or she would on that day, Clarissa's eighteenth birthday, enlighten her.

Ridiculous, he told himself. Like some nineteenth-century novel. Wilkie Collins maybe. But if it was an illusion, it was one he couldn't get out of his head.

19

When for years you have had authority, it is hard to lose it, suddenly to find that powers you took for granted have disappeared overnight and, perhaps more to the point, stayed disappeared. Once he was like the centurion—he *was* the centurion— who says to one come and he cometh, to another go and he goeth, and to a third do this and he doeth it. Once he could have picked up the phone, dialled this woman's number, and told her his name and rank. She would have been overawed —most were—or frightened or, if she was legitimately in trouble, pleased. This one, this V. B. Steyner, was likely to be puzzled by his wanting to speak to her without authority. If she agreed to a talk, she would question him more than he questioned her. Why? Why ask this, do that, be interested at all? He couldn't say, as he often had in the past, "I ask the questions." The call hadn't yet been made, he was still thinking, being indecisive, taking himself out of the house by walking down Queen Street to Kingsmarkham's only remaining bookshop in quest of a new novel that had had good reviews.

The turn into the high street is sharp, rather less than a right angle, and you can't tell whom you may meet or bump into as you negotiate the corner. Wexford walked round without thinking and almost crashed into Maxine Sams. He put out his hands to avoid their faces' actually colliding. She leapt away with a shriek. "Take your hands off me!"

"Maxine, I'm sorry. I'm sorry about that business with Jason too. But I had no choice."

"Don't you call us by our first names. We're Mr. and Mrs. Sams to you."

"All right. If you like. How is—er, Mr. Sams?"

"Thanks to you he's lost his job. He's waiting to come up in court. Unlawful killing, it's going to be, on January twentieth. Pleased with yourself, are you? Oh, you make me sick."

There was no point in lingering. Wexford walked off towards the bookshop, a stream of abuse following him and attracting a small crowd of onlookers. One thing, he thought, being a policeman for all those years, coming up through the ranks, inures you to insult, foul language, accusation, and threat. The fear and ongoing disgust such abuse causes in others—and stays with them, sometimes for weeks—passes over your head and leaves you only reflecting on the unpleasantness of so many people. Anyway, that idiot Jason was going to get away with unlawful killing instead of manslaughter, and he wouldn't be separated from his beloved daughter for as long as he might have been. Wexford bought his book, walked home, and picked up the phone.

An answering service told him that this was Victoria Steyner's phone and asked him to leave a message after the tone. He couldn't do that. What could he say? He would have to try again. But at least he knew it was the right number. Already he was forming in his mind a picture of what she would be like, this Victoria Steyner. Strong, perhaps domineering, used to having her own way, sharp and clever, mentally young for her age. There he stopped himself. He had never even spoken to her or heard her speak. At her age, the chances were that she would be at home in the evening and therefore likely to answer her phone, but not too late in the evening. Old people tended to go to bed early.

A few years ago, when he was still the centurion, he never had time for anything. He was always occupied. Now he hardly knew how to pass the time apart from reading, and even he couldn't read for hours on end. He thought of phoning Burden and telling him what he intended to do, but he knew how that would go down. Crisp was on remand, Crisp had done it, there was no need to look further. Wexford could imagine the tart, impatient note in Burden's voice and his attempt to hide it. At six, when Dora had just come home, they watched the BBC news. Apposite was the item about how people on remand had a worse time while in custody than convicted prisoners. Poor old Crisp, but perhaps he was treated better because of his age. Wexford didn't hold out much hope. At seven, he and Dora had a glass of wine and then the fish pie she had made because he liked it so much. He went to the phone again at eight and she answered.

It wasn't anything like the voice he'd expected but rather high-pitched, feminine, fluttery, and breathless. "Yes, this is Vicky Steyner. Who is it?"

Vicky. The driver of the Jaguar had called her Victoria. "Mrs. Steyner, you don't know me. My name is Wexford, Reginald Wexford. I was a police officer; I'm now retired. I wonder if we might meet and talk."

"Me? Do you really mean me?" The voice was even more fluttery. "Oh, it's such a long time since a man has rung me up and wanted to meet me."

"I assure you I'm harmless," he said, thinking that this was exactly what a man would say if he was not. "It's in connection with the lady who was once your daughter-in-law. There are some enquiries I'd like to make."

She laughed, a shrill giggle. "Oh, how delight-ful! Are you a private detective? I know that gentlemen who've been policemen do that. Will you take my fingerprints? I can lend you a magnifying glass. I've got a new one now my reading glasses aren't quite up to the mark."

"Nothing like that, Mrs. Steyner," he said, wondering if this avenue was a dead end, not worth entering. "If I could just come and see you or we could meet outside somewhere. In a café, say."

"Oh, no! I'd love you to come here. A real man coming to tea with little me! You will come to tea, won't you? Tea at five and then a glass of sherry. That's what I like. Will you do that?"

Her manner had become flirtatious and sud-denly he felt sorry for her. "I'd love to," he said heartily, and they fixed a date and a time. "Tomorrow at five then."

Not a flat, as he had supposed, but a terraced house in a street not far from Holland Park, the only part of Kensington he knew. Though small, No. 12 looked grand from outside, but the interior small and poky when she opened the front door. Her own appearance might have been a surprise if he hadn't previously spoken to her. As it was, he rather expected the pink, flowery garment he thought might have been called a tea gown, the high-heeled, pink satin shoes, and the heavy makeup on her wrinkled face.

She let him in while he was still showing her various items of identification he had brought with him. "Oh, Mr. Wexford, I'm so delighted to see you! I'm thrilled. Now, may I call you Reginald? Please don't say it's forward of me, though it is. But I can't help it. When I meet someone new, I just don't want them to be new for more than five minutes." She showed him into a small sitting room that anyone buying the house today would have combined with the next room by taking down a wall. Furniture was crowded together so that the chair she sat in seemed to be trying to push over the chair he sat in, and his to be thrusting aside a spindly-legged sofa. "I'll tell you something in the strictest confidence," she said in her bird's voice. "If my son knew I'd let a *strange man* into my house, he would have a fit, so I won't tell him! I won't tell him! As if I can't tell when a man is a gentleman, an absolute white knight, a Galahad!" She laid a wrinkled hand on his sleeve. The nails were not red as he would have expected but powder blue. "Now, we'll have tea, shall we? Sugar and milkies?"

Wexford said tea would be nice but no milk or sugar.

"But you don't need to slim. You're just right. A man shouldn't be too thin. A person should have some meat on his bones."

It was the kind of thing men said in defence of their fat wives. But Wexford didn't think Tony Kilmartin would ever say it. Left alone, he peered at some photographs, framed in sculpted silver, of the pale man who had held Victoria Steyner's arm at the memorial service. So this was her son. There were no photographs of the man who had held the car door open for her. She herself was a laughable figure, but how cruel life was to the old. What would she have to do and how would she have to act not to be laughed at, at her age? Wear sober, dark clothes and flat, black shoes, let her sparse but blond hair go back to its natural white, reveal unpainted her creased-up, sunken face? Then she would simply be ignored, so invisible as almost to be tripped over. The way she looked at him, he thought she might be one of those elderly people who hoped that sex might not be over for them. He and Dora hadn't yet left that behind them, but it wasn't in the unthinkable distant future. But this old woman still saw younger men—for he was still a good deal younger—as potential partners, lovers. He was feeling an overwhelming pity for her and knowing at the same time that he mustn't show it. She came back with a laden tray, which he took from her.

"Mrs. Steyner . . ."

"Vicky, please, Vicky."

Immediately, from now on, the other person

could be called nothing at all. "I believe you were very fond of your daughter-in-law, Sarah."

"Oh, I adored her! She was the sweetest thing." He knew a good deal about Sarah Hussain by this time and that *sweetest* was the last adjective to be applied to her. "I expect you know about the accident, don't you?" He nodded. "Of course I was devastated, my beloved husband, my darling son, but I was devastated for her too. Did you know darling Sarah?"

"I never met her."

"She went completely mad, you know. After the accident she was a different person. Turning herself into a vicar! I couldn't believe it when my son told me. But I said to him, the only explanation is that she went mad. When you know she lost her mind through grief, you can understand everything. She used to come and visit me, she stayed once or twice, but she had changed; she was very strange. Obsessed with *God.* She lost all interest in her appearance, and when a woman does that, you know things are very serious. I wouldn't have objected if she'd married again, you know, even though it was my son she'd been married to. I even—well, you'll find this hard to believe, but I even thought she might marry my other son. Leo and Christian were twins, you know, the sweetest identical babies—I thought, why not? Nothing could have made it all right, but if they'd married, what they call the *healing process* might have started."

"But Sarah and Christian didn't go along with that?"

"Poor darlings, I don't think they ever saw each other. Will you have some more tea? A piece of cake? It comes from Harrods."

"No, thank you," Wexford said firmly, though he liked the look of the cake. "Your son doesn't live with you, does he?"

"Oh, no, I'm all on my lonesome." Without actually moving her chair, she edged closer to him. "Did you think Christian was here?"

Starting to feel awkward, he shook his head, then shrugged.

"He lives in Knightsbridge, he's in business there and he's got the most beautiful house he shares with his friend Mr. Arkwright, Timon Arkwright. I expect you've heard of him, he's in the fashion business, according to my son, whatever that may mean, but it sounds very grand, doesn't it?"

Gay, Wexford thought. Not in the closet, though, not these days. Mother has been told but refuses to accept or even take it in.

She laughed a shrill, tinkling laugh. "I tell him—Christian, I mean—it's such a waste of a good man, and so nice looking, staying single, I mean, when the place is simply *brimming* with lovely young girls falling over themselves to marry him. Not Sarah any longer of course. She wouldn't have suited him now. They're the same sort of age, but women grow older sooner, don't they?"

And women like you, he thought, do their own sex no favours, selecting a thirty-year-old as a suitable mate for a fifty-year-old, his contemporary having missed the boat.

"And a vicar!" said Victoria Steyner.

"I expect you saw Sarah's daughter, Clarissa, at the memorial service."

"Oh, yes. Very Indian-looking, isn't she? I never seemed to mind that so much in Sarah. Sure you won't have a piece of cake?"

"Quite sure. I supposed it was Clarissa who'd invited you and your son."

"Heavens, no. I've never spoken to her and I'm sure my son hasn't. It was a Mrs. Bray who told me about it. She wrote. I wouldn't say she invited me, she just said it was happening. I told you, I was absolutely devoted to Sarah and shattered when I heard what had happened to her. My son only went to take care of me, he's wonderful like that, so good, and he got his friend to drive us in that gorgeous old car."

She had not once asked Wexford what his interest in Sarah Hussain was, shown no curiosity in his reasons for asking these questions, barely looked at the ID he had shown her. She was a total egotist, so wrapped up in her own concerns as to have no room for anyone else except a small corner for her son, whom she probably regarded as part of herself. If he, Wexford, had asked her to hand over her credit card so that he could have some detail on it checked and said it would be returned to her in a week's time, she would likely have done so, with a smile and another fondling of his sleeve. He got up to go, knowing she would plead with him not to, and she did.

"But you've only just come."

"Thank you for the tea. You've been very kind."

On the doorstep he thought she was going to kiss him. She brought her face within an inch of his but withdrew it at the last moment. "See you again soon, I hope."

He doubted it but said nothing. She had been useless, he thought as he walked to South Kensington tube station. Yet there were one or two things. She had no interest in Clarissa but she had no interest in anyone. She knew Georgina Bray. How? Georgina must have known her address. He would ask Georgina about that. He hadn't asked Victoria Steyner about Clarissa's father because he was sure she wouldn't know, or if she knew, she wouldn't say. She would have drawn a veil over it; to admit to a love affair would spoil her image of Sarah. Perhaps he would have to see her again. . . .

20

A letter from Thora Kilmartin told Wexford she was coming to Kingsmarkham to meet Clarissa and have lunch with her on January 16. *I didn't want to intrude on her on her birthday.* Thora went on to say that she thought this would be *all right with Mrs. Bray,* as Thora was after all Clarissa's godmother. Thora didn't evidently know that Clarissa had moved out and was now living in Sylvia's house. *Perhaps we could have tea,* Thora wrote, *as I remember we did once before.* She might even stay the night, she suggested, in which case perhaps he and Mrs. Wexford would have dinner with her.

What tale did she want to spin this time? But for a moment he wavered. Suppose she had been telling the truth and Tony Kilmartin was the fabulist? It was the kind of doubt that makes your heart turn over. But no. Kilmartin's story had all the elements of truth while hers was hedged about with caveats and warnings: "Don't see my husband again"; "My husband disliked Sarah." Believing her was to swallow the description of the handsome Indian at Quercum Court, to ignore Clarissa's *blue* eyes, to accept Sarah's refusal either to have an abortion or to go to the police. But still his mind travelled forward to January 20. Absurd as it was, he still seemed to see an emissary appearing on that day, a messenger from beyond the grave, come to the girl to tell her that indeed she was the result of rape.

His phone call to Georgina Bray was welcomed. "I am glad to hear from you. I'm still so ashamed of the way I spoke to you when Clarissa left me."

"Please don't be. I've forgotten it."

"Well, I can't believe that, but if we can both put it behind us, it would be a great relief to me. One thing—I think I must have misled you. I told you I'd been at university with Sarah, and then I told you or I told that nice woman detective Lynn Fancourt that I'd only been friends with her for four years. I didn't mean to mislead. The fact is that I barely knew Sarah at Keele. We only became friends when she came here."

Interesting. He thanked her. A meeting with Burden first, though. Of course Georgina's truthfulness made no difference to Thora's veracity or lack of it, but in a strange way Wexford felt it did. He asked Georgina if they could have a talk about Sarah's family and the Steyners and she agreed. Would he call round at about seven and they could have a drink? She felt strange, she said, a woman asking a man round for a drink. Was that all right? "Quite all right," he said.

It troubled him a little that now Burden had someone awaiting trial for the murder of Sarah Hussain, Burden had no objection to be seen drinking in public. Any press photographer could come into the bar at the Olive and Dove and get a shot of his sitting at a table with a glass of wine in his hand. If they printed it, no one could say he was fiddling while Rome burned. Wexford wondered if Gibbon mentioned that or was it just another myth? For the first time in years, sitting together like this, he and Burden had nothing to say to each other. The weather, of course, that could always be discussed. They were Englishmen. The health of their children, and now in both cases grandchildren, could be enquired after. Desperate for something to say, Wexford mentioned that he was due at Georgina Bray's at seven, and immediately the words were out he could see that this went down badly with his friend.

"It's too late for that, Reg," Burden said. "It's flogging a dead horse. Since I can't imagine that you've started up a personal friendship with that woman, I can only suppose you're drinking with her to manufacture a new perpetrator for the Hussain murder."

"Not manufacture, Mike. I don't believe Crisp did it, and I don't think it'll be long before you come round to my way of thinking."

"I notice you never come up with an alternative."

"Not yet, but I will."

Their meeting had lasted less than an hour, and it was obvious to both that this coolness would resist, at least for this evening, any warming-up attempts. They parted outside the Olive, Burden to take a taxi home—first checking that no reporter from the *Kingsmarkham Courier* was on the watch—Wexford to walk through the lightly falling snow to Orchard Road. A Christmas tree was still standing on a table by a front window in the Brays' house and still hung with fairy lights. It pleased him that Georgina Bray hadn't dressed up for him but was wearing the clothes she had obviously been wearing all day, jeans and the kind of heavy, dark blue sweater that is called a Guernsey. She and her husband, Trevor, were identically dressed, only the colour of their trainers differed, and it struck Wexford that only since the mid-twentieth century was such costume, common to both men and women, possible.

He accepted a glass of Chilean sauvignon, glad that neither of them were wine snobs and about to subject him to a mind-blowingly boring disquisition on the superiority of western South

American wine to southern South American or some such tedium. Trevor Bray seemed to read his mind. "I know it's plonk but it's quite good plonk."

"I'm sure it is."

"You want to talk to Georgie. Would you like me to go? I can take my wine upstairs and watch TV in our bedroom."

Georgina was starting to say that their discussion should be private when Wexford interrupted to ask him to stay. "There'll be no secrets." Wexford turned to Georgina. "Now, Clarissa. We've talked about her before. You think she was the result of artificial insemination and Sarah did it herself."

"That's right. Of course, I don't *know* that. Sarah and I never talked about things like that. I mean sex and bodily functions and biology sort of stuff." Wexford's eye unintentionally caught Trevor Bray's and, rather to Wexford's horror, intercepted Bray's gesticulations, unseen by his wife and aimed evidently at him, the casting up of eyes, the pursing of lips, and the wrinkling of nose. Wexford quickly looked away. "I don't actually suppose she told anyone. Well, she must have told the what d'you call it, the donor."

In a sarcastic tone Trevor said, "Oh, she must, she must."

Wexford was beginning to wish he had taken up the man's offer to go.

"Clarissa's got blue eyes," Georgina said. "I never actually noticed that before, but I did when she was staying with me. So I think Sarah must have picked a donor with fair hair and blue eyes."

This was telling Wexford nothing he didn't already know. Trevor was smiling and shaking his head. "I believe it was you invited the Steyners to the memorial service."

"Well, I don't really know them. All I know is what I got from Sarah. Old Mrs. Steyner was after all her mother-in-law or had been. If your husband is dead, is his mother still your mother-in-law?"

"I don't know."

"It's of such vital importance," said Trevor Bray.

Georgina ignored him but a look of distress came into her face. "I don't think Sarah ever saw Mrs. Steyner after she came to St. Peter's, but she did write to her and phone her. She never saw Christian Steyner or his boyfriend."

"What a word! Don't you mean his catamite?"

Georgina set down her glass so heavily that Wexford feared it would break. She said in a voice as shrill as Victoria Steyner's but firmer, "That's enough. I can't go on with this conversation if you're going to carry on making these stupid comments." She stood up. "If you won't go, I will. I'll take Mr. Wexford into the kitchen and we'll have another glass of wine. God knows I need it."

"I'll go," Wexford said.

"No. Please don't." Trevor Bray was laughing. "My wife isn't endowed with a sense of humour."

"Nor am I," Wexford said, and followed Georgina into the kitchen. She was sitting at the table, crying, her head in her hands. "I shouldn't have come."

"It's not you. It wouldn't have mattered who it was. He's like this with almost everyone. Not friends of his own, just mine. Oh, I'm sorry, I don't mean to call you a friend, that would be presumptuous."

"Not at all."

"He was awful with Clarissa, but still I didn't want her to leave. She was a companion for me and he's not always here. He has to go to work."

She poured more wine for herself but Wexford refused, shaking his head. He had already had a glass here and one with Burden. "You were going to tell me about Sarah's relationship with Christian Steyner."

"There wasn't one," she said, still tearful. "She'd only seen him once or twice since Leo died and that was years and years ago. What's a catamite?"

"A man's homosexual lover of rather lower status than his, maybe a slave."

"Well, Timon Arkwright's not like that. He's a millionaire, according to Victoria. He's got a business making classy handbags. Fifteen hundred pounds apiece they sell for." She dried her eyes on the drying-up cloth. "I'd leave Trevor, you know. I'd love to leave him. He hates all my friends. He dislikes his own children. I think he's a psychopath. But where can I go? And he wouldn't keep me. He'd go to jail before he'd pay a penny for me if I wasn't here in this house. I mean it. I wait on him hand and foot but it's never enough. And when I say I'll leave him, he laughs at me. He just laughs."

The stream of invective and denunciation continued to pour out of her. Wexford felt he couldn't leave while she was like this and the husband in the next room quietly laughing. He could hear the laughter, the soft but penetrating chuckles that reminded him unpleasantly of a demon's mirth in one of those Hollywood exorcism or necromancy films. As he sat there thinking of his dinner which awaited him at home, of his marriage which in spite of vague ups and downs seemed like Eden compared to this one, of his children who never stayed away because of a parent's unpleasantness, she eventually quietened, and he got up to go.

"What you must think of us," she said as he knew she would. There was no reply to that. "You must come back sometime when he's not here if it's not being forward of me to suggest it."

"Not at all," he said, a response he seemed to be making all the time these days.

It was snowing heavily, but he wasn't far from

home. Trevor Bray's behaviour, the wanton cruelty of it, stayed in his mind to the exclusion of all else. He so evidently enjoyed upsetting his wife, it was almost like a game to him, that Wexford saw it as a kind of verbal sadism. Was Georgina alone the recipient of this sarcasm and scorn or were his children also subjected to it? Wexford wondered too if it was exclusively confined to words or if she was made to suffer physical abuse and of a similar kind, an actual stabbing with pins perhaps.

It was next morning before he sat down to write a letter in reply to Thora Kilmartin's. Writing at all, applying, that is, a pen to paper, putting the address at the top and the date underneath it, seemed to him—although he was a stumbling practitioner online—to be archaic, an obsolescent means of communicating that would likely soon be lost to the world. As the old died, handwriting would remain only in documents for scholars to study. Passing away, he thought, as we were now supposed always to refer to death, as if the elderly, faded to shadows, disappeared into the mists where another country existed beyond the crematorium urn. Enough, he said to himself, and laughed as he told Thora Kilmartin of Clarissa's present whereabouts and politely refused for Dora and himself her invitation to have dinner with her. It would be interesting to see if she persisted and, if she did, to find out why.

Dora had a piece of news which she prefaced by telling him that she didn't suppose he would be interested.

"Try me," he said, attaching a first-class stamp to Thora Kilmartin's envelope.

"We've got a new vicar at St. Peter's. A replacement for poor Sarah Hussain."

"Woman or man?" he asked, thinking she would prefer the two sexes placed in that order.

If she did, she gave no sign of it. "Man. He's been a curate somewhere up in the Midlands. The Reverend Alan Conroy, and he's quite old. Anyway, he's retired. Apparently, that's quite common these days. Young people can't exist on the salary the C of E pays—stipend I suppose you'd call it."

"Has he started yet?"

"Next week. They've got people in cleaning the place up but they're not redecorating it. Too mean. That's my opinion, not Mr. Cuthbert's. I've been talking to him and he's delighted. Largely, I gather, because the new vicar's not a woman."

"I didn't know you knew Dennis Cuthbert."

"I know everyone connected with the church."

I think I'll go and have another talk with him, Wexford thought. He was due to vacate the room as Parveen intended to "turn it out." She was at least as good a cleaner as Maxine and far less talkative. She seldom spoke at all and only to request replenishment of polish or bathroom

258

cleanser. He could hardly have said he missed Maxine, and most employers would have found Parveen a perfect replacement, but it troubled him that she looked so sad. Dressed as she always was in a pale blue sari and dark grey veil over her head, she was tall and slender, elegant and upright, the tragic muse, he called her to himself. Dora said she had a husband who was some sort of technician and two children known at Kingsmarkham Comprehensive for their formidable intelligence and Oxford prospects. But her otherwise handsome face looked as if she carried all the sorrow of the world on her shoulders and as if she had never smiled. He told her he would leave her to get on as he was going out, and this she acknowledged with a gracious nod of the head.

He had phoned Dennis Cuthbert and been told that he "could come round" if he could put up with Cuthbert's doing the decorating. There was to be no "electric fire" this time. Wexford drove there, careful of where the snow lay three or four inches deep. Should he mention the discarded lift he had seen in the hallway at the Olive and Dove? Maybe not. A business that was evidently no longer in existence might be something Cuthbert didn't want to be reminded of. The place was ice-cold. The upper part of his body covered in a canvas coat as once worn by assistants in hardware shops and the lower part in the trousers of an old suit, both garments splashed with paint of different shades from the pastel green he was applying to the walls with a roller, Cuthbert descended a few rungs of the steps and extended a hand, not entirely free of green paint spots, to Wexford.

"Take a seat." Cuthbert reached for the cigarette he had left in a saucer on a higher rung. "How are you? All right?" His occupation, perhaps a favourite, seemed to have put him in a good mood. Definitely a bad idea to mention defunct lifts. "Heard we've got a new incumbent, have you? And a gentleman, for a welcome change. He's been here, and d'you know the first thing he did? Called on me and introduced himself. She never did that. And don't say I'm speaking ill of the dead, it's only the truth."

Wexford took a seat in front of the bedspread tapestry, now covered with a dust sheet. This morning Dennis Cuthbert needed no encouragement. "Of course he's not one of these young ones. My age he is, if not a year or two older. None the worst for that. And lost his dear wife to cancer like me. We have a lot in common. He's got one son too, a university lecturer. And that's where we differ. My boy's the reverse of that, what they call a bad lot." Cuthbert gave a final sweep with the roller, surveyed his morning's work, and began to come down. The roller immersed in a tank of paint remover, he sat down and cleaned his hands with rags soaked in the same stuff. "Not to me, though, not to me," he said ruminatively. "Always good to me." Was he talking of his son still? "I'll make a cup of tea in a minute," he said, reverting to the new vicar. "Conroy's his name, the Reverend Alan Conroy. A fine-looking man in my estimation. Gone back to Coventry for a few days now and then he'll be here permanently. He knew her, you know."

"Knew Sarah Hussain?"

"That's right. They met at a retreat. I can see by your face you don't know what a retreat is. Well, I do. I've been at one myself. It's in some country place where the clergy and a few people like me can go and have a quiet time, praying and meditating, most of it in silence and a very pleasant change it is. He told me he met her at a weekend retreat and they talked. There's not much talking at these things, but you can if you want. I daresay they were lonely. People like us are, widowers and widows. I'll go and make that tea."

This was unexpected. Wexford was wondering how well the new vicar had known Sarah Hussain, when Cuthbert came back with tea in two mugs and told him without any prompting, "They met at this retreat, he said, but he already knew her husband or had known him. They were at university together. Oh, yes, I know Mr. Conroy was a good twelve years older but that was because he went there much later than those

Steyner twins; he went to do a theology degree. He told me all this. He was very open. When he and she met at the retreat, I daresay they talked about her late husband, and that would have made a sort of bond, wouldn't it?"

Wexford agreed that it would. He expected Cuthbert to say something about Duncan Crisp, but he seemed to have forgotten the man's existence. He was full of Alan Conroy, and the new vicar had driven everything else out of his head.

"He's going to use *The Book of Common Prayer* whenever he can. He made a point of telling me that. I expect he knew how much it means to me. He said he'd have morning prayer from it regularly on the first Sunday in the month. I could read his mind by then and I could tell he'd like to have all the services from it, but his bishop wouldn't let him. It's going to be such a pleasure to me to have the General Confession again."

"When is he coming?"

"He hasn't got much furniture, but what he has got is coming next week sometime, and he actually moves in on Saturday the nineteenth. He'll take his first matins next day, the Sunday, but it'll be the *Alternative Service Book*, I'm sorry to say."

Wexford drank his tea and left, reflecting that the first Sunday of Alan Conroy's incumbency would also be Clarissa Hussain's eighteenth birthday. It was easy (and absurd) to see the new vicar as representing that messenger from beyond the grave who would bring the girl a revelation. Of course it was impossible. She probably knew of Alan Conroy's existence, but she might never have met him. Wexford began the homeward drive carefully, avoiding the narrow side streets where the snow had settled while he had been in the vicar's warden's house, and making a detour which took him past Kingsmarkham Comprehensive School. Clarissa Hussain, inadequately dressed as most of them were, was coming out of the main gates.

Wexford pulled in and leant across to open the passenger door. "Get in. I'll take you home. I don't mean to be intrusive, but tell me why you teenagers never wear winter coats or even raincoats or sweaters or cardigans. I'm sure you've got them."

She laughed. "It's not cool."

He expected that reply. He wanted to ask her about Alan Conroy but decided not to. Let her tell him without being asked or avoid telling him. He would wait. Instead he said, "Do you ever go to church? I never do but not because I'm not a believer, though I'm not. I'd go to hear the words if they were the beautiful, old ones."

Plainly she didn't know what he meant. "I haven't been since Mum died. I used to go just to please her. Maybe I'll go when the new man comes. I sort of know him. Well, I like met him once." She changed the subject. "Robin's got a job. Did you know? With his First he shouldn't have to stack shelves at Tesco on the minimum wage, but what do you do when there's no work?"

He dropped her at Sylvia's. It was snowing heavily now and he drove home more slowly than he could have walked. His front garden had accumulated a thick white covering while he had been out. He left the snow-canopied car on the snow-clogged drive and waded slowly to the front door, the fall clothing him. Dora had seen him arrive and opened the door. For no special reason, he felt that he wanted to seize her in his arms—because he wasn't one of the lonely, forsaken ones?—but didn't. Snowmen don't.

They each had a glass of sherry, that drink that Clarissa and Robin and their contemporaries had never heard of, while they watched a more than usually interesting weather forecast. Snow every-where: fallen, falling, and to come. Gradually he was realising that what he had hoped for had happened. No messenger from beyond the grave was coming, but an ordinary man, someone who had known Sarah Hussain and might even remember the confidences she had placed in him and have some insights into her past. They had been at a retreat together. If one talked at a retreat, surely that meant any conversation they had had would have been of an intimate and confiding nature. And if it did, would Conroy feel able to disclose it now? This future encounter had the potential of being far better than that with Victoria Steyner; more than that because Mrs. Steyner had been no use at all.

The fate of Duncan Crisp had begun to worry Wexford. A man in his sixties—in his *late* sixties? —shouldn't be in a remand prison even if it was a good one, more like an open prison, according to Burden. Wexford didn't believe this. He had never heard it before. He even thought of going to visit Crisp or trying to. He was sure Crisp wouldn't want to see him, would refuse to see him. If he was no longer a police officer, he had recently been one, a detective chief inspector and for many years. In the unlikely event that Crisp did agree to a visit, what could Wexford do? Only what he was doing now, find the real perpetrator.

Mrs. Morgan, doyenne of Dragonsdene, approached on the phone via her housekeeper, Linda Green, was happy to agree to his request to walk round her garden. That was how he had put it, "walk round your garden," which she translated herself into "see if you can see what poor Mr. Crisp says he saw."

"I didn't know I was so transparent," he said to her when, encountering her in her own handsome drawing room, he was accepting, instead of the eternal cups of tea, a glass of claret.

"Isn't that what we are all supposed to be these

days? Governments are always saying we should have more transparency. Not that they do, they and the banks."

She was a pretty woman in her late fifties, Linda Green much the same age but one of those ultrathin people whose emaciation owes nothing to dieting. She was likely a hearty eater, Wexford thought.

"No one's been here," Mrs. Morgan said, "to check on whether Mr. Crisp could have seen the vicarage French windows from where he says he did. Don't you think that's strange?"

What Wexford thought strange was that Daphne Morgan knew that Duncan Crisp claimed to have done this. When Wexford was a police officer, he wouldn't have asked this question, but he could now. "How do you know that, Mrs. Morgan?"

"What, that he says he saw the French windows and a figure behind the glass when he was coming from my back door? I know because he told me."

Wexford had been sure Crisp wasn't lying but that his memory had been at fault. "May I ask you when he told you?"

"No one's asked me any of this before. Now when was it? Not that afternoon. He didn't come back to tell me. You see, it wasn't at all important then. He didn't know he was probably seeing a murderer. When he came back to the gardening— about a week later—he told me, and I said he should tell the police, but he must have forgotten. I suppose he didn't want to tell them, he didn't want to get any more involved with them. We do forget to do things we don't want to do, don't you think?"

Wexford nodded. "Was there a light on behind those windows?"

"I don't know. He looked at them, I didn't. I'm not tall enough to see over the wall, anyway. But it was a bright, sunny day and the clocks hadn't yet gone back, not on October eleventh, so I don't think a light could have been on. Let me take you outside and show you those windows."

The wall between Dragonsdene ground and that of the vicarage was about five feet three inches high, at present with a three-inch crust of snow. Uneasy with the metric system, Wexford still privately thought in feet and inches. Plainly, Daphne Morgan couldn't see over it, but it presented no problems to Wexford and would probably not have done to Duncan Crisp. Three steps came down from the back door into a paved passageway. But if Crisp had paused on the bottom step and looked to the right, he would have had an uninterrupted view of those windows. Wexford tried it, not even needing to crane his neck to see what Crisp had seen. And more than Wexford had hoped to see: Alan Conroy's furniture was being brought into the vicarage. Wexford had seen a self-hire van parked outside but thought little of it. Now it seemed he was in luck for, as he stood there eyeing the windows, two men appeared behind the glass carrying a table, which they set down near the window.

From the top step Mrs. Morgan could just about see. "So it's quite possible," she said. "It looks as if the new vicar is moving in."

"His stuff is. He's not coming till the nineteenth."

They went back into the house. "Are you a churchgoer, Mrs. Morgan?"

"I was brought up to it, you know. I feel guilty if a Sunday morning passes and I haven't been. I do hope they'll realise poor Mr. Crisp didn't do it, don't you?"

Indiscreet as he had already been, Wexford didn't feel he could openly agree with this. He smiled, lifted his shoulders.

In a burst of confidence, she said, "He's not a very nice man, you know. Quite a good gardener but quite rude too. I think *taciturn* is the word. I don't really like him, but that has nothing to do with it, has it?"

Here Wexford could readily agree that it had not.

21

Rain came and cleared away the snow. Icicles that had hung by the wall fell off and turned into puddles. Clarissa, who had talked about having a party for that significant eighteenth birthday, gave up the idea and did nothing, Robin having taken her to London for the preceding weekend, Saturday-evening dinner at the Wolseley, and a night at the Dorchester.

Sylvia commented that he must be the only supermarket shelf-stacker ever to stay there.

"What a wet blanket you are," her father had said. "They'll have had a lovely time."

The new incumbent had arrived at St. Peter's on the Saturday and held matins at eleven on the Sunday morning. The congregation, often confined to no more than twenty persons, was much larger.

"About fifty, I'd say," said Dora, who had attended. "That Mrs. Morgan from Dragonsdene was there, and Mr. and Mrs. Bray, and who d'you

269

think? Mike and Jenny. I was amazed. Mike's just the sort of man who would have a Damascene conversion."

"No, he's not. I am."

Dora laughed in a derisive way.

While she was in church, he had been reading the *Sunday Times* supplement called "The Rich List," or rather, dipping into it. Somewhere down the list, at No. 88, which still made him very rich indeed, was a name he recognised among all the unknown billionaires: Timon Arkwright. There was a photograph, of course there was, a picture of a tall, handsome man with longish dark hair; too long for someone who was clearly in his forties, one who probably thought that forty-five was the new twenty-nine. But who was he? But of course, the partner of Christian Steyner.

He was reading Gibbon next morning and vaguely wondering how to approach Alan Conroy when the new vicar came to him. It must have been to him because Conroy had already met Dora, exchanged a few words, and shaken hands with her after the service. Gibbon endeared himself even more than usual with a passage in chapter 35 of *The Decline and Fall* and Wexford was reading it again, the more fully to digest it.

The sister of Valentinian was educated in the palace of Ravenna; and as her marriage might be productive of some danger to the state, she was raised by the title of Augusta, *above the hopes of the most presumptuous subject. But the fair Honoria had no sooner attained the sixteenth year of her age than she detested the importunate greatness which must for ever exclude her from the comforts of honourable love; in the midst of vain and unsatisfactory pomp Honoria sighed, yielded to the impulse of nature, and threw herself into the arms of her chamberlain Eugenius. Her guilt and shame (such is the absurd language of imperious man) were soon betrayed by the appearance of pregnancy. . . .*

Wexford was savouring and approving Gibbon's broadmindedness, in the 1770s more-over, his tolerance and great sense of humour, when Parveen showed Alan Conroy into the room. She did it with all the self-effacing meekness of a parlourmaid in Gibbon's own day, and Wexford couldn't imagine where she had learned it.

"The Reverend Mr. Conroy!"

Sneakily shoving the book under a cushion, Wexford got up and held out his hand. It was quite enough impressing a visitor with a perfect domestic without arousing admiration for one's intellectual tastes. Alan Conroy said, "How do you do?"—a meaningless but polite phrase Wexford hadn't heard on a new acquaintance's lips for several years. Conroy wasn't a small man but still wouldn't have been able to see over the wall between Dragonsdene and the vicarage, his reddish hair sprinkled with grey, his face reddish too, and his eyes a clear, bright blue. Blue eyes fade as the years pass but his hadn't. From the moment Parveen brought him into the room, Wexford had been wondering if he was in for a session of proselytising, but the new vicar quickly made it clear this was far from his intention.

"I haven't come to ask you if you believe in God; that would be impertinent when I'm never really sure if I do myself."

"Aren't you *supposed* to?"

Conroy laughed. "Few of us are as devout and —well, committed, as poor Sarah was."

A way in, Wexford thought. "You knew her?"

"I met her at a retreat. Some of these things are very rigid, like a bunch of Trappists, but this one wasn't. Silence wasn't demanded, just quietness and reflection. It was in a very beautiful setting too, in Shropshire. We talked. More than we should have done, but we got on so well. I miss her very much."

This was the retreat Cuthbert had mentioned. "I don't know much about retreats, but I don't suppose Ms. Hussain brought her daughter along, did she?"

"Oh, no. Liberal as the people who ran it were, that wouldn't have been allowed. Sarah talked a lot about her, though. She showed me photographs. I remember she had forty photos of Clarissa on her mobile phone. A very beautiful girl."

"Indeed. She's going out with my grandson."

This piece of information (which might have enraged Sylvia) seemed to delight Alan Conroy but shifted the subject away from Sarah Hussain. It also negated any suspicions Wexford might have. They talked a little more, this time about Kingsmarkham and the surrounding country-side, which the new vicar seemed to know well. How well had he got to know Sarah? The way Conroy talked, it sounded as if quite an intimate relationship had grown up between them. But not sexual, Wexford was sure of that. He was beginning to think that Sarah's only sexual experience had been with her husband.

Dora had sent Clarissa an eighteenth-birthday card, one of only a few which had come that day, according to Sylvia on the phone to her father. "I sent her one, of course, and I think one came from that fat woman. Anyway, it had a Reading postmark." Since losing an alarming amount of weight on the Dukan diet, Sylvia had been inclined to dub all even slightly overweight people fat. "I must say she hasn't paid Clarissa much attention since failing to carry her off to Reading. She had a very nice card from that Mrs. Bray and a package with a pretty silver chain in it. She showed me. And what do you think Robin's given her? An iPad! He's been shovelling snow and cleaning cars to raise the money, not to mention taking her to the Dorchester. But she deserves it; she's a really nice girl." You've changed your tune, thought Wexford, but he didn't say it aloud. "You'll tell me I'm nosy, Dad, but I couldn't help noticing a letter that came for her with a London SW7 postmark. She took it upstairs and I couldn't exactly ask, could I?"

"It will be her mother's former mother-in-law. She lives around there." Only after Sylvia had rung off, he remembered that Victoria Steyner lived in west eight not southwest seven, which bordered on it. Still, people go for walks, they go shopping, and post a letter when they pass a pillar-box. If they indulge in the near-obsolete practice of posting a letter at all. But would Mrs. Steyner know the date of Clarissa's birthday and, come to that, know it was her eighteenth? Perhaps. She had known Sarah quite well, had apparently loved her. There might have been conversations at those meetings they had had over the years very much concerned with Sarah's daughter. There might have been, but the more Wexford thought of it, the more he felt sure there hadn't been. Only the child of her son Leo, conceived within marriage, would have been acceptable to the flirtatious old woman in the pink frills.

Burden was offended with him. He was taking exception to what he saw as Wexford's inter-ference in what was no concern of his. Or that, at

274

any rate, was the idea in the forefront of Wexford's mind. He had meddled—Burden would see it that way—in the whole Duncan Crisp business, in the man's arrest, charge, and detention on remand, daring to be anxious about the conditions in which Crisp, as an old man, was kept.

Wexford was wrong. Like a good 10 percent of the population of Kingsmarkham, Burden had the flu. It was real flu, Jenny said on the phone, not just a bad cold, the authentic virus, not responsive to any antibiotic or antiviral. His temperature had gone up to 102 degrees— translated for Wexford's benefit, for if that had been a Celsius measurement, poor Burden would have been dead, his blood boiling over. Dr. Crocker, officially retired but still seeing favoured patients, said that if Burden's temperature didn't come down by next day, he'd have him removed to the Princess Diana Memorial Hospital.

Wexford went to see him, but Jenny refused to let him get past the bedroom door, making his exclusion worse by telling him that at his age he should be careful to avoid infection. He walked home the long way round by way of Ladysmith Road, hoping not to encounter Nicky Sams but not avoiding the area on that account. If he met with another torrent of abuse—well, so be it. But Nicky and Isabella were nowhere to be seen. Instead he found himself approaching the man he recognised as having seen letting himself into

Nardelie Mukamba's house, tall, dark, in his thirties. They didn't know each other but still Wexford found himself saying good morning.

The greeting was returned, but with a "Hi. How are you?"

Not the words but the accent surprised him, and Wexford immediately reproached himself for making such a judgment. Had he really taken it for granted that a man who had lived in that part of Stowerton, and now perhaps lived here, wouldn't speak with the voice of a cabinet minister?

Burden escaped being sent to hospital, and in a day or two he was allowed visitors. Wexford was admitted to what he called the "pesthouse," his friend's rather beautiful bedroom, as elegant in shades of cream and caramel as its occupant. Burden was up, sitting in an armchair upholstered in autumn-leaf-coloured satin, a fleecy, cream blanket over his knees.

"Crocker's let me get up because I want to get back to work. He says no to tomorrow, but I think he'll let me back on Thursday."

"I haven't noticed things coming to a standstill without your guiding hand," said Wexford.

"That's because I'm guiding them from in here. Thank God for technology. I hate to encourage you, but your pal Duncan Crisp's not well. Nothing to do with him being banged up. Apparently, according to Crocker, he's got cancer. Or he very probably has. At his age it's more than likely, poor devil."

"What sort of cancer?"

"Prostate." Burden reached for the glass of orange juice on his bedside table. "They'll only be sure when they've done some tests."

"Well, I'm sorry. And even I can't blame that on remand prison conditions. People call it prost*rate,* you know. I've heard nurses call it that. And women think they can get it. The other day I heard a woman Dora knows say that a female friend of hers had cancer, and they weren't sure yet but they thought it might be prost*rate.*"

Burden laughed, then stopped as suddenly. "D'you know, twenty years ago if anyone had told me I'd be amused by anything to do with cancer, I don't know what I'd have done. Hit him, I think."

Remembering the death of Burden's first wife from breast cancer, Wexford said, "Why have I escaped that fate?"

"You told me to get over it, but not to laugh."

"Are they going to do these tests then?"

"They are, but not when he's inside. Haven't got the facilities, they say. They'll have to take him to the Princess Diana in an ambulance, or we will, with a guard."

"He's hardly likely to make a run for it," said Wexford as Jenny came in with tea on a tray.

"Mike looks much better, Reg," she said. "Must be your therapeutic presence. I can go back to school tomorrow."

22

The Dukan diet—Wexford said it was much the
same as the Atkins diet of twenty or thirty years
ago—had changed Sylvia's appearance so
radically that he said untruthfully that if he'd
passed her in the street, he wouldn't have known
her. Only because she was sitting with her
mother in the Wexfords' living room did he
recognise her as his daughter.

"You only say that out of envy, Dad."

"If envy means wanting to live on nothing but
protein, no thanks." Cancer was on his mind.
Poor old Crisp. "Too much of that and you'll get
bowel cancer."

"Oh, Reg, really!"

"Really what? She doesn't take any notice of
what her father says, anyway. She'd be an
unnatural child if she did."

"Well, now I'm going to," Sylvia said. "Clarissa
wants you for a go-between, a sort of middleman."

"She what?"

Dora got up. "I don't know what this is about, but I think we should all have a drink. Something white, some of that Cloudy Bay stuff." She went to the kitchen to fetch it.

"You remember that letter I told you about, the one with the London west-something postmark? Well, she told me it was from someone in her mother's past. She didn't say who. Not that it would have meant anything to me, so I don't know why not. Anyway, she wants someone else to meet this person before she does, find out what it's about, and it's you she wants to do this. I was amazed, I didn't know she knew you that well."

"Whoever this person is, does he want a go-between? Does he even know there is to be a go-between?" Wexford paused. "If there is."

Dora came back with the Cloudy Bay.

23

The prison where Crisp was held in Myringham was by no means as unpleasant as Wexford had feared. And the sickroom or san, for "sanatorium," as it was known, was a pleasant enough unit containing five beds, one of which had been occupied by Crisp since he had suffered a haemorrhage a few days before. The prison doctor and the urologist at the Princess Diana Memorial Hospital had consulted and decided to remove Crisp to Stowerton for tests with a view to possible surgery.

Crisp was sixty-nine, not very old by today's standards, but his stay in the prison had aged him, and the prison doctor referred to him as a "poor old guy." His back, never very straight, had become bent, gardening would no longer be possible for him, and it was hard, even for Burden, to imagine him having the strength to strangle a strong woman in the prime of life. It was easier to picture death coming before justice caught up with him. The doctor, a cheerful soul, said that surgery and hormone treatment would likely make a world of difference to his health and appearance.

The ambulance, driven by one paramedic and carrying another, arrived in Myringham at nine in the morning of Monday, January 28. It was cold, several degrees below freezing. Not on a stretcher but seated in a wheelchair, Duncan Crisp, wearing a thick wool dressing gown over pyjamas, wool socks and slippers, a wooly hat, and wrapped in a blanket, was brought out and lifted, still in the chair, into the ambulance. Accompanying him was a prison officer. The paramedics introduced themselves to Crisp and his guard as Michelle Fox and Keith Turner, and the prison officer said his name was Dave Cresswell and, for some reason, known to no one but due perhaps to the prisoner's age or perhaps because he was on remand, presented him as "Mr. Crisp."

Little snow was lying but the grass verges along the country roads were white with frost. Hoarfrost, that Christmas-decoration-like silvering, coated the tree branches, while on the lanes where old, melted snow had frozen on the road surface, care had to be taken to avoid skidding. Keith, who was driving, did avoid it; they moved onto the bypass and proceeded in silence towards the Stowerton exit road. Keith and Michelle would have had no objection to a chat, but Dave made it plain silence was preferred. Duncan Crisp, swathed in his blanket, had pulled the wooly hat down to cover his eyes and appeared to have fallen asleep. At more or less this point, Jeremy Legg had been in that collision that resulted (or didn't result) in Isabella Sams's fit and ultimately in Jeremy's death.

Half a mile farther on, Keith turned left onto Stowerton Road. A nondescript green van overtook the ambulance, raced ahead, and pulled sharply to the left, creating a barrier across the road. Keith hooted. No notice was taken. He stopped and got down from the cab as Dave moved towards the rear doors. Two men got out of the van, both wearing masks, and one of them wearing gloves. Keith stood still and shouted at them as to what was going on. He said afterwards that he was lucky they didn't kill him for before they grabbed him and bundled him into the van, he saw that each had a gun.

Dave too was seized. He was armed but he had never used his weapon. He did not use it this time for he was seized, his wrists handcuffed behind his back, and a sack pulled over his head and upper body. He staggered, fell, and was lifted into the van along with Keith. Michelle showed more enterprise than the men, calling 999 and asking for the police before she got down from the ambulance. Using the doctor's words, she said to the two men with the guns, "He's a poor old guy. He can't do any harm. You leave him alone."

They took her phone from her but not before she had told them she'd called the police. One of them, the bigger of the two, punched her in the face, breaking her jaw. She fell on the roadway where they left her, then went into the ambulance and brought Crisp out. He was screaming but they didn't attempt to stop him, pushing his chair to the back of the van. They lifted him out and threw him in along with Keith and Dave. Two miles down the road they turned into a farm track and drove up to a barn. Keith and Dave were taken out and dragged into the barn, where they were blindfolded and their ankles bound together with rope. The barn door was slammed shut but, as there was no key or padlock, not locked. The two who had left them there returned to the van and out onto the road.

The police arrived quite quickly, and another ambulance. The first thing they did was lift Michelle up from the frozen ground and carry her into the new ambulance, though the one the four had been in was still there, undamaged. Because her jaw was broken, she could tell them nothing. The ambulance took her away to the Princess Diana Memorial Hospital, where Duncan Crisp should by now have arrived.

Burden had no fear for Crisp's life. He

wondered what the motive could have been for taking him but reached no conclusion. Crisp had been "sprung," but why? Were the men who had taken him mates of his, the whole thing a setup? He must be paying them and paying them handsomely. They had guns. They were risking, if not their lives, their liberty. Duncan Crisp had only his pension and what Mrs. Morgan paid him and would by now have ceased to pay him.

The snatch was the lead story in the *London Evening Standard* and the lead item on the BBC's regional news at six thirty. By this time it was as dark as midnight and very cold, the frost returning with ferocity. Keith Turner and Dave Cresswell were rescued about ten minutes later by the farmer on whose land the barn was. He had driven down there to fetch a bale of straw for a farrowing sow and found the two men, both of whom were rushed to hospital.

They sat in Burden's office, which had once been Wexford's office and was now minus the rosewood desk that had been his pride and joy. Its present home was in his house, filling almost a whole wall in the tiny study. Since he was last there, Burden had got a new calendar, which appeared to be of Cornish pondlife.

"In this age of technology," said Burden, "we've no need to be here. We might as well be down the pub or at least in the Olive. We might as well be at home. But somehow I know I'd feel guilty if I were not here awaiting news."

"You can have a drink. *We* can have a drink. We're not going to drive anywhere. On the last day this office was mine I left a bottle of amontillado in that cupboard. I suppose you've drunk it by now."

"I certainly have not. You have a glass if it's still drinkable. Go on. I won't. I'll get someone to bring me a cup of tea."

"Potable," said Wexford. "That means 'fit to drink,' doesn't it? It's not a term anyone uses anymore."

The bottle was still there and two sherry glasses. As Wexford was pouring the pale-golden wine into one of them, Burden's tea arrived. The landline phone was ringing but it was only Karen Malahyde to say that Keith Turner and Dave Cresswell would be fit to talk in half an hour's time.

There was no news of Duncan Crisp, and the green van had not been traced. Wexford said that the sherry was indeed potable, in fact improved by its sojourn in the cupboard. "I wish there was something we could do. But short of roaming about the countryside looking in barns and abandoned vehicles and catching hypothermia like those two, there isn't."

"You can go home, Reg. You might as well."

"Not yet. I'll wait a bit longer."

"Tell me a story. Tell me what's happening with that girl and what she was supposed to be told on her eighteenth birthday. It's not in the least relevant to Crisp, I'm sure, but it might be a distraction."

So Wexford told him about Christian Steyner, whose partner, Timon Arkwright, was a wealthy tycoon (or something of that sort) and on the *Sunday Times* "Rich List." Christian's mother was a flirtatious little old woman who lived in South Kensington, and Christian's twin brother, Leo, had been Sarah Hussain's husband. Wexford told him about the car crash that had killed Leo and his father, and that Wexford had learned only that day from talking on the phone to Victoria Steyner that her daughter-in-law had been pregnant when Leo was killed but suffered a miscarriage two days after the accident.

Burden picked up on Arkwright. "Must be awkward being called Timon. Everyone will call him Simon by mistake and he'll spend half his life correcting them."

"Yes, well, I think Christian wants to tell Clarissa that Leo died in possession of a sum of money left to him by some relative and wanted him to pass this on to Sarah's child."

"But as it happened there wasn't a child. Or not that child."

"No, but maybe he said 'Sarah's child' and that could be stretched to any child."

"A bit far-fetched, isn't it?"

"You always say my ideas are far-fetched," said Wexford.

Burden laughed. "Why not make a will?"

"Why not indeed. Of course he can't have known he was going to die. He was only about thirty. I may well be wrong. But I can't think of anything else he could have to tell her."

"Thanks, anyway. People are weird, as we've remarked before. It's good to hear something that has nothing to do with Crisp, though more than anything I want to know where he is. I think I'll go home now. It's nearly midnight. Donaldson can drop you off and take me home. I might as well get the enlightening phone call there as here."

24

No phone call came, enlightening or otherwise. Karen Malahyde kept what Turner and Cresswell had to tell her until the following morning, when she passed it on to Burden face-to-face. He wanted to know what the men who had taken them away looked like, but Turner and Cresswell had only been able to say that they wore masks and one of them was tall and heavy. She had a better result from her visit to Michelle Fox, who was still unable to speak but put down some interesting information on a sheet of paper.

The one that punched me has a tattoo on his right wrist. He lifted his arm to punch me and I tried to duck but still I saw the tattoo. It is of a woman in a long dress with a hat on and sort of rays coming out of it, maybe supposed to be an angel.

Karen read it to Burden, then handed him the sheet of paper. "They're going to operate to mend the jaw today, but it'll be a day or two before she can talk."

"Have any of these people you've seen got a clue or a theory as to why anyone would want to snatch Crisp?"

"Not that they told me and of course I did ask them."

A search had started. Not just for the green van but for Crisp himself, "the poor old guy," as everyone now called him, even though he had been awaiting trial for murder. As many officers as Burden could muster were set to search every barn, garage, and outhouse in an area of about sixty square miles, a gargantuan task.

Wexford had his own idea of the reason for the snatch. It had nothing to do with setting free a man whom many people thought innocent. These were not just deliverers and were no friends of Crisp's. Wexford had his own idea and a grim one, but he told no one. What would be the point of telling Burden? Everything was being done to find Crisp, and revealing a theory the detective superintendent would only call far-fetched would do nothing to aid the search. Michelle's note was read to him over the phone, and he got himself into a bad temper by brooding on the way people thought angels were female—the influence of Hollywood, no doubt.

A chance meeting with Dr. Crocker in the high street had resulted in an invitation to call in for coffee. It would be something to do with his blood pressure, Wexford thought, for although Len Crocker was retired and Wexford was registered with a young GP, his old friend still took a keen interest in his health. In accepting, Wexford had forgotten Maxine still worked for the Crockers, but even if he had remembered, he wouldn't have avoided the house in Wessex Road. That was no way to live. Such hazards had to be faced up to and a confrontation, if it came, taken in one's stride.

It came sooner than he expected. He walked up the Crockers' front path, admiring the Christmas roses and the daphne in the borders, and rang the bell. The door was answered by Maxine. The anticipated torrent of abuse or even spittle never came. She stood staring at him in silence. He said nothing. She stood aside and moved back, holding the door open for him to pass into the hall. By this time Dr. Crocker had appeared from the living room. Wexford said because it amused him to say it, confronted by Maxine's stony face, "Mrs. Sams and I are not on speaking terms."

Maxine made a snorting sound. Inside the living room, the door closed, Dr. Crocker asked what "all that was about."

"I revealed to the law something about her son she thought she had told me in confidence and maybe she had."

"Oh, dear. Would you rather have a drink than coffee even though it is only midday?"

"Yes, please," said Wexford. "I've been thinking how much easier police work must be in a warm climate than here, for instance. Not to mention in Scandinavia, so fashionable at the moment for crime and crime TV and crime fiction. I'll tell you what I mean."

"I'll take your blood pressure first." The doctor was waving his sphygmomanometer about. "Before you raise it with alcohol."

His blood pressure satisfactorily showing a measurement of 130 over 70, Wexford went on, "In California, for instance, or practically anywhere in southern Europe, not to mention Africa, people have big areas of skin exposed. They wear vests or T-shirts with short sleeves, women have bare legs and short skirts. While here, from October till May everyone except teenagers cover up. Scars are hidden, hairiness is hidden, and tattoos are."

"It's worse in Moslem countries," said Crocker, bringing Wexford a glass of Cloudy Bay. "Women veiled from head to foot with only the eyes exposed. What's the point of this anyway?"

"A tattoo. You'll have seen about the abduction of a man who was in prison on remand."

"Crisp, yes. Poor old guy."

"Well, the paramedic who got punched in the face saw a tattoo on the arm of one of the men who took him. A picture of some saint or Madonna, it sounds like. She only saw it because, although it was freezing cold, he rolled up his sleeve before he hit her. The chances would be that this tattoo would be hidden all through the winter. I suppose he forgot about it."

If Wexford had hoped that Crocker would say, Why, yes, he knew who that was, it was one of his patients, Wexford was disappointed. In fact, he thought he had seen the tell-tale arm somewhere himself, exposed in some setting where the cold wouldn't be felt, but he couldn't remember where. He had tried and tried but couldn't remember.

"What do you think this Madonna man has done with Crisp?"

"Nothing, I hope," said Wexford. "But where is he? We always bear in mind that it's much harder to hide a living man than a dead body. He's been gone two days now."

Dr. Crocker saw Wexford to the front door and let him out. There was no sign of Maxine.

Clarissa had told Robin all about the coming meeting with Christian Steyner, his grandfather's role in the encounter, and details of her specula-tions as to what this could be about. Wexford had given her no clue as to his theory of the matter Steyner might wish to impart to her. He was possibly wrong anyway. He had suggested to Clarissa that he and she should meet in advance of Friday, the eighth of February, the scheduled date, but he hadn't expected she would bring

Robin with her. He should have known, Wexford told himself. Those two did everything together, being apart only for Clarissa to go to school and Robin to stack shelves.

"Have you, like, any idea what it's about?" This was Clarissa. "It would be good to have—well, a clue."

"I know nothing as yet," Wexford said, dispensing wine. "We have to wait and see. If I were to suggest anything, it would only be guesswork."

"You mustn't worry," Robin said, putting his arm round Clarissa. "Remember, I'll be there."

"I'm afraid you won't," said his grandfather. "We don't know this man, we know very little about him, but we do know that he wants just Clarissa to be there and one witness or arbiter, and that's me. Sorry about that, but that's the arrangement."

"You'll be able to wait outside or just downstairs." She gazed adoringly into Robin's eyes. "There'll only be a wall and a staircase—well, a lift—between us."

"So Tesco are going to pay you for taking the day off, are they?"

"I'll take the day off pay or no pay," said Robin, the unpleasant look he gave his grandfather making Wexford laugh.

He saw them out, on their way to Kingsmarkham's only club, and remembered suggestions he had heard of matchmaking. She was only in early middle age herself but she hadn't moved with the times. Robin and Clarissa had probably never thought of marriage in connection with themselves, or if they thought of it, it was as something for "old" people, those in their thirties, for instance. Any money that might come to Clarissa as a result of Friday's disclosure, she would likely think of as useful for buying a flat after she had graduated from university, while her counterpart of fifty years before might have contemplated sharing it with the funds of a husband-to-be.

He put them and the ways of youth behind him and set his mind on Duncan Crisp, what his kidnappers wanted him for and what they had done with him. If things were the way Wexford believed they were, the Madonna-tattoo man and the one with him would want Crisp dead. Alive he was always a threat, and that threat increased as the time of his trial approached. They would want him dead for their revenge and their protection.

He had seen that tattoo somewhere. But where and when? Since October certainly, and that meant that when he had seen it the weather was cold. Only foolhardy teenagers needing to prove how cool they were went about in vests or T-shirts when snow was on the ground, and this man was no adolescent. So where had he seen him? Sleep on it, he thought, and he went to join Dora, who was riveted to a television programme about childbirth. Men are parents as much as women, but few men want to watch babies being born on film, while the woman who doesn't is an exception. Wexford fell asleep after two minutes of it.

"You talked in your sleep," Dora said when he woke. "D'you want to know what you said?"

"Tell me." Maybe it was the name or even the address of the Madonna-tattoo man.

"You said, 'Man that is born of a woman hath but a short time to live.'"

"Did I really?"

"Spare me the funeral service next time I'm watching TV."

In the morning he remembered something about the man and the tattoo but not enough. For some unknown reason he connected it with Mrs. Mukamba, the young and pretty Congolese woman who lived in a poor and run-down area of Stowerton. A house in Oval Road it was. If necessary he would knock or ring at all the doors in the street. It wasn't necessary. He knew the house as soon as he saw it from the bags of rubbish and the two broken-down bikes in what had once been a front garden. Nardelie was her name, as pretty as she was. Nardelie Mukamba, the pious young woman who had attended Sarah Hussain's memorial service. What decree or rule (or chance rather) had set Victoria Steyner in charming and elegant South Kensington and Nardelie Mukamba here in this tip? Still, it was probably an improvement on backstreet Kinshasa. The bell being missing, he clattered the letterbox. She came to the door, as lovely as ever, in a thick, wooly cardigan over her floral dress, with a fat baby on her hip and holding a toddler by the hand.

"Good morning," she said, all smiles. "We have met. How are you?"

Wexford said he was well, he hoped she was, and what beautiful children she had.

"A handful." She laughed. "A lovely handful. Please come in."

It must be the wrong house, he thought as he followed her into a living room cluttered with toys. That man has no place here. It was clean and the room was warmed by a single mobile electric radiator. The only warm room in the house in February, he guessed. She began to talk about the new vicar. She liked him, he had told her to bring her children to church if she liked, and if they ran about a bit and made a noise—well, they were children, weren't they? What did the people expect? But I like to bring them up right. They must keep quiet and be good when I tell them.

"What can I do for you?"

"I don't know," Wexford said. "I don't even know if this is the right house, but one day a couple of months ago I called here—I think—it was very cold. A man came up to the door and opened it with a key. His arms must have been bare because I saw a tattoo of a woman, saint with a halo maybe, on his right wrist. I really do need to know who he is, but I don't suppose you can help me."

She was laughing by now. "He lived upstairs. Not a good man, but a lovely voice he had, and my boys loved what they called 'the lady.' You did, Jacques, didn't you?" The little boy nodded enthusiastically. "What was it? Do you remember?"

Jacques said promptly, "Saint Catherine, the man said."

"That's right." Nardelie showed no dislike or disapproval. "Good boy. He'd been a bouncer in a nightclub, he told my boys. I was glad when he left, went to somewhere in Kingsmarkham. There was always people coming here, up and down the stairs. After drugs, I think, and I didn't like that around my boys."

"Do you remember his name?"

"Marty," said Jacques. "He said, 'You call me Marty.'"

"Martin Dennison, he was called, but everyone called him Marty."

So he had been a dealer. Or had he? Wexford, walking back to his car, thought that he would not have jumped to that conclusion just from a number of visitors to the upper floor, though he might have done if he had had small children. A parking ticket on his windscreen caught his eye almost before the car itself did. What had he done or left undone? Stowerton still used old-fashioned parking meters, and he had duly put in two exorbitant pound coins. But it hadn't been enough. It was the first time ever that he had received a parking ticket, and remembering a lifetime of being protected from such persecution made him laugh. Well, he would pay the fine, of course he would.

He wasn't going to risk another by somehow parking in the wrong place outside the police station. He drove home and decided to walk to the high street.

"A call came for you, Reg," Dora told him. "A Mr. Steyner. Why use the landline?"

"God knows. I didn't know he had the number."

Maybe he got it from his mother. Dora had written down the number Steyner left and Wexford called it, but from his mobile.

"Very good of you to call back." The voice was upper-class. The kind of voice Marty Dennison had? More a superior banker's voice, Wexford thought, though he didn't know if banking was Steyner's occupation. He also detected in it an undercurrent of nervousness. It was slight but there, trepidation rather than rank fear. "I wonder if I may ask you a great favour?"

Wexford's reaction to this sort of thing was

always an abrupt or stiff reply. This time it was a cold "Of course."

"I believe you and I are due to meet Miss Hussain, Clarissa Hussain, on Friday."

Steyner knew very well they were. Wexford said nothing.

"It seems rather awkward meeting like that, all strangers to each other, as I don't imagine you know Miss Hussain very well."

"That isn't so. Clarissa rents a room in my daughter's house. I've known her for nearly four months. She chose me to be present at this meeting."

This Steyner ignored. "So I thought it might be a good idea for you and me to meet first. I mean, prior to the three of us meeting. I could come to you in Kingsmarkham, and we could have a talk about what I have to tell her."

Why? Wexford didn't say it aloud. "I think the whole thing, whatever it is, can wait till Friday. I hope I'm not being discourteous, but I don't see the need for a prior meeting. If you will go ahead with booking a private room, we'll all meet at the Olive and Dove at eleven a.m. on Friday. I will call for Clarissa and bring her with me."

Steyner's tone changed. He suddenly sounded weak and much younger than he was. The words he chose were strange. "I hope it will be all right."

Making no attempt to decipher this, Wexford called Burden and asked to see him.

"I'm having lunch sent in," Burden said. "Shall I double the order? It's just sandwiches from the Italian place, but nice ones."

Poor Mike. No newspaper spy could catch him in his office and find fault in print with his daring to eat or drink while Duncan Crisp was still missing.

The sandwiches had just arrived when Wexford got there. "Smoked salmon. For once they haven't mixed it up with mozzarella or put it in focaccia." He stopped, met Burden's eyes. "Am I becoming an old curmudgeon?"

"Yes."

"I will strive to be tolerant and easygoing. Now, I've found the tattoo man. His name is Marty or Martin Dennison, and he may once have been a bouncer in a nightclub. I think he lives somewhere in Ladysmith Road but I don't know where."

"Well done," said Burden. "Have another sandwich."

Wexford told him about the house in Oval Road and Dennison's visitors while he lived there, his move to Kingsmarkham. "He's a dealer, I think, among his other charming habits. I went to the house to see a woman called Nardelie Mukamba. I hope she'll be OK. I don't want him finding out she helped me."

"You think he's dangerous?"

"Well, don't you?"

"Where is he? And come to that, where's his

mate and poor old Crisp? What do they want Crisp for, Reg?"

Wexford said slowly, "Crisp knows something. He's in possession of a vital piece of information. I've spoken of it before, but when I do, you don't want to hear. You don't believe in it. You think it was Crisp's invention, a ploy to get him off the hook. But Marty Dennison believes it and the man with him does, and more to the point, absolutely to the point, whoever is employing them does."

"Someone is employing those two?"

"Of course. They're just your run-of-the-mill villains, aren't they? They're thugs. An ex–nightclub bouncer and his pal. This won't be new to them, they'll have been involved in something like it before. I think Crisp is dead."

Wexford stayed for a while, repeating his story until Burden admitted to a grudging belief in it. While he was there, news came in that a silver Vauxhall Astra had turned up, half-sunk in a horse pond on a farm near Forby. A man's tracksuit was in the boot, and immersion in half-frozen water hadn't removed all the bloodstains on it. Soaking wet, it had previously been soaked in blood. The car was stolen and reported missing a week before.

"You may have been right all along. It looks like it. We've got samples of Crisp's DNA to check against that on the tracksuit. That poor old guy."

"Your sympathy comes a bit late in the day," said Wexford nastily.

25

The search for Crisp continued. The weather changed, warming up, rain starting. The rain fell heavily, raising the water level of ponds, swelling the rivers. Meadows were waterlogged, some turning into shallow lakes. The Kingsbrook became a torrent, carrying with it the body of an old man, not naked but dressed only in underpants and a vest, and depositing it on the riverbank under Kingsmarkham High Street bridge.

Of course it was Crisp. There was never much doubt of that and none after the body had been identified by his landlord and a prison officer. His throat had been cut, the deed probably done in the Astra, which would account for the excessive amount of blood on the tracksuit.

"It shouldn't be hard to find this Martin Dennison." Burden scorned to use a nickname or diminutive employed by such a thug. "We've got a house-to-house going on in Ladysmith Road now. No, it shouldn't be hard to find him."

But it was.

26

Robin had changed his shift at Tesco and worked
Thursday night to have Friday free. He opened
Sylvia's front door to Wexford. She had left for
work an hour before. Clarissa came downstairs,
not exactly dressed up but wearing a skirt (short
and black) and a sweater (long and black) under
a faux-fur coat.

"It was Mum's. D'you think it's all right?"

"You look lovely," said Robin. "It's more than
all right, it's perfect."

He'd have said that, Wexford thought, if she'd
come down in a burka or bikini. Wexford said
nothing. Ever since he'd woke up that morning,
he had been troubled by misgivings and wished
that he had never taken on this task but had
refused at the start. Too late now, much too late.
Steyner's fault, of course, setting up for a
melodrama when all of this could surely have
been done on paper.

"We'll have to walk," he said, "or call a taxi.

304

The Olive won't let me into their car park as I'm not a resident."

"Let's walk," said Clarissa.

Robin and she held hands. They invariably did. No one speculated any longer on what might be the purpose of this meeting. They walked in silence until Robin spotted a friend on the other side of the street, raised his hand, and called out, "Hey."

The friend said, "Hey," and after he was out of earshot, Clarissa asked who it was.

"Guy I was at school with," said Robin. "Jonathan something."

The high street was busy, as it always was on a Friday morning. They went into the Olive and Dove, and Wexford asked at reception for Christian Steyner. He was told that Mr. Steyner had a private room on the ground floor, down a passage where the cloakrooms were and the Internet room. Wexford told Robin to stay in the reception area, which was also a kind of lounge with sofas, a couple of coffee tables, and a newspaper rack, and, passing into the passage, noted the name on the foot of the doors on the new lifts: Luxelevators Ltd.

"I'll be right here," Robin said to Clarissa, taking both her hands. "I won't move. If you want me, whatever it is, and I mean whatever, call me on my phone. You'll do that, won't you, sweetheart?"

Wexford restrained himself, said nothing, but thought a good deal. If Robin had been going to the wars and Clarissa left at home with a couple of babies, the two of them on a railway platform in 1914, the parting could hardly have been more fraught. Wexford shook his head, said, "Come along, Clarissa," and headed down the passage for the private room, the girl reluctantly trailing him.

The door was ajar. The room was as such rooms always are, beige, with beige carpet, floor-length beige curtains, a bowl of glass fruit on a coffee table, a vase of artificial lilies on the windowsill. There was a brown tweed sofa and three beige-and-brown-patterned armchairs. Steyner looked as if he had been pacing up and down, though he was standing still when they came in. Wexford expected him to shake hands, it would be the normal thing to do, and it occurred to him that whereas Steyner would have had no objection to shaking hands with him, he wanted to avoid doing so with Clarissa. He said, "Do sit down. It's good of you to come."

If the three of them had never before met, they had all seen each other before. On that occasion, Sarah Hussain's memorial service, Steyner had looked a normal, healthy man, if rather pale, his hair prematurely white. Today he looked unwell, rather as if he were recovering from flu. Perhaps he was. Many people were. Once Wexford and Clarissa were seated, Steyner too sat down, but immediately got up again and walked across the room to stand in front of the girl.

"When I asked if you would name someone to be with you here, I really meant a woman. I think it would have been more suitable."

Clarissa said gently, "Why didn't you say so then?"

"I don't know. All this has been a great strain for me."

Neither of them knew what he meant. "I didn't want a woman," Clarissa said. "I haven't got any relations. Mr. Wexford is the nearest I've got. He's my fiancé's grandfather."

Wexford started at the word but managed not to show his surprise. Were those two really engaged? Surely not.

Steyner made no comment but returned to where he had been sitting. He was looking at Clarissa, his pale blue eyes meeting her deep blue eyes. "You don't know me. I had better tell you something about myself. I am fifty years old and a doctor of medicine, but I have never practised. I sit on the board of one of our major medical charities. Your mother's husband was my twin brother. We were identical twins.

"I am homosexual but my brother was not. So much for identical twins having everything as well as their appearance in common."

He paused. Wexford noticed that he hadn't referred to himself as *gay* but used the formal, correct word. Wexford wondered what all this was leading up to. Not what he had imagined, certainly. Clarissa had begun to look frightened. She looked as if she knew that something alarming, even deeply disturbing, was about to be said, and Steyner's tone was certainly ominous.

"Obviously I have never married. I live in a civil partnership. Your mother and I met soon after Leo, my brother, first met her. They were very happy together. Perhaps to say 'happy' is inadequate. They adored each other." He paused again. "I need a drink." Both Wexford and Clarissa thought he meant alcohol, but he helped himself from a carafe of water that stood on one of the tables.

"I don't know why Leo went to a football match. He had never shown the least interest in football. It must have been his first time. I don't even know which teams were playing. I think one was Manchester United. My father was a supporter and I suppose Leo went with him because Dad asked him to. It was his birthday, my father's, I mean, and Leo didn't like to say no. There was a pileup on the motorway and a lorry crashed into them. Both were killed instantly."

Clarissa, who had been silent up to then, said, "Oh, awful. Poor Mum."

"Yes. Your poor mother. Poor all of us. I'm making too much of a speech of this. I must get to the point. After that, your mother went on seeing my mother for a few years. She and I met once or twice. Leo had no money to leave. Sarah—your mother—was earning, but my mother worried about her and wanted to make her some sort of allowance, but she wouldn't take it. You've met my mother, I think," Steyner said to Wexford. "She's in the early stages of dementia and she's very different from what she was then."

Wexford nodded, said nothing. Christian Steyner went on, "Then one day I had a letter from Sarah. She wanted a meeting. We met after not having seen each other for two years. She was very direct, she always was. She said she would never remarry. More than that, she would never have a relationship. She supposed I would never marry or have a relationship with a woman, and there she was right. I remember she looked hard at me, harder than anyone had ever looked at me, and she said that though I and Leo—she called him 'my beloved husband'—were not alike in character, I was practically a carbon copy of him or he was of me." Steyner began to speak rapidly. "Therefore, would I be a sperm donor so that she could have a child that would be as near as possible Leo's. Eventually, not that day but later, I said I would. I did."

As rigid and as pale as a statue, Clarissa stared at him. Then, staring, she screamed.

Her screams came quickly, one after another, the classic hysteria. To stop them you were supposed to slap her face. Wexford couldn't, he dared not. Christian Steyner was aghast. He made a little sound of pain or dismay. Wexford stood up, spoke to the screaming girl, but afterwards he couldn't recall what he had said to her. Someone came to the door, knocked at it, called out, "Is everything all right?"—as if it could possibly be.

"There's a man called Fairfax in reception." It was the first time Wexford had ever referred to Robin as a man. "Ask him to come here, would you?"

Clarissa was sobbing now, throwing herself up and down against the back of the armchair she sat in. On an impulse Wexford added, "And brandy. Would you bring some brandy?"

Robin's footsteps sounded as he ran down the passage. He burst in, drawn by the sound of Clarissa's crying. "What have you done to her?" he demanded of Wexford as a waiter or barman arrived with a glass of brandy on a tray.

"Don't be stupid," Wexford said, and to Steyner, "Let's go outside somewhere."

Clarissa was in Robin's arms. Wexford led the way out and Steyner followed, the two of them finding their way to the lounge.

Steyner was visibly shaken. "I didn't expect her to take it like that."

"It's not every day you're told by your father that he was presented to your mother in a bottle."

"Don't."

They sat down. Wexford took his eyes from Steyner's face. Now, for the first time, and oddly it was when the girl was out of sight, Wexford saw the resemblance. The same blue eyes, but hers brighter; the same features, the same smooth and rather shiny skin, though hers was darker.

"It was like that, though," Steyner said. "The bottle, I mean. I never saw her again. She wrote and told me she had had a daughter born on twenty January 1995. She would tell her about her—her origins—on her eighteenth birthday. I never had a description of the child, I never had a photograph. But I never wanted any of that. As far as I was concerned, I was just a—well, a producer of a biological constituent. I told no one but my partner, and that was years later."

Wexford nodded. He could think of nothing to say.

"My partner told me to forget all about it. He advised me not to make contact with the girl, to keep out of it. He said the chances were that Sarah would fabricate some story of a love affair when the time came, but I knew Sarah. I knew that wasn't on. And then Sarah was killed and what was I to do?"

"What you did, evidently. Tell me something. If we'd had that meeting you wanted, the one that was to be prior to this one, would you have told me what you told Clarissa?"

"I don't know."

Wexford shrugged. "I've never in my life advised anyone to lie, but I think that's the advice I'd have given you. Lie. Say her mother had confided in your mother that she'd had an affair. Something like that. It would have been better than this."

"It's too late now."

A waitress appeared from somewhere, came up to them, and asked Wexford if she could bring them anything. An enquiring glance at Steyner fetched only a shake of his head.

"I may as well disappear." Steyner took a mobile phone from his pocket. "Tim? It's all over. See you in an hour."

Not until Steyner had gone did Wexford realise *Tim* might well be a diminutive of *Timon*. Steyner's partner had advised him not to make contact with Clarissa. If the outcome of their meeting had been different, if the girl had accepted the test-tube truth of her origins, she might have entered the closed world of their partnership, have become a daughter. Was that what Steyner had hoped for? It sounded as if it was what Timon Arkwright had feared. Or had neither of them cared much either way? It might be that, like most people, Arkwright wanted to avoid trouble and change. Lie to her, tell her her father is a onetime lover of her mother's, and forget all about the girl who is a purely biological offspring of yours. Now or soon he would be saying to Steyner, You see what all this honesty does, stirs up a can of worms or a glass of sperm.

Wexford went back to the room where all this had happened, but it was empty. Robin and Clarissa had gone out by a back way.

27

The result of Burden's house-to-house in Ladysmith Road was the discovery of the room Marty Dennison had rented. It was on the third floor of one of the taller houses in that street. Janet Corbyn-Smith, the woman who had been his landlady, told DI Vine an interesting story. Dennison had given her three hundred pounds in cash as a deposit on the room and said he would want it for six months at two hundred pounds per week. He then asked firstly if she had another room his friend could have and, when she said no, asked if the friend could share his for a week. Miss Corbyn-Smith said that would be OK, but it would cost him an extra two hundred pounds for that week. The friend had an unusual name, Arben Birjar, which was why she remembered it.

Birjar arrived a week later in the evening in a white van, which he parked outside and drove away before eight thirty next morning when parking restrictions began. She never saw the van or Birjar again, but all the rent she was owed was paid by Dennison and the two hundred pounds for Birjar's share of the room, even though he had only stayed there one night. Martin Dennison told her he was going away for a week, but he wanted to keep the room, where he was leaving clothes and other pieces of property. She assumed he would be going abroad because when he paid her, he took a handful of notes and papers, among them a credit card and a passport, out of his pocket and put them down on the table while he counted out the money he owed her. He was quite a pleasant fellow, she said, and he needed to be, being so big and powerful and with that tattoo on his right arm. He had a "posh" voice. Money seemed to be no object with him, he flashed it around in a way you wouldn't expect from a guy who wore a torn T-shirt and a jacket of mock suede.

No, she never saw him drive anything. She never saw a silver Astra outside. Apart from Birjar he had no visitors, but he was only using the room for a week and a half. Vine and DC Laura Bird went up to the third floor to look at Dennison's room. The clothes he had left behind would not be missed by a man who threw money about the way Dennison had. It looked as if he had simply dumped them there, the way he had dumped a stack of magazines, a couple of CDs, and a dirty sleeping bag. Fingerprints in the room and on these objects would be taken later in the day, Vine told Miss Corbyn-Smith. Prints on the silver Astra had largely been obliterated by its immersion in water and melted snow and ice, but some kind of comparison was worth a try.

Where was Martin Dennison now? Nardelie Mukamba remembered someone telling her that the club where he had been a bouncer was the Anaconda in Brewer Street in London. Her brother, a waiter in a restaurant nearby, had told her.

Barry Vine and DC Laura Bird found the Anaconda closed. Its windows were covered in white blinds with a discreet silver pattern. In spite of its name, no snake logo or motif was in evidence. It looked tasteful and even respectable from the exterior.

"There's never trouble," said Andre Zewnu. "It's always all quiet on the Western Front." Mystified, Vine wondered where on earth a Congolese twenty-five-year-old had picked up the phrase. Was there an old film? "Course they don't open till eleven p.m. and that's when we're closing up. May be pandemo-ni-*um* by midnight. You want to know about Holy Marty? We called him that on account of him having that angel on his arm. He was OK though. What d'you want him for?"

Laura nearly said, "Murder." And would have but for a warning glance from Vine. He never answered questions from the public.

"Because if there'd been anything wrong with him, would I have told him the flat above my sister's was vacant? They thought a lot of him next door. One time I saw the boss stop outside in his beemer and drop him off."

"Who would that be then?"

"Don't ask me. A toff. Typical of next door. Celeb-land is what I call it. I've seen royalty go in there. Princess someone and one of them Spice Girls as was."

"Where d'you think he is now?" Laura asked.

"Marty? Down your neck of the woods unless he's moved again. Never stayed long in one place did Marty."

"And what about the other man?" asked Laura when they were in the train going home.

"You mean the one with the Albanian name?"

"Is it Albanian?" Laura was quite excited.

"I looked for it online and there it was, Birjar, Albanian apparently."

"D'you think he's an illegal?"

"I wouldn't be surprised," said Vine.

"He's left the country," said Burden. "Why else have his passport lying about at Corbyn-Smith's place? There was nothing to stop him going. Maybe he and Birjar went together. For all I know they'll be in Tirana now. It is Tirana, isn't it?"

Wexford nodded. "When I was young, when I was a child, that is, you called them 'double-barrelled names.' I mean, names like Corbyn-Smith. The possessors of them were upper-class or toffs. That's all changed. Ms. Corbyn-Smith is very far from a toff. She's called that because one of her parents was Corbyn and the other was Smith. What puzzles me is what happens when a Corbyn-Smith has a child by a, say, Morton-Jones. Does the child take all his or her parents' names? Persephone Corbyn-Smith-Morton-Jones? And if not, which ones do you drop?"

As usual, Burden was uninterested in specu-lation of this kind. Wexford adverted to it only to annoy. Childish, he told himself severely, don't do it again. "I know you're not much interested in motive, but just the same, you're not assuming that Martin Dennison and Birjar had any personal reason for killing Sarah Hussain?"

"As things stand at present, I've no idea."

"There's no evidence, is there, that either of them knew her or had ever been to the vicarage?"

"No-o," said Burden in a tone both grudging and cautious.

"Because you take it that they're hit men? Or Dennison is the hit man and Arben Birjar his henchman? Good word *henchman,* don't you think?" Wexford was doing it again in spite of intending not to. "*Accomplice,* I mean."

317

Burden said coldly, "I am quite well aware of what the word means."

"I'm sorry, Mike. So are you thinking that poor old Crisp saw one of them through the vicarage French windows or saw their employer, whoever that may be? Saw and could identify him?"

"No, that's what you're thinking."

In the ensuing silence, Wexford thought that because of his friend's continued refusal to recognise that Crisp had been telling the truth about what he saw or if he even saw anyone at all, the dead man had never been asked to describe the man he saw through glass. Once Crisp had been known to have lied about having tea with Mrs. Morgan and Miss Green on the relevant afternoon—or, as Wexford preferred to see it, simply forgotten where he had been— Burden had assumed him to *be* a liar and that nothing he said could be relied upon as truth. But even a habitual liar must in the nature of things more often tell the truth than lie. Besides, though Burden took it for granted that Crisp had invented seeing the man in the vicarage living room where Sarah Hussain had died, no evidence either proved or disproved that.

"You see," Burden said suddenly, "I don't believe, I never have, that a man arrested for a crime and with no defence or alibi will remember that he saw a better candidate for that crime at the scene of the crime just when he most needs him."

"'Old men forget.'"

"Yes, and I know where that comes from. *Henry the Fifth*. I googled it. But Henry goes on to say that though they forget a lot of things, they won't forget the battle they fought that makes them heroes. In other words no matter how old they are, people don't forget vital events in their lives, something that makes them heroes or could rescue them from ten years in prison."

"He did remember eventually."

"Or invented eventually," said Burden.

"Then why did poor old Crisp have his throat cut? I stick to my guns. Because he saw, not one of them, but whoever hired them. According to Ms. Corbyn-Smith, Dennison had plenty of money to splash about. He had been paid or partially paid in advance. I should think throat-cutting a revenge activity practised by Albanians, wouldn't you?"

"Who's a racist now?" said Burden.

The house was one of those newspapers call a mansion and carry stories about them as on sale for more than any London house has previously fetched on the market. Twenty million, twenty-five, over thirty. They are bought by sheikhs and IT billionaires, their forty-bedroom interiors sometimes gutted and rebuilt according to a more trendy design than that fashionable when the last makeover took place two years before.

Emerging from the park at Queen's Gate and turning into an exquisite street where he knew Christian Steyner lived, Wexford remembered when the record asking price for a house in London had been twenty thousand pounds. He had been young and the price of that house had seemed enormous to him. The one he was seeking this morning was so much the finest in the street that he knew which it was long before he reached it. Standing alone, it was that rarity, a West End detached house with front garden and garden surrounding it on all sides, white stucco, Georgian so-called but really mid-Victorian with bow windows on each side of the porticoed front door. A pair of amphoras, each carrying a February-flowering scarlet camellia, stood on the steps. Not wanting to be seen—for he had no intention of calling at the house—he walked past it on the other side, round the block, if such a term could be used of this august area, and through the mews at the far end.

Now it seemed as if he was to be rewarded. A BMW, not the Jaguar that had brought Mrs. Steyner and her son to Sarah Hussain's memorial service and was driven by Timon Arkwright, had been parked outside Carroll House. Its driver, a small, thin man, could just be seen sitting in the driving seat and seen too to be eating what looked from this distance like a large sandwich. Wexford had read somewhere that women over fifty pass unnoticed in the street. Could that also be true of men over sixty-five? If the women hated being thus ignored, he would welcome it. Of course it is generally true that police detectives don't want to be seen. He wished he had some reason to go into one of the houses opposite, where he could watch out of a front window, but he had none. Not for the first time but perhaps more positively and tellingly than before, he was realising how insignificant he had become in the great scheme of law and order, of lawmaking and law-implementing, of having nothing to do in a society where doing things was all-important.

But still he waited, standing this time a little way down the street outside a huge house, which, from the series of bells by the main entrance, seemed to be divided into flats. In case anyone was watching him—in the unlikely event—he put on a small show of impatience, looking at his watch several times and then, as if unable to wait any longer, he took out his mobile phone and made a call.

Dora spoke rather irritably when he told her what he was doing. "For heaven's sake, Reg, give it a rest. You're retired. You don't have to do it anymore." Inspiration came to her aid. "Gibbon misses you."

That made him laugh. "Tell him I'll soon be back."

He stopped there. Someone had come out of

Carroll House and was walking down the steps between the red camellias. For a moment Wexford didn't recognise him. Since the memorial service Timon Arkwright had grown a beard, a small, dark, pointed beard, and really only because the man at the wheel of the BMW jumped out and came round to open a rear door for him did Wexford know who it must be. He was quite a long way off, but even from where he stood he could see what a wonderful work of art the suit Arkwright wore was. It was the kind of suit billionaires wore (as he knew from photographs in newspapers), smoother, with a softer, silkier sheen, a sharper cut, a perfect, more creaseless fit than anything Wexford had ever bought or even seen on Burden. Where did they get them? What insignificant, retiring tailor, hiding behind an eighteenth-century window in Savile Row, could produce this creation of genius? He watched the car go and thought he might reverse his intention and venture to ring the bell at Carroll House for the sake of talking to Christian Steyner.

Crossing the street, he wondered if Arkwright was the kind of man who grows a beard and shaves it off and grows it again. Those who do this are usually young, he thought, like Robin, who had already done it once, and Wexford rang the bell.

An Asian woman in a dark blue tracksuit came to the door. She showed him into one of the bow-window rooms. Done up in blue and white and gold, it had white and yellow roses in blue vases. Christian Steyner kept him waiting but a short time. Also in a tracksuit, but a light grey one which made him look paler than ever, he was shaking Wexford's hand almost before he held it out.

"Sit down, please. Do sit down. It's good of you to come. How is she?"

He could only mean Clarissa, but still Wexford was surprised. "I hardly know," he said, suddenly aware that this was something he should know. "She has a room in my daughter's house." He felt unable to give his support to this engagement story. "I'm sure she and my grandson are looking after her." He added because, perhaps unjustifiably, he felt that Clarissa's highly emotional reaction to Steyner's revelation shouldn't be encouraged, "She's not ill, you know."

"I didn't think I would feel like this. My feelings are a complete surprise to me. I thought our meeting would be almost a business thing, setting the record straight, that sort of thing. Instead I felt an enormous emotional sort of pull towards her. Believe it or not, Mr. Wexford, but I *loved* her. I do love her. I can't account for it unless it's somehow my blood calling to her blood."

Rubbish, Wexford thought, or, in the current expression he never used, bonkers. He said in a

323

calm, level voice, "She's very good-looking, very charming. I expect that accounts for it. It will pass."

"I love her. I can't get her out of my head. I want her to live with me and be my daughter. That's what she is, my own child."

"You'd seen her before. You saw her at the memorial service."

"It didn't affect me in the same way. If she wasn't my daughter and I wasn't gay, I'd think I was in love with her. But that isn't so. I love her as a father loves his girl, I'm sure of that. She lived with her mother. I'm as much her parent as Sarah was. Why can't she come and live with me?"

"Maybe she can." Wexford was wondering how he got himself into this. He had called—why had he? Not because Steyner had invited him. Simply perhaps to be polite, ask how the man was after what had been an ordeal for him, see him close to, see his partner—because people were an abiding, a consuming interest? No, there had been something else, which had slipped his mind.

"You mean I should ask her? She screamed when I told her who I was, who *she* was. I've said some of this to my partner. Not all of it. After all, it's he I love. I'm utterly committed to him. Can't there be room in my life for both of them?"

The man was opening his heart to an unprecedented degree. Such a release of feeling was the last thing Wexford had expected. "Your partner doesn't care for the idea?"

"He thinks I should have some sort of counselling, maybe psychotherapy. He's a very cool, rational man, very different from me. Perhaps that's why we get on so well. He says it's too late, Clarissa's grown-up, she's even thinking of getting married—"

"I don't think so," Wexford interrupted. "You can put that out of your head. But you can ask her. Obviously it would be better for you and her to be on good terms, just visiting each other from time to time. Can you imagine that? Would Mr. Arkwright agree to that?"

"Oh, he'd agree. It's just that I don't think it would be enough for me. I know it wouldn't be. I've even thought of moving out of here so that I could be on my own and have Clarissa with me."

Wexford got up. "I've told you what I think. This will pass, especially if you don't see her. Take your partner's advice." He moved towards the door. "I hope all goes well for you."

Walking down the street towards South Kensington tube station, he asked himself why all these people had begun confiding in him. How he would have welcomed it when he was a policeman! Now, unasked, they poured out their hearts: this man, Georgina Bray, Clarissa, Tony Kilmartin. Possibly the cool and rational Arkwright would be the next one. Suddenly he

remembered what he had intended to ask
Christian Steyner. What, if anything, did he know
of Duncan Crisp? Was he, could he be, the man
Crisp said he had seen through the glass of
Sarah Hussain's French windows? But he was
fair, not dark, and there was no way, Wexford
thought, as he waited for the Circle line train, that
he could imagine this pale, worn, yet passionate
man as Sarah's murderer.

Among those who unexpectedly confided in
Wexford was one other, Mike Burden, who had
seemed, if not invulnerable, self-confident enough
to withstand attacks from those he thought
ignorant and publicity-seeking. But now the
media onslaught, increasing almost daily, was
affecting him so badly as to threaten his health,
and in his office—because the Olive and Dove
was a dangerous place to be—he poured out his
fears to Wexford.

"I expected them to accept Crisp as the
perpetrator. Is it my fault that Dennison and Birjar
murdered him before he came to trial?"

"No, obviously not. But it would help if you
could find either of them."

"The *Mail* says I should resign, and the *Sun*
says I was always unfit for the job."

"At least they can't say what the *Star* said of
me, that I was getting senile." Strange, Wexford
thought, how words which when uttered or
written pierced to one's very soul could later on

not just be reflected on with wry humour but actually make one laugh. "You won't resign, will you? If ever there's an admission of failure, that would be it."

"I won't resign."

"Is there any more of that sherry left?"

"For you," said Burden, "but better not for me."

In calling on Sylvia on his way home, he hoped to see Clarissa. Robin he had already seen when going into Questo for a cut wholemeal loaf. But asking after her seemed clumsy. She must be asked herself and answer herself. All the news Robin had was common to every employee in the store. Their sometime manager, Jason Sams, was being, if not released, given a temporary freedom on police bail until his trial in April.

"With a tag on his left ankle," said Robin, but Wexford didn't believe this. It brought him unexpected pleasure to think of Jason, tiresome and absurd though he was, being reunited for a while with his baby daughter, Isabella.

Robin wasn't yet home when Wexford got to Sylvia's house.

"She's been in a bad way," Sylvia said, "but Robin's done her good. He's altogether good for her. I'm not sure I can say the same for her—that she's good for him, I mean."

"Their engagement is all nonsense, I suppose."

"We've heard no more about it. She's upstairs,

you know, if you want to see her. She absolutely adores you now. You're her flavour of the month."

Wexford's silent reaction to this was to note how this metaphor or rubric had simply disappeared from contemporary usage. What had it been the flavour of? Some kind of sweet or chocolate bar, he thought vaguely. The unwelcome thought came to him that his daughter was middle-aged. "There you are," she said, "I can hear her coming down. She must have heard your voice."

Clarissa came in. If anything could have deprived her of all attraction and beauty, the clothes she was wearing did. She had on torn jeans, the knee parts missing, a whitish, frilly blouse almost covered by metal chains, the familiar black leather jacket, and on her feet dirty grey trainers, their laces undone and flopping. But her head covering was in both senses the crowning horror. There must be a name for this style of headgear, but he didn't know what it was. A spirit-something? The knitted cap was a cloche that covered her whole head, concealing her hair, and with long flaps that hid her ears and fell several inches below her neck. Wexford wanted to laugh or simply stare to take it all in. Instead, he greeted her and asked how she was.

"I'm good now," she said in an earnest tone,

"I'll be OK," as if she were recovering from a life-threatening illness. Of her adoration of him she gave no sign but said, "I couldn't have done it without Robin. He's been so lovely."

Wexford found himself adopting the role of peacemaker without really intending to. After a small hesitation in which he wondered how to refer to Clarissa's father, he began, "I've been to see Christian Steyner. I went to his house in London—"

"It's not his house. Robin says it belongs to his partner."

Wexford nearly said, then home is my house, not my wife's, but decided to let it go. "He talked about you a lot. He wants to see you, Clarissa." Should he say more? Should he say he wants *her?* No, let Steyner do that if this meeting could even be achieved.

She was silent, staring at him, Christian Steyner's blue eyes wide. Then she said, "What's the point? I think it's creepy. I know it happens all the time, IVF and stuff, but it's like science fiction. I don't want to have been born like that."

What to say but that she had been and nothing would change that? "If Robin says I ought to, I will. I really trust him, you see. Well, I trust you and Sylvia, but it's not the same, is it?"

"No, I don't suppose it is."

"If I went up there to see him, would you come with me? I mean, would you go and take me?"

He was touched. "Of course I will. Do you want me to tell him?"

On his way home he encountered Georgina Bray. He would have liked to avoid her, but there was no hope of that as she came homing down upon him, running across the road almost in front of a minibus and causing the driver to scream imprecations.

"Just the language Trevor used to use to me" was her greeting. "All over now, though. I've left him. At last. No more insults, no more sarcasm."

Wexford, not knowing what to say, said, "Congratulations."

"Yes, well, thanks. It was this change in the law, you know, that did it. I mean the law against domestic violence now to include *psychological* violence. I thought, but that's what he's been doing to me all these years, so when he started on one of his sneering campaigns, I upped and said, 'That's it, I'm going, I'm out of here in the morning,' and I was."

"But you're back."

"Only to fetch my stuff. I've got a man with a van and we're taking it to my daughter's in Myringham. Just for a week. I've found a flat and a job."

He said he was pleased for her.

"It's good seeing my kids again. They've hardly been home for a long time, couldn't stand their father's nasty tongue."

• • •

Dora knew all about Jason Sams. The latest installment in the Sams saga had been told her that afternoon.

"Maxine and I are bosom pals now. We ran into each other—almost literally—outside Questo, and she was all over me. It's you that's persona non grata. She'll never feel the same about Mr. Wexford, she says. I'm afraid that's something you have to live with, darling. She wanted to tell me the whole tale, and it was so freezing cold outside that I took her into the Questo cafeteria and she ate two slices of carrot cake. Jason's going to be charged with unlawful killing, and the chances are he won't do any more time. He's been in prison three months already."

"How does he like it in Ladysmith Road?"

"Oh, you know what he's like. Anywhere would be paradise so long as he's with his Isabella."

"I hope you're not having Maxine back."

"Oh, no. Trust me. I couldn't do without Parveen. Oh, and Reg, Parveen and I are turning out your study. I know no one's supposed to go in there, but this is a rule that's made to be broken. It can't be cleaned properly, it's so cluttered. There are a whole lot of newspaper cuttings I've found, they're all old, and I want to know if I can chuck them. I've put them on your desk. Would you have a look at them and see what you want to keep? And soon, please, darling."

He sat at his desk, looking at this stack of newsprint. What had he kept all this stuff for? He'd look through it, but not now. It was wiser, he thought, to take his time about calling Christian Steyner. Wiser too to make that call in the morning when Timon Arkwright would likely not be there. The number he had was recognisable as a landline. If Steyner had a mobile phone, Wexford hadn't been given the number. Wexford began to see that the situation might be awkward if he turned up with Clarissa when Arkwright was at home *in his own house* and this girl he had made clear he didn't want to know arrived to be reunited with his partner. It seemed important to know if the house was Arkwright's and Steyner a beloved guest, or if it belonged to both of them and was shared, or even if it was Steyner's and Arkwright just visiting. This, after all, was how Victoria Steyner had put it. "My son has a lovely house in Knightsbridge" was what she had said or something like that, adding that he shared it with Arkwright. Could Steyner just bring his daughter to live there if he wished? All speculation, Wexford told himself. The girl will never consent.

Next day was Sunday, and after morning service the new vicar was having a prelunch drinks party in the vicarage. Because Dora was invited, Wexford was too. He drew the line at going to matins, not so much because he wasn't and had never been a believer, but for fear of being made to wince at the inelegant language of the *Alternative Service Book. Alternative,* he thought, it wasn't. *Default* was more the word. The officiating cleric was expected to use it unless he had a good reason for putting *The Book of Common Prayer* in its place. It was absurd really for Wexford to care that one generation after another of possible church attenders was growing up without the least knowledge of that beautiful work, probably without even knowing it existed. So he didn't go to church but met Dora at the vicarage afterwards.

The living room where it had happened had been recarpeted and its walls repainted. On the walls were photographs of rows of undergraduates sitting cross-legged, the tall ones standing behind, and a cricket team, its captain holding up a trophy. He was wondering what had happened to the portrait of Clarissa when a voice behind him said, "I've got it. They gave it to her and she gave it to me."

He turned to say hallo to his grandson. "She isn't here?"

"Oh, no. She couldn't bear to see people—well, merrymaking—in this room. Can I come with you to Christian Steyner's place?"

"Better not. Anyway, I don't intend to stay, just to leave them together if it looks like it's working out."

"Did you know his mother had died?"

That pathetic bedizened woman . . . "No, I didn't."

"There was a death notice in yesterday's *Times*. Mum told us. I mean, it's weird, but she was Clarissa's grandma."

Wexford went to make his presence known to his host, who was talking to Dora. Alan Conroy said, "I invited your grandson really because I couldn't have invited poor Clarissa. Now I understand she's had another bereavement, her mother's mother-in-law."

So he didn't know the facts of Clarissa's provenance. Just as well if it could be kept that way throughout Kingsmarkham society. Wexford went off to get himself a drink from a tray being carried round by a boy who introduced himself as the vicar's nephew. Conroy was probably gay, a thought which brought Wexford back to Christian Steyner. Not a good idea to phone the man so soon after his mother's death. He had better wait a day or two.

He was savouring the rather good burgundy the nephew had provided when Dr. Crocker came up to him. "I hear your grandson's got himself engaged to little Miss Hussain."

"They're going about together. I doubt the engagement."

"Maxine tells us she's the product of insemination by her mother's husband's twin brother. Can that be anything but fantasy?"

"I wish it was. Naïve of me, but I thought it was a secret. How does Maxine know?"

"What a question. Maxine knows everything. In this case it's through the boyfriend of her daughter Kelli with an *i* being a bootboy, dishwasher, or some such at the Olive, where your transactions apparently took place."

"Behind closed doors," said Wexford with a sigh.

"If walls have ears, doors have keyholes."

It was another four days before Wexford phoned Christian Steyner, beginning by sympathising with him in his loss.

"Yes, thanks," Steyner said. "It comes to us all, though. She was very old."

It sounded callous. What do you say to that but agree or keep silent?

"Clarissa wants me to bring her to your house."

"Oh, right. That's fine with me."

They arranged a day. Steyner sounded subdued, as perhaps was to be expected from a man who had just lost his mother. Wexford could think of nothing else to say, but the conversation left him feeling uneasy. He told Burden about it, but his friend greeted it with little interest and no enthusiasm. The calendar on Burden's office wall had been turned to the month of March and a photograph of a disused police station, overgrown with ivy, in a Manchester suburb.

"Dennison has disappeared," Burden said.

"You'd think disappearing was impossible these days. No matter where anyone had got to, he could be tracked down. But not so. We know all about Dennison. Where he's lived, where he's worked—when he has—his wives. He's had two and two divorces. Both of them would like to shop him but they don't know where he is. The same goes for girlfriends. If he's left the country, he must have done so immediately after he killed Crisp and well before the body was found. Arben Birjar is probably in Albania, but how can we know? If he came in illegally, he went out illegally. Probably the man or men who employed him are hiding him. Until we have him, we don't know who they are."

"One of them is the man Crisp saw through the window."

"I'll need a good deal more evidence before I accept that," said Burden.

Wexford thought of driving to London. He regularly did so when he and Dora were spending a weekend at the little house Sheila had put at their disposal. But it was one thing to come off the westbound M25 and dip down into Hampstead where he had a garage to put the car in, another to make his way through the park to Knightsbridge and there find somewhere to park, no longer needing small change to feed a meter but making phone calls to a local authority while the car sat guiltily on a double yellow line.

"We'll take the ten-oh-eight to Victoria. I don't suppose we need to book ahead."

"I'll do that," Clarissa said. "I'll book online."

Robin, who knew his grandfather's technological limitations better than she did, said they could pick up the tickets when they went for the train, instructing him how to do this and adding that it was simple. When they got there, it was.

Wexford had expected Clarissa to be dressed as usual: the torn jeans, the leather jacket, probably the wooly hat with the long, knitted lappets. But something had impelled her to dress up—her realisation that this was an occasion, her first real meeting with her father, a meeting that might change her life? She wore a short, black dress but not too short, black shoes with high heels but not too high, a red jacket inadequate for the time of year and the icy wind.

The journey was short, less than an hour. He had a book with him, a paperback Gissing novel, but only because it was habit to go nowhere without something to read. He thought it would be rude to read it in her presence and attempted a conversation, a few words on the early signs of spring which could be seen from the window.

She interrupted, "You won't go, will you? You won't leave me with him?"

"He will expect me to go, I'm sure."

"If you get up to leave, I'll leave with you. I

will. He'll be glad if I do. He'll just think of me as the girl who, like, screamed when he said who he was. This is a waste of time, isn't it? It's not going to work. Say we'll leave if I say so."

Helplessly he said, "I will do whatever you say, Clarissa."

The woman in the seat in front of them turned her head to stare but said nothing. All the other people in the coach were too busy on their mobile phones to take any notice. He knew enough about the London underground system by now to escort her into a Circle-line train without having to check the map. Clarissa had conjured it all up on her mobile anyway. Having enlarged the map, marked it with something that looked to Wexford like a lollipop, she moved away from it and called Robin. Reception was bad but not impossible. She told him where they were and repeated what she had said to Wexford:

"It's not going to work. I know it isn't."

When she saw the house, she stood still and stared. Her comments were exactly what he would have expected from an intelligent young woman of her age with a social conscience. "If the government had done what they said and brought in a sort of mansion tax, the man who lives there would have had to pay millions. Instead of taking it from the poor like they do all the time."

Wexford said, "Come along," and headed

across the street. He clearly remembered Sylvia and Sheila saying the same sort of thing all those years ago when they were this girl's age.

"It's that house?"

"I'm afraid so."

The red camellias were still in bloom. They walked up the steps and Wexford rang the bell. Another bell also rang, that of a church clock somewhere nearby. It was eleven thirty.

In the big bow window on the left-hand side he had seen the figure of a man. As Crisp, in the account he gave Burden, had seen the figure of a man through the vicarage French window. Could it possibly be the same man? Dark, tall, clean-shaven, middle-aged. For a moment he appeared sinister, moving about, frowning as if searching for something he couldn't find. Then he looked up at the sound of the bell and, seeing them, smiled and raised his hand. The door was opened as if by someone who had run to it.

"Hallo. Come in. It's pretty cold out there."

They stepped over the threshold, Clarissa first, of course, though diffidently.

"I'm Timon Arkwright. How do you do?"

Christian Steyner was in the enormous drawing room. He gave no sign that the last time he had seen Clarissa she had collapsed in screaming hysterics but stepped forward and took both her hands in his. Don't kiss her, Wexford thought, not yet. "Tim," Christian said, "this is my daughter."

After that everything became pleasant. Clarissa spoke politely to Timon and shook hands with him. At his invitation she sat next to her father, and all screams and horror looked likely to be forgotten. She talked about school and her coming A-levels and where she would like to go to university and then about Robin and how wonderful he was. To his relief, Wexford felt he wasn't needed. He wanted to be on his own to think about Arkwright and what, fantastically, had crossed his mind. Both men thanked him quite effusively for bringing Clarissa. No, he wouldn't stay to lunch. Would Clarissa be happy for him to go?

"How shall I get home then?"

"My driver will take you whenever you want to go," said Timon, laid-back. "But we hope you won't want to go too soon. I've taken the day off work to meet you."

Wexford wondered what *work* meant and what Timon would fail to turn up to: a board meeting, a conference, a meeting with some other tycoon? Wexford got up. Clarissa amazed him by holding up her face for a kiss—a first time, that one.

Christian took him to the door. "I think Timon's going to love her as much as I do."

Wexford wasn't so sure about that. Wasn't this exactly how Arkwright would behave if he had killed Sarah Hussain? If he had killed her to prevent her telling Clarissa the truth about her parentage, but now, finding that his action had failed, could only make the best of a bad job?

"We're going away to our country place for the weekend," Steyner said. "It's in Cornwall, and we're hoping Clarissa will come with us. Do you think your grandson would come too?"

"I can't speak for them, not for either of them. You ask her."

Wexford sat in the train. He had no evidence for what he had half believed unless seeing a dark man through glass was evidence, and the hearsay evidence of that man's love for another man. If Wexford was right, wasn't he wrong to have left that girl in Arkwright's company? Wrong to have put up no objection to Clarissa's spending the weekend with Christian and Timon? He couldn't have stopped it, he thought. He had no power.

28

The last volume of *The Decline and Fall* lay on his desk next to the pile of newspaper cuttings he still hadn't looked at. Nor had he read a word of Gibbon since getting home. I shouldn't have left her there, he kept saying to himself, and over and over, how long was I to stay, then? The whole weekend? I shouldn't have left her. Stop it, don't do this. He opened volume six at the place he had marked and began to read of the great khan of the Tartars.

It is the religion of Zingis that best deserves our wonder and applause. The Catholic inquisitors of Europe, who defended nonsense by cruelty, might have been confounded by the example of a barbarian, who anticipated the lessons of philosophy, and established by his laws a system of pure theism and perfect toleration. His first and only article of faith was the existence of one God, the Author of all good, who fills by his presence the heavens and earth which he has created by his power. The Tartars and Moguls were addicted to the idols of their peculiar tribes; and many of them had been converted by the foreign missionaries to the religions of Moses, Mohammed and of Christ. These various systems in freedom and concord were taught and practised within the precincts of the same camp; and the Bonze, the Imam, the Rabbi, the Nestorian and the Latin priest, enjoyed the same honourable exemption from service and tribute. In the mosque of Bochara the insolent victor might trample the Koran under his horse's feet, but the calm legislator respected the prophets and pontiffs of the most hostile sects. The reason of Zingis was not informed by books; the khan could neither read nor write. . . .

He hadn't been sure that Timon Arkwright was guilty, but it still seemed to him that everything fitted. There was more to discover, of course. What was Arkwright's connection with Marty Dennison? Wexford remembered what Nardelie Mukamba's brother had said about those who visited the Anaconda nightclub, among them the rich and famous. He wouldn't be surprised if Arkwright had been one of them. He might even have had a share in the club's ownership. But find out, it shouldn't be difficult.

Should he have left Clarissa alone with the man? Not alone exactly. Christian Steyner was there too. Her father was there. It was five past four. He called her mobile number, wondering what to do if she didn't answer.

"I'm in Timon's car." They moved on to first names very fast these days. "I'm on my way home. What do you think about me, like, going away for the weekend with Christian and Timon?" She left him no time to reply. "I'd sort of like to but I'm going to ask Robin. Ask his advice, I mean."

"Of course."

The dryness in his voice went undetected. "I'd love him to come too but maybe it's a bit soon for that."

Wexford had no opinion to offer on this example of belated caution. He ended the call, still wondering, though she was safe now, how safe she would be on further contact with Arkwright. If he had killed her mother to prevent the girl's having any contact with Steyner, how much more of a menace to him was she herself? All that bonhomie and effusiveness could be a front. This place they had in Cornwall, was it by the sea, were there high cliffs, disused tin-mine shafts? An accident could be arranged that Steyner knew nothing about. Oh, nonsense, he told himself, people don't do such things, as Ibsen had it. But they do. All the time.

He had better go through this pile of newsprint, cuttings he had made and now forgotten what for.

Each separate column or half page must have seemed worth saving at the time. Here, for instance, was one from the *London Evening Standard* headed "Murder of Woman Vicar" with a picture of poor Sarah Hussain, another about rural housing, and a third on some new model Audi. Why he had kept those two he couldn't imagine. He had a house and he didn't want a new car. All the papers went into the black plastic bag Dora had left for him. The face of Timon Arkwright came as a shock. It stared out from the group he was standing in front of so unexpectedly as to seem unreal, something Wexford *had* imagined. He shut his eyes, opened them. The photograph of the man was still there, still in one of his beautiful suits, presenting an award to a woman in a trouser suit and hat and surrounded by half a dozen men. The caption read, "Arkwright Associates chairman Timon Arkwright presenting the City of London's major Industry Award to CEO Jennifer Carpenter, the first time the award has gone to a woman." The hands on a clock on the wall between their heads pointed to three thirty.

A kind of coincidence but of no further interest to him. He had picked it off the pile and was about to drop it into the bag when the date on the top of the page caught his eye. Thursday, October 11, 2012. He read the date again slowly. It provided a simple but perfect alibi for Timon

Arkwright. If he was in a building in Finsbury Circus that afternoon, there was no way he could have been in Kingsmarkham vicarage. Wexford had been libelling the man in his thoughts. Probably Arkwright had never set foot in the Anaconda Club, still less been associated with a villain such as Martin Dennison.

It was a relief too. He didn't want to be right, and now thinking that he had been right, thinking that no more than ten minutes ago, seemed absurd. It was all very well to tell himself that people do such things. It still remained true that people like Arkwright don't. In any case, Arkwright would not have killed Sarah from such a motive, and he could have had no other. He, of all people, would have known that his lover was Sarah's child's father and that, once Sarah was dead, Christian Steyner would tell Clarissa the truth. He, of all people too, would have been told by Christian all the details of Sarah's intention to tell Clarissa that truth on her eighteenth birthday. Timon Arkwright was nice and polite and pleasant to Clarissa because he loved Christian and wanted above all for him to be happy.

He, Wexford, had been fantasising, and as a fabulist he wasn't a patch on Thora Kilmartin. Reality was Martin Dennison and Arben Birjar. His phone was ringing. Burden. He was on his way home. Could he pop in for a chat? Wexford welcomed the prospect of a visit, all the more because he could no longer make a fool of himself proposing an eminent and respected company chairman as Sarah Hussain's killer.

"He hasn't left the country," Burden said. "We know that. Border Control have kept a watch for him and there's been no sign. A new development, if you can call it that, is that Janet Corbyn-Smith—remember her?" Wexford nodded. "She called us, said she'd just remembered seeing Dennison's passport. He left it in his room one day and she looked inside. Not that it's been much use."

"What's new about it then?"

"He really is called Martin Dennison. As you know, you don't have an address in your passport or the names of your parents. His date of birth is 1981. All those interesting things that used to be in passports like hair colour and height aren't there anymore, haven't been for ages."

"So all your new development has told you is his age and that he really is who he says he is."

"That's right," said Burden. "He's got two previous convictions, which the passport of course didn't tell Ms. Corbyn-Smith, but records did tell me. Actual bodily harm in twenty-oh-seven and breaking and entering a year later. You know, people think that with all the technology we've got now, it's impossible to hide for long. A car can be traced in seconds, a mobile phone locates you, innumerable records list you. Your name is on various databases. But suppose you're not what we'd call respectable. You've no fixed abode, any car you drive you've stolen. You can change your name when you like, there's nothing to stop you, you're free to call yourself what you choose. Pity we don't have what they have in the US, where it's extremely difficult and time-consuming to change your name. You can't even change the spelling of your Christian name without a lot of bother. Taking it that you're a man, and you're more likely to be, there's always some woman somewhere who will give you houseroom. You can get in your stolen car and drive off up some motorway until you come to a turnoff that goes to a place you've never been to but like the sound of. Find a Holiday Inn, for instance, dump the car, and drive off next day to find another place and another car to nick. It's advisable to pay your hotel bill, of course. . . ."

"Yes, Mike, right, I get the picture." I'm not yet in my dotage, Wexford thought. Most of this has been true since I first got the job you've got now. "We do have one advantage," he said, hoping Burden wouldn't object to that *we*. "We know what he looks like. We know about the tattoo on his hand, we know he's a tall, big man with dark hair. I don't suppose Ms. Corbyn-Smith thought of taking a photo of the passport on her phone, did she?"

"It would be difficult with an ordinary mobile. Anyway, she didn't."

One or two things Burden had said alerted Wexford, but he said nothing about them. He had to think, maybe write those things down and give them some thought. They might mean nothing. He gave Burden another drink—he would be walking home—and they talked some more about hiding places for those seeking bolt-holes.

"If you hid with an old girlfriend or a relative, all you'd have to fear would be recognition by a neighbour."

"And that's no small thing, Mike," Wexford said. "Few people will give their support to a neighbour who has a suspicious friend staying with him or her, someone they've never seen at the house before but who's now there all the time."

"And if that suspicious friend never goes out once he's arrived? If he's not been seen when he arrived? What then?"

This was what Wexford wanted to think about once he was alone. He called Burden again to ask if Janet Corbyn-Smith had been questioned in the past few days. Not since Dennison's disappearance, he was told. What exactly had her relationship with Dennison been?

"Just landlady and tenant," Burden said. "What are you suggesting?"

"You know what I'm suggesting, Mike."

"There was nothing like that, any more than there was with Arben Birjar. Barry and Laura have been all over the house. She's not sheltering him."

Someone was. Wexford had always been interested in the reasons people have for choosing the names they do; choosing names for their children, for instance, and choosing an alias for themselves. These choices were seldom if ever arbitrary. In the case of Christian or given names, the choice was often that of a celebrity, a television personality or a pop singer. The characters of novels and films provided names, think of *Emma, Shirley,* and *Alfie.* But what of surnames as aliases? People used the phone book when phone books were in constant general use. But all those who had no landline might never see a phone book. Where then would you get an assumed name from? The title of a book? The name of an author? Not if you lived an itinerant life and possessed no books anyway. He wrote down the name *Dennison* on a sheet of paper, then *Martin Dennison,* followed by *Marty Dennison.* This told him nothing. Then he began to make a list of all the people he and Burden's team had spoken to in the investigation, starting with Georgina and Trevor Bray.

A long list followed. He had made notes of each interview he had carried out, most of them made after the meeting was over, and from these he picked out names: the Kilmartins, Duncan Crisp,

Daphne Morgan, Linda Green, Clarissa Hussain, Dennis Cuthbert, Nardelie Mukamba, Alan Conroy, the Sams family, Christian Steyner, Timon Arkwright. Watson and Mrs. Steyner were dead, the women who had alibied Crisp seemed too long a shot, Janet Corbyn-Smith was no longer in the running. He ran his eye down the list but the names told him nothing. He didn't even know what he expected them or one of them to tell him. Perhaps he meant not what he or she would tell him, but what he could deduce from what the name said. And was that deduction that one of them was hiding Marty Dennison?

How long could you hide someone in an ordinary dwelling house? He thought of all those cases of men who had abducted women and kept them prisoner, often for years. This would be easier because whoever was sheltering Dennison had his cooperation. Whoever it might be must live in a big house. Hiding someone in a small flat would be impossible. He looked up from the list when Dora came into the room.

"Just to remind you, we're having supper with Sylvia."

"Five minutes and I'll be with you," Wexford said.

Ben was home from university, and rather to Wexford's surprise, Robin and Clarissa were both there. Less surprising was Clarissa's announcement, before they sat down to eat, that she would be going to Cornwall with Christian and Timon for the coming weekend and Robin would be with her. That she had told Wexford only a few hours before that it was too soon for that made him smile, but he suppressed his laughter. Perhaps Robin, in his role as adviser, had changed her mind. The list Wexford had made kept appearing word for word before his inner eye. Maybe what he really meant was that he knew it by heart. He resisted thinking about it, talked as his social duty required him, but wasn't sorry when just before ten Dora suggested they leave. This was early evening to the three young ones, but they were all too polite to comment on it. Once the grandparents had said good-night, they were off upstairs to Clarissa's room, where some new variety of music transmission was awaiting their attention.

At home Wexford looked at his list again, a needless exercise as all the names on it were committed to his memory. He dreamt about it, the dead Watson coming back, a pale and diminished ghost, saying in a horror-film voice that he would have the law on anyone who took his name in vain. In the morning Wexford read through the names once more, stopping halfway at the one name on the list that might have a connection with Martin Dennison. He phoned Burden, who took his suggestion grudgingly.

"But do people find pseudonyms that way?"

"Why not? It sounds likely to me."

"D'you want to go round there?"

"Can I?" Wexford didn't quite want to articulate the correct *May I?* "If I may, with Barry, say, or Karen . . . ?"

"Are you thinking about a search?"

"I'm thinking about a talk."

Wexford met Barry Vine on the police-station forecourt. "Dennis-son, you see. Is it a long shot?"

"I reckon the boss thinks so."

They had never called Wexford the boss, but he acknowledged that the title seemed to suit Burden. "But he's letting you go. And he lets *me* go."

"Sure, but for now we're only talking."

They walked. Wexford had often noticed that the weather conditions which were said to be the perquisites of certain months, rain in February and April, sunshine in May, heat in June, continuous greyness in November, were seldom accurate. Today, for instance, and for the past week, where were the sharp and icy March winds? It was a mild, still day, blue-skied, the sun a gentle harbinger of spring to come. Their walk took them through the old parts of Kingsmarkham, the little streets and alleys that lay between Queen Street and York Street. The tall nineteenth-century house stood alone, too narrow for its height, too ugly for this area of stucco or stone or half-timbered dwellings.

Wexford, who had never taken much notice of it before, observed as if for the first time the disproportionate windows, the clashing yellow and purplish red of the brickwork, the steep, tiled roof more suited to a house in a Belgian or northern-German street than an English country town.

If he had thought that Dennis Cuthbert suffered from parkinsonism on the previous occasions they had met, he now saw that he had been mistaken. Cuthbert no longer shook but he smoked as heavily. Allowed to enter grudgingly, they stepped into a grey fog, reminiscent of a pub's public bar in days gone by. If possible, the clouds of it were even denser in the living room. Repainted not long before by Cuthbert, the pale surfaces (apple white) were already stained yellow by smoke, while the skin of Cuthbert's right forefinger was dark brown.

He made no attempt to deny that Martin Dennison was his son, even saying, "I thought you knew." Then he said, "You expect me to be ashamed of him, don't you? I'm not. Whatever he's done, he's been a good son to me. I don't suppose you people ever read your Bible." He paused, perhaps expecting rebuttal or agreement. When none came, he said, "In the parable of the Prodigal Son, our Lord tells how the father forgave his son for his iniquity and made a feast to welcome him home. He even said to his good son that he mustn't be envious of his brother because 'all that I have is thine.' We're all forgiven, you know, no matter what we've done. No matter how bad it is."

Neither Wexford nor Vine commented on this, but after a few seconds of silence Wexford said, "Where is your son Martin now, Mr. Cuthbert?"

"I don't know."

"He doesn't live with you, does he?"

"He does sometimes." Cuthbert lit a cigarette from the stub of the last one, and this time the inhalation set him coughing. He repeated what he had said. "He does sometimes."

Wexford had the curious impression that he had had before in questioning people who had a deep aversion to lying. They were jesuitical in that they would tell a truth they intended to be perceived differently from the usual meaning of the words. For instance Cuthbert's "I don't know" might mean not that he didn't know where in the country or the world his son might be, but that he didn't know in which room of the house he was at that moment. And Cuthbert now came near to confirming this conjecture by looking up at the ceiling and, realising what he had done, jerking his head down again.

"Martin Dennison, otherwise known as Martin Cuthbert," said Vine heavily, "is wanted for murder. I think you know that, don't you?"

"Even for murder," Cuthbert said, "we're forgiven."

They crossed the street and stood behind the rear wall of a bus shelter, from where they would be invisible from Cuthbert's house.

"I'm going to call someone to take over from me," Vine said, "keep the house under surveillance. Rouse, I think. I'll wait here till he comes."

"And I shall go back and talk to the boss," said Wexford. "If Marty's not in there but staying with a girlfriend in the Isle of Man, I shall look rather foolish, but never mind. It wouldn't be the first time."

Having rejected Wexford's theory of alias selection, Burden was now impressed that what he called his friend's "guesswork" turned out to have been right.

"You'll get a warrant?"

"I'll have to," Burden said. "From what you say, Cuthbert's not likely to welcome us in to search his house without one. The prodigal son, indeed."

The warrant secured, Burden announced his intention of being present while the search went on. David Rouse, who was already outside the house, Barry Vine, Lynn, and Karen were joined by two uniformed officers. Wexford thought he would be expected to go home, but Burden said, "Stay," which Wexford said made him feel like an obedient dog. Both men had looked up to the steep roof, which would certainly house a loft.

Indoors, they all left the silent and stony-faced Cuthbert to "smoke himself to death" in the living room, as Burden put it, and began the climb up the steep flights of stairs.

Everyone seemed to have decided Martin Dennison's favoured hiding place would be in the loft. As Burden said, the loft was "a gift" but also too obvious. Still, he sent Rouse down to ask Cuthbert if he had a ladder. At first Cuthbert said no, a refusal which only aroused suspicions once more. Vine came down to join Rouse and say that if Cuthbert refused the loan of the ladder (which "you must possess"), they would send out for one and that would only delay things. Cuthbert produced the ladder, and Rouse and Vine carried it up four flights of stairs. Karen climbed up into the loft, saying indignantly that just because she was a woman, there was no reason to keep her from this vital area of the search. She was a lot fitter than most of them, she said nastily. But in the loft all that was to be seen were two water tanks, no piles of old newspapers, no defunct machinery, no crates full of broken crockery, and no Marty Dennison. The trapdoor was put back and the ladder taken down.

As was usually the case with houses of this age, all the rooms were small. Cuthbert slept on the first floor, and a room above it on the second floor looked as if it might sometimes be occupied. Like all the other rooms in this bleak house, these had the bare minimum of furniture: single beds, marble-topped tables with metal legs, upright chairs with broken cane seats. In the second-floor bedroom some clothes hanging in a cupboard and a couple of crumpled shirts in a drawer suggested that it was occasionally occupied, as did the sheets on the bed.

"I didn't say he never slept here," said Cuthbert. "I said he wasn't here now."

An Authorised edition of the Bible was in the drawer of the bedside table in Cuthbert's bedroom.

"Hotels used to do that," Wexford said. "Maybe they still do."

The only furniture apart from bed and bedside table was a cupboard and a chest of drawers Wexford thought might be called a tallboy. It reached up to his shoulder, and above it was a picture, the lower edge of whose tarnished gilt frame reached within an inch of the top of the chest. The picture was a reproduction of a nineteenth-century painter's rendering of the marriage at Cana with a bearded and robed Jesus turning water into wine amid a crowd of wedding guests. Wexford gave the tallboy a shove, moving it a few inches away from the wall. He lifted the lower edge of the frame so that a darker rectangle of wallpaper, brown chrysanthemums with bright green leaves instead of yellow flowers and grey leaves as papered the rest of the room, was revealed. He looked more closely, then Burden did, then Vine.

"The paper has faded," Vine said, "but they kept a bit of the original stuff and pasted it on over—what?"

The pasted-on rectangle was the size of an interior door. Vine measured it. The house was damp in places, and Vine was able to peel a section of it away from the upper right-hand edge, but underneath was no door or doorway, only the same sort of plaster as the rest of the wall.

"It doesn't make sense," Vine said.

Wexford had an idea, but that didn't really make sense either. "Let's see what's directly underneath."

Underneath was the living room. Cuthbert was there, sitting in front of the electric heater, extinguishing his most recent cigarette in a pottery bowl that was already half full of stubs. He immediately lit another. It was as if he had set himself a target to fill the bowl by a certain time, say twelve noon. The police officers made no attempt to suppress their coughing, and Burden coughed more loudly than any of the others. Cuthbert inhaled deeply, took *The Book of Common Prayer* off the table, and began to read it, causing Wexford to reflect there must be few occasions when these two activities were practised simultaneously.

Directly underneath the chest of drawers, the

painting, and the mysterious sheet of wallpaper hung the bedspread Wexford had noticed before but had barely registered. Burden said, "What's behind that?"

"A door," said Cuthbert without laying aside his book. "A cupboard."

"Would you remove the curtain, please?"

"Do it yourself." But now Cuthbert got to his feet.

The bedspread was hung from a wooden curtain rail and could be drawn back. Behind it was a metal door. For a moment Wexford thought he was looking at the door to a large safe. He realised, almost incredulously, that he knew what it really was when Burden opened the door and revealed another inside, one of metal mesh. It was a lift, an old and old-fashioned Cuthbert and Son lift, which had perhaps been in this house for a century.

Cuthbert seemed to have given up the struggle. He said, "Sorry, son," and put his head in his hands.

The metal-mesh door slid aside to disclose a man slumped on the floor. The lift, no more than a box large enough to hold two people, was lined in wood-grain wallpaper that was peeling off in places. The man on the floor, unmistakably Marty Dennison, was dark with several days' growth of beard. His short-sleeved T-shirt, a faded green with a turtle pictured on the front, revealed the tattoo that identified him. The half-empty bottle of water on the floor beside him was no surprise to Wexford. Even the incarcerated, even the fugitive, seemed to need perpetual water these days. Dennison stood up and, in that public-school accent that went so incongruously with his appearance, said, "My great-grandfather put this in. His wife got ill and couldn't climb stairs. Handy, isn't it, even if it doesn't work anymore?"

His father stood up. Marty Dennison, who had once been Martin Cuthbert, put his arms round him, laid his head on his shoulder, and held him. "See you, Dad."

29

Wexford was thinking of a line from somewhere about two thieves kissing, Shakespeare probably, but he couldn't place it. "I shan't get sentimental about a couple of villains who appear to be devoted to each other."

"Nor me," said Burden when they had both Cuthberts at the police station. "A Cuthbert has lived in that house since it was built, apparently. One of the first of them had a factory in Stowerton making lifts. They've still got one of their lifts in the Golden Lion hotel in Myringham. Got a modern one as well, of course. The one in the Olive and Dove has just been taken out. If you heard that Marty speak and couldn't see him, you'd think you were listening to a cabinet minister."

"I know. Would you call yourself an accentist?"

"A what? Oh, I see, like a sexist or a racist. I don't know. Would you?"

"I talk Sussex," said Wexford, "so I couldn't."

"Do you think the media would get wind of it and say offensive things about me if I suggested we went out for a late lunch?"

"You must learn to ignore them, though I never could."

The newly opened Persian restaurant called Halle was Burden's choice. It was on the opposite side of the high street to the Cuthbert house, with a smart frontage all polished wood and gilding and a menu in an ornate gold frame beside the entrance. A single white calla lily that looked and felt real decorated every table. No one was there, though several tables had a reserved sign beside the calla in its crimson vase.

The dishes on the menu were different from anything they had eaten before. Burden chose a yoghurt dish to start, and Wexford *kashke bademjan,* which was eggplant.

"I daren't have anything alcoholic." Burden was cautiously eyeing a weedy little man with red hair and a green pullover and his companion, a small, thin girl who wore shorts over black leggings, moving towards one of the reserved tables. "One if not both of them look like journalists."

"I'm going to have Persian wine," said Wexford. "It will make me feel like Omar Khayyám. What have you done with those two Cuthberts?"

"Barry and Karen are questioning the so-called Dennison now. He's asked for a lawyer, who has probably arrived by now."

"You haven't charged him?"

"Not yet. He'll be charged with just one murder and I'll keep the other in reserve."

Wexford looked at him speculatively. "That's how you see it, then? Marty Dennison is the perpetrator in both cases?"

"What else?"

The wine came; almost immediately afterwards, the *mast va khiar damavand* and the *kashke bademjan* arrived. "I sometimes wonder what the vintners buy," quoted Wexford, "one half so precious as the goods they sell."

"Never mind that, Gibbon or whatever it is. What did you mean about Marty Dennison being the perpetrator in both cases?"

"I thought you knew. I mean, I thought you'd seen it too. It wasn't Marty but his father who killed Sarah Hussain."

Burden said nothing. He ate nothing either.

"It was Dennis Cuthbert that Duncan Crisp saw through that window. And Cuthbert saw him. They didn't know each other you see. Each of them just saw a man he'd never seen before. Crisp was new to the place, he'd only been there a few weeks, and Cuthbert seldom went to the vicarage. He hated Sarah Hussain for all the changes she was making in the church services and the liturgy and more that she threatened—well, promised, she said—to make. He went there that afternoon to tell her she mustn't change any more of the old hymns."

"Are you saying Cuthbert killed her for that?"

"I don't think he meant to kill her. She must have said that she meant to go ahead with her plans. I'm sure she said it nicely. After all, she'd always been nice to him. On a previous occasion—to his rage—she'd kissed him. I think that rage sort of rose up in him again, he threw himself at her and put his hands round her throat."

Burden nodded. "I think you're right. D'you know, I hate having to admit it, but I think you're right. Where does Marty Dennison come into all this? Only as the killer of poor old Crisp, I suppose?"

Their main course came. Both were having the *koofteh berenji,* meatballs with rice and split peas and plums. "I like meat with fruit," Wexford said.

He started to eat, leaving further explanation for a few minutes. Burden too began on the meatballs. The couple at the reserved table were evidently not interested in them, and by this time more lunchers had arrived. Wexford thought how much he would have liked to drink the whole bottle of wine and how much he would regret it later.

"Marty Dennison is devoted to his father," he said. "You will tell me they're a worthless pair of villains and I'd go along with that, but even men like that can have a selfless love for each other. Marty Dennison would do anything for his father and he did. When he wanted a tattoo, he even had a picture of a saint. He carried out a brutal abduction of poor old Crisp, followed by a brutal killing, so that Cuthbert could never be identified as Sarah's murderer."

"They're very different."

"So are most fathers and sons, I'd say. Dennison's devotion shows in his taking his father's name as his alias. He needed an alias not to bring shame on his father. But he'd gone to the bad, it was a life that suited him, and his father never blamed him or even showed his disappointment. That's what I think, I don't know. Marty went home from time to time and he always had a room or a flat in the neighbourhood. One day when he was at home, Dennis Cuthbert told him Duncan Crisp hadn't killed Sarah Hussain, *he* had, and that he was sure Crisp had seen him through the vicarage French window. Marty said to leave it to him. Did he know what Marty planned to do with the help of Birjar, whom Cuthbert had probably never heard of? Very likely Cuthbert knew nothing about it. He would only know that just as he had never reproached or threatened his son for the way he behaved, so his son said nothing to condemn him for the murder of Sarah Hussain."

"I shan't threaten or reproach you for seeing what I didn't," said Burden. "Not that I wouldn't like to."

"You're tired. You look worn-out. You could go home now."

"No, I couldn't. There'll be two lawyers to deal with, I suppose. One each. I have to be there. I have to put up with them asking if I'm going to charge 'Mr.' Cuthbert and 'Mr.' Dennison, and then I have to do it and be sure to be bright and early tomorrow morning when they're up in court."

And I may have a lie-in with Gibbon or Tom Holland, thought Wexford, saying good-bye, saying, "See you," as he started on his walk home. All those people who had come into his orbit in the past few months, some such as Thora Kilmartin, that he'd be glad never to see again, or her husband that he'd rather liked; that other couple, the Brays, now mercifully for her at any rate split up; the Sams family, which he was sure had not made their last appearance in his life; Nardelie Mukamba, who could obviously have no place there but for whom his feelings had been tender; Clarissa Hussain, who would, if this were a Victorian novel, be sure to marry his grandson, but, because it wasn't but was reality and today, would soon find someone else if she hadn't done so already and would like the rest depart.

"Ah, make the most of what we yet may spend," he said aloud, having an Omar Khayyám moment as he inserted the key into his front door, "before we too into the dust descend," and walked in to meet and kiss Dora, who stood on the other side of it, waiting for him.

About the Author

RUTH RENDELL has won numerous awards, including three Edgars, the highest accolade from Mystery Writers of America, as well as four Gold Daggers and a Diamond Dagger for outstanding contribution to the genre from England's prestigious Crime Writers' Association. A member of the House of Lords, she lives in London.

Center Point Large Print
600 Brooks Road / PO Box 1
Thorndike ME 04986-0001 USA

(207) 568-3717

US & Canada:
1 800 929-9108
www.centerpointlargeprint.com